BLOOD OF BELLADONNA

Blood Of Belladonna

A NOVEL

J L Rehman

A Division of Rehman Technology Services, Inc.

COVER DESIGNED BY J L REHMAN

Manufactured in the United States of America

ISBN-978-1-607710059

www.partnersincrimepublishers.com

To all the old guys
who refuse go down without a fight.

CONTENTS

1

gatorland

ROLLING ALONG THE Florida turnpike in a Lincoln town car limo, not the late model stretch variety, but smaller—one a good fifteen-years-old in need of a paint job, the chassis rusting out beneath, pushing two hundred thousand miles on the odometer—Joe Salas sits confined in used luxury in the back with Pop, his eighty-year old father, and Julio, threatening car sickness.

They're being chauffeured by some guy named Fred-or-Frank-Something hired by the art gallery because Joe is their newest star and the humble winner of a once-in-a-lifetime art showing at Art Basel Miami. He's given up on a nap thanks to Julio's incessant Cuban rambling.

Julio got a ride-a-long for being the gallery assistant and it's his job to take care of the lodging and any needs of Joe and his father.

Limo passes landfills, the excrement of greater south Florida, tons of discard from wealthy and poor, seasoned with occasional crime evidence and body parts. Joe notes great raised mounds with neatly leveled tops, seeded with green grass to give the illusion of rolling hills above the flat lands of swampy Florida.

In the air above, seagulls and vultures swarm the carrion truck stop, seduced by metal pipes spewing methane gas like a neon beacon for fast food. Joe wonders if the vultures at home have moved on, or await his return in hopes of a fresh meal. He'd expect raccoons, opossums, even the occasional fox to hang around for handouts, but vultures? He wonders if vultures can acquire a taste for humans the way tigers in India, or polar bears do. But those are predators, not scavengers. Aren't they? He can't remember ever hearing of vultures moonlighting on the side, stalking kills of their own in the dead of night or back alleys, and if they did, would it be because of him? Could he have started something in the food chain, forced a connection to an easy food source? Joe doesn't want to dwell on it.

Pop blurts, "Castro dead? Heard he died. Heard they had him freeze dried so's they make folks think he's still alive. Been dead for years. What I heard."

Julio raises an eyebrow. "Chew wash too mush TV."

"I like The Guiding Light."

Julio scoots closer, suddenly animated, "Ooo, I love that one, too!"

Pop shakes his head because he knows every detail of the story line. "Hand me a Dr. Pepper, will ya, Jo?"

Joe cranes his neck to see the driver. "You smell somethin' burning?"

Pop sniffs, "Not my fault. Not cookin'. Remember when I just about set the kitchen afire? You slapped that smoke alarm clean off the ceiling. And the trash you slung at the dog. Damn dog. Just about ate me up, but JoJo took care of that, too."

Joe shoves a Dr. Pepper from the mini bar at Pop's gut. "That's enough, Pop. Don't think he wants to hear it." Just what he needs now. Pop to re-enact the shuffle back and forth over things done in the shed.

Pop taps a finger to his lips, "Oops, sorry." Imitates zipping his mouth.

Limo pulls from the herd of traffic and exits the turnpike. Driver calls on the intercom. "We're having engine problems, folks. I'll need to pull over and check her out. Should only be a slight delay."

Other than the silhouette of the back of his head, they can't actually see him.

Julio beats on the glass partition. "Hey, hey, driver man!"

Joe pulls a mint from the small leather bag on his belt, pops it in his mouth, "Can't hear you. Got the speaker on the one way."

A slow surging starts. Even without being mechanics they all know it's just a matter of time before they're thumbing a ride down the turnpike.

Landscape goes by. No buildings, no cars. Pop thinks getting to Miami is gonna take longer than he thought and they should have flown—just get Joe drunk and shove him on a plane. "You'd think there'd be a station or some kind of life around here. Where the hell are we?"

Joe gestures to the back of the driver's head. "I don't know, Pop. You see me talkin' to him?"

DRIVING EAST KEEPS the light at their back, the encroaching ominous darkness ahead. Talking stops—Joe and Julio stare out the window—Pop contemplates his shoes. Surging morphs to a weird heave with an intermittent engine cough. Another left turn and the hard road turns to dirt, narrow, overgrown with weeds, the complimentary glassware chiming in their luxury cubby. Steam bellows from under the hood.

The limo stops and Frank-or-Fred-Something gets out. Joe opens the door, takes his time surveying their surroundings. Twenty feet from the limo is a canal—dark, murky, sort of place gangbangers like to dump stolen cars. The dirt road seems to run parallel, but ends farther up as if someone forgot what the road was for. On the other side of the road drape trees and shaggy overgrown vegetation in various stages of freeze-burn and re-growth. Bigger stuff snapped at the top by the hurricanes. Wild grape and potato vine snake through suffering branches.

Fred-or-Frank-Something pops the hood, sheds his jacket to use against the intense heat of pressurized steam. Sweat bleeds through his starched white shirt. Never occurs to anyone to actually ask the guy's name.

"Got a hole?" Joe stretches his neck as if he doesn't need to get involved.

"A slow hole. I warned them it was piddling water like an incontinent old woman. Cheap bastards. We'll need to get her filled. Damn!"

"How long will it take for a tow truck, you suppose?" Joe asks, slaps a horsefly-sized mosquito off his neck, blood staining his hand.

"Tow truck? Now wouldn't that be nice? Not likely. Cell phone has no range and can't call out, can't call in."

"Will any water do?"

"Anything other than pissin' in the radiator. I'd even do that if I thought it'd help."

Joe looks at the murky canal. "Plenty of water here."

Frank-or-Fred-Something steps back and props his hands on his hips. Spits. "It'll have to do. I'll check the trunk for something to put her in."

As far as Joe can tell, Pop and Julio are still catching up on stories. Figures it'll help them pass the time and keep the little gay one from whining. Nice enough fella, but whiny.

In the trunk are various containers and duffle bags stuffed for emergencies—first aid, snack foods, blankets, Pop and Joe's ragged forty-year-old luggage and Julio's pristine blue oversized *Coach Bag* wrapped in a white garbage bag to keep it clean.

Frank-or-Fred-Something comes back with a plastic thirty-two-ounce *Circle K* cup and steps down to the canal, refills the radiator cup by precious cup, grumbling between trips about the state of government and social security.

Joe stands at the engine listening to cool water boil from the hot radiator, then quiet. Smacks another mosquito on his forearm and smears it on his thigh.

Fred-or-Frank-Something—rehearsing a tirade in his head for when he gets the piece of crap back to the shop—pushes the cup under canal water. A ripple expands from the other side and laps at his wrist. Just as he pulls the cup from the water, teeth grip his arm and yank him hard enough to pull him off his feet. He lands hard on his left side, arm under water, feels he's being dragged in.

Joe thinks the guy fell in, can already imagine the wet bitching when he comes back. It's the scream that tells him something's happened. Something *bad*.

At the edge of the canal, a gator's got Frank-or-Fred-Something up to the shoulder in a death roll so he won't fight so much. The gator doesn't seem intimidated by the screaming.

Joe stands frozen and useless, his mind trying to engage, sees the starched white shirt turn crimson, covered with mud and rotted vegetation. Thinks he sees *bone*.

He doesn't remember running, doesn't remember his hands diving into the trunk yanking out the tire iron, or the sprint back. He's vaguely conscious of repeated blows to the gator's head, the déjà vu of pulverizing human skeletal remains at the base of the dead pine behind his house. He blows out the gator's eye with the tire iron. That causes it to retreat without its meal. Breathless, Joe tries moving through the numbness, his brain soggy with adrenaline, the blood coated tire iron shaking in his hand. Not until Pop screams at him does reality sharpen again.

More screaming. Joe wonders how the poor guy can still manage to do anything, then realizes Julio's the one screaming—a high pitched wail of terror and drama that aggravates the whole thing. Joe shoves the tire iron in Julio's face.

"Shut the hell up or you're next!"

Julio slaps his hands to his mouth, swallows a scream, eyes saucer. Instant quiet. Except for the moaning coming from Frank-or-Fred-Something's direction. Pop's already at him, pulling off his belt for a makeshift tourniquet, knowing the arm's probably gone. All Pop's missing is mortar fire and he could be right back in Korea.

"Get some towels, JoJo. He's hurt bad. We gotta get him off this bank before the gator comes back. Might have friends. Go!"

Joe returns with the towel, complete with limo company logo, glances at Julio, hands to his face, still holding in screams. "You just gonna stand there!?"

"What chew wan' me to do?!" It comes out screechy and hysterical.

Joe doesn't answer, really doesn't expect him to do anything. He just can't stand the sight of him wringing his hands like the driver's about to die. Maybe he is.

"Deesinfecen!" Julio yells running back to the limo. He grabs a bottle of Absolut from the mini bar and runs back to the confusion by the canal bank to pour a good three cups of high end vodka onto the gaping wound.

Fred-or-Frank-Something screams and passes out. Pop and Joe look at Julio as if he'd poured on battery acid.

Joe grabs the bottle from Julio's hand, "What are you doing!?"

"To stop infeshion. Chew don' know the germs in there."

Joe's confused, asks Pop, "That true?"

"Don't think that's his biggest problem, boy. He's likely to bleed to death first. Now he just smells liquored up," Pop says. "We gotta get him outa here. Julio, go open the back door. Joe, help me get him to his feet."

Joe shoves the bottle at Julio and wraps a towel around the gaping wound. Hopes the arm won't fall off. Hopes even more the guy can make it to the car so they don't have to drag him—worries about the logistics of dragging a guy a good three hundred pounds by one arm in the dark and stuffing him in the back of a limo.

They get him to his feet and back to the car, barely. Blood, that at any other time would send Fred-or-Frank-Something into a tirade, smears the pristine white seats. Doesn't seem to care so much now. He's more or less out of it, eyes, at times, rolling to the back of his head or staring a hole through anyone he can focus on.

Joe looks at Pop hoping for good news like, *Yeah, boy, he'll be just fine—once I figure out how to clamp this artery.* There's an awful lot of blood. Joe thinks that maybe the guy can afford to lose more blood than the average man because of his weight and all. Doesn't know that's true, but sounds reasonable. Thinks about asking Pop if it's so, but thinks the timing's off.

"What's his pulse, boy?"

Joe shoves his fingers in Fred-or-Frank-Something's neck. "Goin' really fast. Could just be me, though."

Pop grabs Joe's hand and slaps it on the wound. "Push down hard. *Real hard.*"

Pop checks Fred-or-Frank-Something's pulse, shakes his head. "He ain't gonna last long like this. We gotta get him outa here."

Joe looks at the empty driver's seat. "I think the car can move now. Maybe enough to get to some help. I'll drive." Joe slides from the backseat.

Julio is still standing by the car, hands to his face, shaking—whimpering escapes in *peeps* and *hisses.* Doesn't dare scream out like he wants to, and suddenly realizes he's still got the bottle in his hand and takes a drink.

Joe yells at him, "Get in the back there and help Pop with the guy!"

"Wha' chew wan' me to do? I get sick. All that blood. I thin' I'm gonna pass out."

"You do and I'll sling your ass into the canal and let T-Rex finish his dinner."

"You name *him*? I get in the back," Julio whines flapping his hand, "but I get sick at the sight of blood."

Julio collects himself and sits on the very edge of the back seat trying not to get contaminated, shoves the bottle of vodka between his knees. The center partition rolls down.

Pop looks up, scowls, notices that Julio quietly dry heaves whenever he glances at the wound. "You're about as useless as tits on a boar, boy. Joe, change of plan. I need you back here. Let him drive." Turns to Julio, "You can drive, right?"

"Oo yes, I drive." Julio sounds happy for the alternative to hardcore field medic work, and doesn't share that he really doesn't drive all that much because he's terrified of heavy traffic and aggressive drivers and multi exits and large semi's and lane changes and… "Yes, I get us out of here."

Joe practically shoves Julio in the front seat, slams the driver's door and crawls in the back.

Julio places both hands on the steering wheel and freezes the way a fifteen-year-old might the first time behind the wheel. Brain goes blank like nothing's up there at all. No step one, step two, only a vast emptiness with nothing but fear to keep him company. He takes another drink and wedges the bottle between his thighs.

"Step on it!" Joe screams.

"I'm goin'!!" Julio screams back. Remembers the ignition and turns the engine over—a small but fulfilling victory.

"Go!" Joe yells again.

Julio drops the transmission into reverse and stabs the gas. The limo lurches slinging dirt and gravel, hardly moves as the tires spin underneath. Tires catch and the limo swerves backward and to the right. Julio shrieks and slams on the brakes. His vodka bottle pitches into the passenger seat. Pop and Joe are slung to the floorboard. Julio shoves the transmission into drive, turns the wheel, and stabs the gas. The limo fishtails down the dirt road in a cloud of dust and broken saplings unfortunate enough to be in the limo's way.

Could be because of how well Lincoln Town Car limos are made, or because they're all pumped up on adrenaline, they don't seem to notice how smooth the ride at sixty-five miles an hour on a pocked dirt road is. Slow moving opossums and armadillo are in peril trying to move from one side of the road to the other. Julio doesn't even notice them—tunnel vision, eyes straight through the windshield on the path ahead, nothing to the left or right. And he's not screaming any more, either. Teeth are clenched like his white knuckles around the steering wheel. He knows the hard road has to be coming up soon and when it does, brakes come to him as an afterthought. Applying the brakes after he hits the shoulder on the far side sends the limo into a slide, flushing mud and vegetation in the air. Limo jumps back to the hard road and Julio stabs the gas again roaring away in the dark to the next expressway entrance.

drinking peach cocktails with troopers

ON A WEDNESDAY night, traffic isn't so bad. Pop and Joe sway in the back as the limo weaves between motor homes, semis, and confused tourists. Julio's picked up a tail hugging his rear bumper, headlights high and blinding the rearview. From the side mirror, Julio sights Hummer H2 logo on the grill—sticks to the limo like a remora on a shark. Julio doesn't care; he's only vaguely concerned with a growing knocking in the engine.

"Find someplace with people and stop so we can get a medic," Pop yells, his hand in Fred-or-Frank's Something's bloody arm trying to clamp the wormy artery with his fingers.

Joe's got his fist pushed down on the guy's arm just below the shoulder, his own elbow aching. He glances up just as a blue sign flies by and yells, *"Rest Stop!"*

Julio cuts across three lanes of sporadic traffic and blows through a road construction barricade—*Ed's Signs* blinking orange lights—to catch the exit. Orange cones get sucked under the car and wedged under the chassis leaving florescent orange skids on the roadway. The bumper makes contact with two construction barrels. One bounces into the ditch and the second flies into traffic, glances off Hummer Boy sending the barrel to the other side of the road like discarded road kill. Hummer Boy doesn't slow down, doesn't stop.

Knocking in the engine gets louder like pigmies announcing the arrival of fresh heads for the stew. Steam drifts over the hood.

The rest area's full of tourists, mini vans, SUV's, pickups, folks desperate for the cruddy bathroom, maybe a quick burger or slice of hard pizza. Some guy's closing down for the night at a nice fruit stand of fresh Georgia peaches, Plant City strawberries, and Ruskin tomatoes set up out front of the main building all displayed in cute wooden baskets.

The knocking under the hood stops briefly, then like a missile, a piston rockets through the hood. The latch pops blowing the hood back against the windshield. Julio can't see a damn thing—screams and slams on the brakes. Limo jolts and slides to the left, collides with the fruit stand and all those cute baskets go airborne spewing produce.

ALL THE FAT trooper wanted was a nice dinner and a little peace and quiet. Standing out front, toothpick between his teeth, he surveys the disheveled parking lot. Doesn't seem to be any injuries except to the fruit. A crowd has gathered behind him peering through the glass, pointing, speculating cause. Those who were stretching and loitering in the parking lot, pick shreds of fruit guts from their vehicles, claim the five second rule and grab up what fruit they can for the trip home. Figure once it's out of the basket it's free.

Joe kicks the back door open and steps out. Under high wattage sodium parking lot lights onlookers grouped around the limo step back and moan. Covered in blood, chest to hands, Joe steps up to the trooper and asks, "Need an ambulance! Guy's hurt bad."

Pop's too busy to notice the irony of car crashes and fruit stands. His hip's seizing up and he no longer has feeling in the finger tips pinching off Fred-or-Frank-Something's artery. Thinks maybe the guy's just about dead by now.

Julio's still in the driver's seat in shock mumbling in Spanish. Could be praying. Through the windshield he notices people milling around staring at him. He checks his reflection in the rearview, notices the mess his hair's in. Smoothes it down at the sides, smiles and opens the door to address his *people.*

Trooper leans in the backseat, sucks his teeth, shakes his head, but doesn't touch anything. "What happened to the fella?" Looks at Joe because he seems to be in charge.

"Gator got him. Can you get an ambulance coming?"

"Looks like the old boy's gonna need more than that," Trooper says. "Who's the old man with him?"

"My father."

Pop looks up, sees the badge. "*Need a medic, Sarge!*"

"Who was driving?"

"Him," Joe says pointing to Julio standing at the front of the limo.

Trooper sniffs, "You all been drinking?" Sniffs again. "I smell an alcoholic beverage."

"Tried to clean him up. Not much in first aid, at least not for something this bad," Joe tells him. "Poured vodka on him. Don't know if it worked."

"That's your story? How do I know you all weren't drinkin' and didn't have some sort of fight? You say a gator. Got proof?"

"Wasn't exactly thinking about proof for the cops when the gator was dragging him into the canal. Thought it more important to get him help." Joe sees the panic sweeping Pop's face, looks back at the trooper. "Help's coming, right?"

"You say the little guy was drinking?"

"No, said he was drivin'."

"I'll have a talk with him."

"Got help comin' or not?"

"Air rescue quick enough for you, boy?" Trooper calls on his shoulder mic for Medi-Vac. Never takes his eyes off Joe while he does it.

"Sarge, I need a medic! Need cover fire while we pull him out."

"It's okay, Pop. He's got help comin'." Joe gestures to the trooper to do something. "Don't you guys have medical training?"

Trooper hikes his duty belt up as far as the muffin top gut overhang will allow. "First responder. Looks like your father has it under control. No need for me to interfere. Medi-Vac will be here before you know it."

Joe spins on his heel, slaps his thigh exasperated, "Great!" Mumbles, "Wouldn't want you to get your uniform dirty."

"What's that?"

"My shirt's dirty. Mind if I go clean up?"

Trooper glares at him in long exam kind of way just in case Joe flees the scene and he needs to remember details. "Don't make me come looking for ya. Come right back here with the old shirt. It's evidence. Got a report to fill out."

They're the same everywhere, Joe thinks. Cops looking to nail someone for something.

A pimply teenager runs up and snaps Joe's picture with a cell phone, runs to the car and takes a couple of shots of Pop with his hand in shoulder meat, then Julio who has his arms wrapped around himself enjoying the attention of strangers trying to console him after his harrowing experience.

By the time Joe comes out wearing a cheesy Florida Sunshine T-shirt and shorts, his bloody clothes wadded in a bag, the Medi-Vac helicopter has landed in an open field by the rest stop. Air from the rotors slings dried cut grass and dirt into a swirl and blows plastic bags aloft from the busted fruit stand, like balloons with handles. Dozens whip and drift across the parking lot, some all the way to the expressway. Pop's sitting hunched over on the edge of the back seat bloody from neck to knee. Joe's heart sinks at the exhaustion on the old man's face.

Medi-Vac boys work pretty quick. They get Fred-or-Frank-Something's artery clamped off for the trip. He's packed up and shoved into the helicopter as the crowd stands in the parking lot to watch it lift off and disappear in the dark.

Other than the limo and fruit stand, everything else goes back to normal. Sort of. Until a TV news truck with telescoping satellite rolls up with a fake-tanned reporter who jumps out and quickly checks his hair-do in the side mirror.

Pop's sitting on the sidewalk in a metal chair provided by the burger joint sipping a soda. The reporter shoves a mic in Pop's face, "Is it true you were directly involved in the incident?"

"You catch on fast, young fella." Pop says, pulling at his shirt. "Looks like I'm gonna need a new shirt. Pants, too. Don't think the blood'll come out. Good and set now."

"What was it like having your hand inside another human being?" reporter asks. Folks standing around move closer to listen in. Camera guy adjusts the lighting.

"Nothin' new. Did it in Korea. When I was under fire! Got hit, too. Want to see the scar?" Pop starts unbuckling his pants. Reporter waves him off and quickly moves on to Julio.

Joe shakes his head. He's perched on the trunk lid of the limo eating a bruised peach and watching Julio entertain a small crowd with his dramatic rendition of events. From what he can hear, Julio's explaining—through exaggerated hand and facial gestures—how he's more or less the one to save them all and trying way too hard to sound humble about it.

"Got a helluva mess. I do that?" Staring at Joe, Pop's clutching a soda with an outstretched hand towards the parking lot disaster. Cup quivers in his boney grip hard enough Joe can hear the rattle of loose ice.

It dawns on Joe that Pop's seriously convinced the whole mess is his fault. "Can't blame you for it, Pop. Julio did it."

"Who?"

"Julio." Joe says pointing to the front of the limo.

Pop stretches his neck examining the six or seven folks clustered in front of the limo. "Which one?"

"Squirrelly little fella in the middle there."

"Oh yeah. Gay guy. He drove. Glad it wasn't me."

"So am I. Come on. Let's get you in clean stuff. You're startin' to stink."

Pop slowly pulls his legs from the chair, stands stiff and wobbly. Leg's gone bad. Joe grabs his arm and helps him into the shop worrying about what's going on in the old man's head.

3

the difference between goats and humans is the lack of horns

DETECTIVE DENNIS CROY'S desk stands out. It's fastidiously neat. There are no personal effects like coffee mugs, photos, toys to play with. The desk represents the best of a Martha Stewart *good thing* work station right out of a magazine. In the top drawer, a can of linen scent Lysol and a container of disinfectant wipes used each time he leaves for the day.

He works at the desk the same way. A single notebook, report sheets with copies, an expensive ink pen bought at Office Depot. He liked the way it looked in the display case and when he held it in his hand in front of a mirror, liked the way it looked on him, so he bought two more in different colors to coordinate with his wardrobe.

No cups, no bottles, nothing to sweat or to stain the paperwork. Nothing, God forbid, to leak on his clothes. He gets ragged about it. Now and then someone plays tricks just to annoy him like leaving sweaty soda cans on his desk, or shoving everything out of order. They have fun watching him scurry about to make it all neat again—clean, wipe, polish. Cheap thrills when it's been a long day and they need a laugh.

But they don't laugh at his work product. And they don't laugh at the scale of his investigations, either. They figure he's probably one of those savants, but without the idiot part. He's got the OCD thing, instead, but with a little medication, keeps it in check. *Mostly.*

Tailored suits, crisp shirts with razor sharp creases, manicured nails: Croy's a walking bill board for harassment. Anyone can see it.

A decent TV sits on a console table against the wall. The breaking news story flashes across the screen in bright red text catching Croy's attention because he's always on the alert for breaking news. If it isn't local, it's CNN or FOX or CNBC to catch his eye. He sees Joe Salas' face on the screen, remembers him standing in front of a limo shoved nose first into what's left of a rickety wooden fruit stand. Joe's a prime suspect in several murders that Croy just can't find enough evidence to arrest him on.

Croy turns up the volume and squats in the closest chair, pulls it along under him to lean over until he's almost nosed into the screen.

Reporter's got a mic in Joe's face, camera going for the head shot. "Why didn't you call 911?" reporter asks.

"No cell coverage," Joe explains. "If we had waited, he'd be dead for sure. Didn't think we should chance it. My dad held him together as best he could."

"Pulling a man out of the jaws of an alligator and getting him help makes you a real hero, Mr. Salas. Your father, is that him?" reporter asks. Camera pans over the reporter's shoulder to a shot of an old guy sitting in a chair picking his nose.

Croy pushes back in his chair rubbing his forefinger and thumb together. He stands up watching the interview, the finger rubbing becoming more intense, a signal that his brain's calculating bits of facts, hoping for information big enough to feed a lead. "Yeah, you're a real hero, all right."

Back at his desk, Croy pulls the missing person file on a possible murder suspect, Ricky Vega and flips to Ricky's Department of Corrections file. Runs his finger down the page to family contacts. Ricky's wife, Betty Vega, name and address at the top—Betty, who'd been beaten to death at the hands of "Someone Unknown." Ricky Vega, top of the suspect list. There's also a mother and two brothers three counties north. They hadn't heard from Ricky, or so they said when Croy called, and they're not likely to tell him anything if they had. Mother, Bella, and brothers, Roy and Eddie all have records. Petty stuff mostly, except for Ricky who went felony for the armed bank robbery. They could be hiding Ricky out. Means a road trip for sure.

Croy closes the red file and opens a blue file with Joe Salas's name on it and re-reads his interview. An idea surfaces. It's a long shot, but the idea is so brilliant he can't help but smile because any time he can get to possible evidence without needing a search warrant is a good thing indeed.

Tapping on the computer keyboard, Croy waits as the printer hums and pukes the print out. An unintended blank sheet lies stuck to the first. He throws the blank sheet in the trash, because, in his mind, if a paper goes through the printer and comes out blank it's used. It's been pressed on, made contact with a foreign machine. It's fouled, tainted, and no longer clean. It must be thrown out. If any paper is wrinkled or torn it must be thrown out, never allowed to contaminate the pure.

When writing narrative reports he uses only fine tip pens. Each suspect file has a matching color pen. If the wrong colored pen is used with the wrong colored file, the entire report is thrown out and re-written with the proper colored pen. No red pen with the green file! And all files must be in sequential order and exactly one quarter inch apart. No one else in the department touches Croy's file cabinet. Ever.

He closes the file, carefully places it back in the cabinet, one quarter inch from the one next to it and heads out the door.

HER STINT IN jail hasn't helped her attitude much. Dee Dee Turner sits at the kitchen table sulking like a dog that's been dumped in the pool against its will. Before her are six bags of various snack foods, two boxes of Cheez-its, two cartons of Krispy Kremes, a liter of orange soda and a large bag of peanut M&M's.

She's naked. Being a home nudist, she's naked most of the time and intends on sitting in this very spot until she's eaten everything on the table. Damn her gall bladder. Damn the doctor's opinions. Damn the cops. Damn them all. And it's a rude interruption to her day when Detective Croy comes knocking.

Dee Dee pays no mind to her lack of attire, opens the door with one hand groping a bag of Hot Tostitos crushed between her breasts.

"Whatcha want!"

Croy steps back and spins to his left. "Ms. Turner, I'm Detective Croy and I'd like to ask you a few questions about your neighbor."

Dee Dee examines Croy up and down, rubs spicy salt across her hip. *Nice suit. Clean hands. Well groomed.* She's smiling without realizing it. "Yeah? And who'd that be?"

"Mr. Salas. But if it's a bad time I can come back," he says to the porch column.

"Oh, no. You don't want to hear what I got to say about that little mother—" She crams three chips in her mouth while overtly inspecting Croy's ass.

"Do you have something you can put on? Or I can just come back."

"Oh, now you're interested. Didn't care when he kilt my dog. Come on in and I'll find me a robe."

Croy can hear her move from the door and chances a quick glance to be sure she's out of sight. Despite being invited in he feels safer on the porch. First time in fifteen years someone's come to the door naked.

"Come on in!" She's moving through the living room wrapped in a brown fuzzy robe resembling a bear pelt on a fur trader— as if she tackled and killed it herself and relished the skinning. Dee Dee wanders back to the kitchen barefoot. Croy drifts behind.

House is dark, curtains closed, lamps layered in dust. There's a weird sour yeasty smell drifting through the air. And mold. Croy's hand dips inside of his jacket searching for the little bottle of hand sanitizer. Notebook. Pen. No hand sanitizer. *Damn!*

There's an audible *crack!* from the kitchen chair when Dee Dee plops down on it. She doesn't seem to notice. His detective eye watches the weak third leg, senses one more time and it'll probably splay out from under her. Prays it doesn't happen while he's here. The thought of trying to get her off the floor and having to touch her sweaty doughy flesh…he'll make the interview quick.

"How long have you known Mr. Salas?"

"Long enough. Kilt people. Lots of 'em," she says pouring orange soda into a dirty glass. Holds the bottle up, "Want some?"

"No thanks. How do you know he kills people?"

"I seen 'em. Draggin' 'em back in that shed out there to whack their heads off."

"Did you call the police?" He knows she did, but wants a cold reaction.

Dee Dee looks up at him as if he's insulted her dead dog. "Did I call the PO-lice? Had 'em out here three or four times! And they put *my black ass* in jail 'cause they were too damn stupid to find anythin'." Shoves her hands on her hips, tilts her head, "Does he give a lot of money to the Police Benevolent Association? 'Cause if it gives him a free ride, I'll tell you now," she says pushing boxes aside with her forearm, "this here bitch's not giving one more damn dime to you people." She grabs the box of Krispy Kremes, digging her stubby forefinger into the lip of the lid until it shreds.

Croy watches her stuff a donut in her mouth. It's like watching a car crash.

Flipping the cover to the back of the pad, Croy jots a note. "How many people do you think you saw?"

"Think! I didn't *think* I saw nothin' no matter what those cracker ass doctors try to make me believe. I *seen* him drag one guy in during the hurricane. Then…" elbow propped on the table, donut icing dripping through her fingers, "there was some other poor fool, but didn't see him come in. Just his head up on that work bench wrapped in plastic like some God-awful Easter ham." Dee Dee shoves the remaining donut into her mouth and stands up. Chewing thoughtfully, she nods so she doesn't lose her train of thought while talking through the side of her mouth. "A woman, too. But she wasn't dead." She swallows. "Not yet. Had a towel over her head. And I just had to peek. Lord a' mercy."

"Have you ever seen these people before?"

"Didn't know 'em from a damn hole in the head." She pours the rest of the orange soda in the glass. "Sure you don't want some? Almost gone."

"That's very kind. Restricted diet," he tells her flipping another page.

"Whatcha got? The sugar? Or somethin' worse?"

She's interested. He can see it on her face. Thoughts skitter through his mind on what to call it. "Allergies."

"Allergies? What to?"

"Everything." Hopes that ends the diet inquisition.

"Everything? I got me some allergies, too." Pulls another donut from the pack and squeezes it in half seemingly entertained as it's crushed between her thumb and forefinger.

"Allergies to what?" he asks halfheartedly, just for something to say while he finishes writing his sentence.

"To not eating. Bet you couldn't see that," she chuckles, cramming donut in her mouth.

Croy gives a quick smile. "What do you think happened to them?"

"What you mean?" she asks out of the side of her mouth.

"With the bodies? How do you suppose he disposed of them?"

The tie on her robe falls loose and Dee Dee's large boobs swing freely. She purposely slow-licks the icing off her fingers and pulls the robe back together as an afterthought.

"Hell if I know. Drove 'em off somewhere or maybe dumped 'em in the cans. I'm not the PO-lice. Just know what I seen and you're not tellin' me no different." She plops down on the chair again. "He knows what he done and knows I know it."

"Well, if you think of anything, give me a call." He hands her a card. "Have you ever seen any of those people at his house before?"

"You mean 'fore he slaughters 'em?" She takes the card, reading. "No. Only one I ever seen there was that spic chick a his. She hasn't been around in awhile. You married?"

"No. That must have been Betty Vega."

"She got my dog."

"I thought you said Mr. Salas killed your dog." Croy jots notes.

"Yeah, but I can't prove it. He more or less said so."

"How's that?"

"During the hurricane. I snuck out to his shed," she says hunched over as if re-enacting the event. "But a big old bolt a lighting struck and I *hollered!* Tipped him off, don't you see. I tried to get back to the house but he was too quick. Caught me by the fence and said, 'You spying on me?' And I says, 'Leave me alone!' Then," she cowers and hisses, "he says, 'keep outa my business if you don't want to end up like your dog!!' What do you think a that?"

Croy's staring at her trying to connect that whole rendition of events to a murder plot. "Well, it must have been frightening for you." Jots notes on his pad and stuffs it back inside his jacket with the pen, fights the overwhelming urge to wash his hands.

Dee Dee pops out of the chair and is in his face before he can turn for the door.

"You say I can reach you at this number?" She's smiling hopefully holding the card as if a prized possession. "You believe me, don't ya?"

"If you have information, just call," Croy says heading for the door. She's on his heel as if trying to beat him to it. He turns to ask another question and she is practically on top of him. "Ever notice anything going on down in the woods behind the house?"

She's so close Croy can smell the remains of donut on her hot breath. Her ample breasts have him pinned to the door.

"You thinkin' somethin's going on back in there?"

"If you don't think so, then it must not. If you'll excuse me."

"If you ain't busy, come on over and we'll get us a bite to eat. Could use a little meat on them bones." She's got her hand on the door knob, gooey donut icing glistening at the edge of her full mouth. She isn't pulling the door open like Croy's expecting and he feels a little trapped.

"I have a very busy schedule. Going out of town," he tells her stuffing his hands in his pockets. Fears he'll have to fight his way out.

"Call me when you get on back now. I make me a mean banana puddin'."

The door whooshes open and he feels the fresh air like a bird released from the jaws of a cat.

"You have you a good day!" she yells after him on the porch. She's got her robe bunched tight at the top, but the bottom separates and the brown bear pelt reveals a frightening black muff. All he can do is raise his hand and get the key in the car door as fast as possible. Realizes giving her his number was probably a really bad idea.

CROY'S STANDING JUST outside the property line at the Salas's back gate that leads to the pond, squirting hand sanitizer in his palm. He's watching the department's best K9 cadaver dog work its way around the pond in a three-hundred-foot radius. Croy's watched the dog work before, but on this particular day, the dog is displaying the erratic behavior of a crack addict. It hits on a plot, digs, runs to another plot, digs, runs to another plot, on and on for the better part of an hour. At each site tagged, some poor academy recruit shovels away sifting for remains only to give up in frustration. Until the last hole that yields a bone.

"Got something!" Recruit gently extracts the bone from its resting place, cradles it in his two hands like it's the Holy Grail.

Croy's heart races, imagining the arrest, the televised coverage, a book deal, maybe a position as a paid consultant for CNN.

The kid's face beams a reflected dream of by-passing the tedious road grunt work of patrolman and going straight into the detective division—getting all the big homicide cases or probing deep in the guts of some white collar political conspiracy case. Drug cases don't interest him so much. Smoking dope and experimenting with various white bread drugs have left him apathetic for drug stings and small-time dealers. Lived too long around people like that in his neighborhood.

Both are almost shaking as the recruit hands Croy the bone. Croy turns it over. Examines the length. The shape.

"Not human." Hands it back.

"What? How do you know?"

"Shape. Size. Probably goat. Dig deeper and you might find the rest of it."

"Aw, man." Recruit withers and returns to dig in another hole less enthusiastically.

All in all, the dog hits on almost fifteen plots until it lies down exhausted at the handler's boots. Handler looks in Croy's direction and shrugs.

Croy yells, "What does that mean?"

"Hell if I know. Something might have been here, but I can't say with certainty. How do you want me to write this up?"

"Training exercises. Does this happen very often?"

"What?"

"The dog going nuts like that."

"It's an animal, not a machine. Has bad days and good. Having a bad one. He's shot for the day. You need anything else?"

"Yeah, a body."

"Good luck with that." Dog handler pulls on the lead. The dog looks up, tongue hanging, panting. Handler pulls again, gives a command. Dog reluctantly crawls to his feet and obediently follows. Jumps in the back of a marked Ford Explorer.

Croy wanders down to the lone recruit still digging by the pond. "How many holes does that make?"

"Too many," recruit mumbles, sifting through muck. Suddenly dawns on him he's not going in as a detective and one bad word from Croy and he can forget getting hired at all. "I mean, there's nothing here, sir. You want me to dig further down?" He's sweat soaked his once crisp white T-shirt and his black BDU's. Mud greases his face.

"How far down did you go?"

"A good two or three feet, but when the dog passed over it again, it didn't seem interested anymore." Recruit surveys the land. "Was old grove land once. Who knows what's out here."

"We know goats for sure," Croy says. "You can take off. Be sure to fill out a special detail sheet."

"Yes, sir. Have a nice what's left of your afternoon."

Croy moves back to the Salas' back gate. Uses a branch to scrape mud off his shoes. Thinks about how Joe could have gotten rid of so many bodies without leaving evidence. At least evidence he can use in court.

He flips the branch to the ground and walks back to his car. Pops the trunk. Takes out another pair of shoes, slips out of the dirty ones, slips into the clean ones and places the muddy ones in a plastic bag. Carefully sets them in the trunk. Squirts hand sanitizer in his palm. "Stupid dog."

4

two-headed demon of the moon stop

EDDIE LIKES TO sit in the car out in the parking lot and watch women as they pass his car, a white Pontiac four-door with a cool spoiler on the deck lid, his chick magnet, chicks that think he's younger than thirty. Doesn't tell them any different.

He's in the car because he hates the grocery store, leaves it for his older brother Roy to push past the brain-dead old people clogging the aisles, vapor locked on coupons, two for one sales, or where they parked the car.

Eddie checks his reflection in the rearview, staring back in mirrored sunglasses—mirrored, the best kind so no one can see what he's watching. Adjusting the left earring, he inspects the mirror again to see if the gold chain draped around his neck looks as cool as it did at home. He sweeps his hand over the shellac hair hoping no one notices the bald spot that he hides with that late night-infomercial spray-on fake hair. Thinks it works pretty good.

His favorite song on Rock Radio gets him moving, his head bobbing and weaving, and he rolls down the window, cranks up the sound, and starts singing out loud—secretly hoping people will notice and compliment him on his talent and ask why he hasn't tried out for American Idol. He'll say because he's got serious business deals going on and maybe when things slow down, he'll give the public a treat and show them real talent.

A broad in a Mustang pulls in next to him and he watches her step out, fiddle with her purse to press the alarm button on her key chain. He considers whether she's married or not, a game he plays in his head, sometimes with Roy, and so far, he's three for three. Married ones walk different. Those that don't want to be married anymore walk like those who aren't. What he told Roy.

This one, she's single and with lots of junk in the trunk, just the way he likes it, and he turns up the radio hopeful she'll glance his way. Maybe she'll notice him and be totally captivated by what she sees, won't be able to resist engaging in small talk or at least an exchange of phone numbers. It can happen.

He runs his hands over his bare arms to feel the flex of his biceps, glad he wore the wife-beater T-shirt today because no woman can resist that look. He can barely handle it looking at himself.

So, she doesn't look his way, but he watches her bend over to check her lipstick in the side mirror, bound in super-low jeans, shifting ever so slightly as she wipes the corners of her mouth. Never gives a look in his direction as she slips into the Walgreens. In his book, that makes her a bitch.

He beats his fingers on the steering wheel to the rhythm on the radio, lost in his head to some rock concert he imagines being the headliner in, dreaming of panties and bras flying at him from the crowd, lots of hot chicks waiting backstage. They crawl all over him begging they can't get enough. At least in his mind.

Eddie watches Roy come back weaving through parked cars, the weight of grocery bags and a gallon water jug straining his stringy biceps, a cordial grin easing people he makes eye contact with along the way despite the shoulder length white hair and skull tattoo on his bare forearm. Eddie cocks his head out of the window and says, "You get everything? We're not comin' back."

Fingers on the door handle to the backseat, Roy suddenly stops and considers.

"Better pop the trunk."

Trunk opens and Roy drops in supplies. Slams the trunk.

"You get the duct-tape?" Eddie's head's in a strange position because he's looking straight up at the sky with his head twisted half out the window like he's not talking to anyone in particular. "Don't have enough for the next one."

"Shut up," Roy sighs. "That's your problem. You never know when to shut up." Roy slides in next to Eddie and opens the glove compartment, pulls out a thirty-eight and tucks it in his belt at the small of his back. Turns the radio down. "Run by the bank. Need to cash the check. Found some of those small bungee cords, too. Took all they had."

"Good for you. Can we go?" Eddie's impatient and starts beating on the steering wheel again. Nervous energy. Hyperactivity the doctor said, among other things.

"Didn't take your pill, did you?" Roy rotates his hand as a gesture for Eddie to start the car and get going.

"Ran out. Got beer, right?"

"And everything else on the list. You not being on your pills sucks for all of us."

"Don't sweat it, Roy boy, haven't let you down yet, have I?"

Roy turns to the backseat and grabs a handful of crumpled blanket, flips up a corner exposing a petite white female maybe twenty, but not over. She's crouched on the floorboard, trembling, her face tearstained and ruining what was perfectly applied makeup. A strip of dull gray duct-tape seals her mouth, and somewhere underneath, her hands are bound with cord from a pair of Roy's pajama pants.

"After this one, I need a break," Roy says. "What do you think about Vegas? Take a couple a weeks off?"

"I don't know, Roy. It's up to them. They just can't seem to get enough of me."

A ONE CAR dirt road winds through thicket and stunted oaks that open up on a small secluded single story in need of paint. A blue 1972 Chevy Suburban is parked lopsided next to the house, the tires on the right side flat down to the rims. Left to weather, sun scalded and frozen, a tattered tarp hangs precariously over the backend.

Roy and Eddie drive like they know where they're going because going is home. Eddie doesn't waste anytime getting out of the car and is on the top step before the car door slams.

Inside, dinner's stewing, frying, smoking on the stove, things in the oven, food enough for an army. Eddie and Roy have done a hard day's work and barely give a glance to the old woman at the sink, dirty dish towel slung over her shoulder, smears of flour, gravy, and beef blood across her cheek and right breast. They sit at the table and take careful inventory—not much said other than Eddie's remark it all looks pretty good.

At the sink, Bella pulls plates from the drainboard and sets one each, flicks stray hair from her face back behind her ear. Doesn't say anything back until they're all well into eating.

"How'd it go today?"

It's an honest question, if not without a tone of suspicion, and she looks up into each man's face taking her own inventory for lies and decadent behavior because all men lie and wallow in decadent behavior, it's just a matter of catching them at it. She doesn't smell whiskey, Satan's brew, the elixir of the devil, and that lets them eat in peace. *For now.*

They know she's prying, watching, as if each bite is a test and if they fail she'll be sure they choke on it. It's what they believe. They believe it because Roy and Eddie came from her womb. Hard to believe looking at them—she appearing older than a mother, more likely grandmother.

"Got those supplies, Ma. And Roy here, he cashed the check. Show her, Roy."

Roy's head pops up and starts nodding like one of those bobble head dolls, mouth full of chicken fried steak, too full to swallow, but not enough room to speak. So, he bobbles, first at her, then back at Eddie so she doesn't think Eddie's pulling a fast one. If Eddie pulls a fast one, they all suffer.

Still chewing, Roy slides the cash from his back pocket and shoves it at her plate like an offering. Avoids eye contact and goes right back to cutting meat.

"It all here?" she asks looking up from the multicolored twenties spread by the tea glass. "Don't look like it's all here."

"Supplies," Roy chokes out, grabs his tea and washes stuff down before it jams in his throat.

"He found it all, Ma. Everything you wanted. Every bit."

Before Eddie can fork a green bean, a steak knife stabs the table inches from his wrist.

"You know what I want!" Bella stands up. Not quick, but slow, like a cobra standing its ground, weaving, eyeing one to the other. "Moon's full," she whispers.

"We got it all."

"Where is it?"

"In the car. We knew we'd be late for dinner if we waited."

She turns to the window and stares. Just stares, off in some world of her own, maybe taking her own inventory. Eddie glances at Roy but neither speaks. They keep eating. And waiting.

"Got the tape?"

"Fresh roll. Still wrapped up in that cellophane. Got cords, too. Thought you'd like that, Ma," Roy says to his plate. Won't look at her. Senses she's drifted into the *black mood* quieter than in the past, wonders if it means some sort of change is happening and if it is a change, then what does it mean for him and Eddie, because they got a long night ahead depending on that *black mood.*

"I don't know I'm feelin' so well today," she says in a soft melancholy voice. She turns back to the table and sits back at her plate sipping her tea.

Eddie and Roy look at each other, but only briefly. Any longer and it might set her off and away from this softer side, a side that might let them go to bed tonight or watch a movie, maybe play a hand of cards. She used to like the cards, but not so much now. Her needs changed. About the time of the *moon stop*. Calls it the *moon stop* from the translation from the doctor down the road there. Not a real doctor like what you'd find in a hospital, but the spiritual ones that know the herbs and poultices to cure things. Menopause-moon stop, whatever you call it, it's like living with a two-headed demon, and wherever the old Bella is, it won't let her out.

Roy's thinking about all this when he looks up and sees she's staring right at him and he looks over at Eddie who's staring at him too, but his face has panic in it, and it's too late as a plate sails past his head. Didn't even see her hand move.

Eddie's finished and gets up from the table, thinking while she's distracted with Roy—poor Roy—he can give her the slip and hit the woods for the night, but she's quicker than that and has him by the wrist with a death grip like when he was little.

She hisses, "You're goin' *where?*" Her eyes still fixed on Roy who's picking green beans off his shoulder.

"Just gonna put my plate in the sink, Ma." Eddie lies. Suspects she knows he's lying, but telling her he was gonna make a run for it would just piss her off. Not as if she's not pissed off now and he can't remember why. At least not for sure. Hard to keep track. The *black mood* isn't so soft anymore and that shoots the night off right in the head.

"Did you bring me one? It got to be regular. 'Cause if it ain't regular—"

"Got it in the car, Ma. Told you so."

With the last word barely out of his mouth, her hand hits his cheek. She loses a nail in the process and that'll stew in her craw for days. It'll be his fault.

"Don't back talk me, boy. You go out an' get it. Put it in *the bunker* there and start digging the hole. Go with him, Roy. Neither one of you is worth a shit, but I can't dig the hole."

Eddie wants to say he doesn't want to, but keeps his mouth shut. The last time he told her he didn't want to do something, she stuck him in *the bunker* and he's hated small confined spaces ever since.

"Gotta do something with it even if I don't feel right," she says.

And that gives Eddie hope. He could just drive off a few miles and dump the girl off by the woods to find her way home and that'd be the end of it.

Bella's looking at him, straight in the eye as if she can read his mind, "Don't start getting' no ideas, neither. She's mine tonight and she'll end up like the last of 'em so don't start gettin' ideas. *Roy! Start on the hole!*"

The plate slips from Roy's hand and it lands on the table, wobble-spinning as if he's practicing a trick. Everyone stops to watch it. His heart's pounding in his chest as if the wobble plate's an omen and depending how it stops could mean the difference between life and death—his.

Killing and planting women has been going on way too long, he knows it, just can't figure a way to stop it without getting implicated, not to mention the things he did for Bella when she got done with them. Stupid Eddie, calls him stupid Eddie, but not to his face because he'll run and tell Bella—stupid Eddie who thinks up shit on his own without telling anyone until it's too late.

Almost cost them when some damn girl mentioned Eddie coming on to her in the parking lot of the grocery store to the cops canvassing information about missing women. Stupid Eddie never could keep his dick in his pants, his dick that does all the thinking and now here he is cleaning messes up after the both of them.

All this time while Roy's thinking, Bella's signaled for Eddie to get the girl out of the car, still staring at Roy, who's forgotten time is passing, and she's suspicious thinking he's hiding something, something like decadent behavior only because she's seen Eddie do it. Caught Roy once as a kid, but all men are the same, and he was in close enough proximity to be involved and in her eyes, that made him guilty.

"Forgot where the shovel is?"

The word "shovel" catapults him out of his thoughts and Roy bolts for the door, needs to get through it before Eddie. Doesn't know why. Practically knocks him down going for the door knob, and when he swings it open, it knocks Eddie in the knee. Gives Roy enough time to slide past him to the shed, hears Bella yell, *"I'm needin' my vision!"*

Eddie doesn't know what the hell's going on other than they ain't going to get to sleep tonight while Bella does her thing. They'll have to stand around outside *the bunker* and wait. They fell asleep one time while waiting and when he woke up Bella had set a severed head on his chest. Then he had to stay in *the bunker* there with the body while Roy dug the hole and thinks to this day Roy took his sweet time knowing he was in there waiting with the head.

Roy skulks out to the shed and pulls the shovel from the corner. Out back beyond the woods line he walks measured paces so he doesn't dig into a grave already full. After years of this crap it's getting hard to keep track. Should of wrote it down somewhere, but didn't think Bella would keep doing it. But she does seem much better after and stays that way for a good six to eight months. Thinking about it, he realizes it's only been three months since the last one and that the two-headed demon has an appetite that rivals a jackal's.

In the dark where sound carries better than in the day, Roy can hear squeals and cries coming from the front of the house. Knows Eddie's pulled the poor thing out of the back seat, ripped off the tape, and handed her over to Bella. Poor thing probably thinks she's safe looking at Bella's face, until she looks deeper or just waits and realizes Bella isn't giving her comfort or motherly concern. She'll discover the true threat just like he and Eddie did, but won't have anything to bargain with. She isn't related to Bella. Too bad.

He remembers some of the girls in the past begging, yelling, swearing. They all tried something a little different. This one, she sounds like a sheep. Not much fight at all. And he wants her to fight, fight hard because he's sick of it, sick of the routine of feeding Bella's demon.

Bella wasn't a dream to live with *before* she met with the doctor, but at least they didn't have blood on their hands. Not sure what the doctor told her, and Roy will never know since the old quack died mysteriously soon after. Whatever was said, stuck. It seared into Bella's head and she took it on as religion, and her common sense died as mysteriously as the doc.

It's never going to end, he thinks, and digs relentlessly in the dark. Doesn't even use a flashlight.

An hour passes and Eddie never does come back to help, which makes Roy think Eddie's gotten his once Bella was done with her, and for some reason it pisses him off. As soon as it pops in is head, he hears something being dragged through the woods. It's Eddie, pulling the girl behind by one arm because he's too damn lazy to hitch her up over his shoulder and carry her, probably because he doesn't want to get blood all over himself. He'd bitched on and on once about how hard it was getting dried blood out of the prized gold herringbone chain he wears around his neck.

Eddie lets the body drop at his feet and sighs as if he's had to work hard, brushes his hands off, and turns back to the house.

Roy looks down at the poor thing, exsanguinated and pathetic, black mascara smearing her cheeks like War paint.

Pulls the thirty-eight from behind his back and says, "You're an asshole, Eddie. Any one ever told you that?"

Eddie turns, thinking how stupid Roy is to pick this time of all times to start a fight. At least it won't be him sitting in *the bunker* alone in the dark. And Roy has to finish burying her, too. Never gets to say it out loud.

Roy pulls the trigger and Eddie goes down right on top of the girl.

Roy grabs Eddie's arm—not sure he's even dead yet and doesn't care—and rolls him into the hole. In the distance he can hear Bella yelling for Eddie, because Eddie's taking too long to get back, and if he wasn't dead, he'd be going into *the bunker* for the night. Roy yells back at her knowing she won't be able to understand a word he's saying from this distance, but it's okay. Just needs her close. And it works. He can hear her rustling through the brush, the two-headed demon in full control of her mouth, speaking in tongues. By the time she gets to him, she's in full fury.

"No one makes me wait!" she shrieks. She's blood-covered from head to toe, would do a wash down with the garden hose, but Roy has no intention on letting her leave to do it, he has other ideas.

"Where's Eddie? That boy run off? He bring you the body or is it missing too, you deviant perverts straight from hell, should of slit your throats the day you was born, not like I'm gaining a thing but hole diggers," she rambles on.

"You remember that old hound we used to have? The one Davis gave us a few years back?" Roy interrupts.

Just asking the question shuts her up because she can't think on two things at once no matter how many heads the demon has—probably just one brain—and she stops talking and starts thinking and says, "The one that kept killin' the chickens?"

"Yeah, that one."

"What about it?"

"Remember what happened to it?"

"Shot it."

Apparently two-headed demons are easily confused because that's how Bella looks, even in the dark under a full moon. Roy's seen her plenty of times under a full moon and knows she looks the same every time, and in the morning, she'll be sweet and calm and they'll have months of peace until, like a werewolf, she'll start to change again and make him drive out somewhere to snatch some young girl off the street to feed the two-headed demon of the moon-stop.

"Well, what about it?"

"We knew that dog would never stop killing them chickens, that's why. Sometimes you just have to put 'em down."

The wind rises and Bella's clutching a sapling with an outstretched hand, her dress hem, weighed down with blood, drifting around her legs.

Roy can't speak. Can't move. Could be fear instigating tricks in his head. Thinks she's turned into Medusa, her long, blood-soaked, hair twisting in sections floating around her face like snakes. Her eyes shine like black onyx.

For a moment he swears he can see it, the demon inside, just a glimpse, or shadow, the soul of it staring back through her eyes, a look that turns him cold to the marrow. He thinks of the girl lying under Eddie in the hole, shuts his eyes, raises the gun and pulls the trigger.

Bella drops, and at that very moment Roy's free. He thinks he hears her voice, but it's just the wind whispering past his ear. He dumps her in the hole and covers them all up. He washes up at the house, starts packing his stuff, and slings his duffels in the back of Eddie's car. At some point he'll dump the Pontiac, hitch to another state and start over. Maybe Vegas. And maybe he'll find a good woman to share his life with. One not in menopause.

LUCKY FOR DETECTIVE Croy, old Roy, worn out from a hard night, has fallen asleep during the process of packing up—a good twelve hours of sleep, stretched sideways on the bed, fresh grave dirt caked to his boots. Bella would have had a fit if she was to catch him like that. Otherwise Croy would have missed him for good.

Walking up the dirt drive, Croy notices the Pontiac's rear door wide-open with a couple of duffels on the backseat, dew settled on the interior door panel which he takes to mean it's been open like that all night. Weird. Whole scummy place is weird and unkempt by way of crap strewn in the yard and the dilapidated Suburban leaning by the house, the tarp now blown off and crumpled in a heap on the ground.

Banging on the screen door thunders through the house and Roy dreams Bella's come out of the grave for him. Wakes with a start and slides off the bed still in his street clothes, dried sweat refreshed by the nightmare. Doubles his stink factor.

Screen door swings open ahead of the stink and he sees Croy standing there all crisp and shiny, fresh as a…doesn't know what he's fresh as. The guy's either government or a real estate broker, not sure which, but either way he intends on sending him on his merry fresh way.

A gold badge pops in Roy's face, Croy holding it there long enough for him to read the credential's fine print. Most people don't, but Roy's been around the block a few times and was born with a suspicious gene directly from Bella.

"Who the hell are you?"

"Detective Croy. I believe I spoke to a Bella Vega a couple of weeks ago. She in?"

"She is not. Spoke to her about what?"

"Her boy Ricky. Who are you?"

"It matter?"

"You're either Eddie or Roy."

"Housekeeper. All you need to know."

"Okay, housekeeper. I've been trying to locate Ricky Vega. Seen him around in the last couple of weeks?"

"Nope."

Croy pulls a scented hanky from his pocket and furtively covers his nose. "Has he called or sent anything to the house?"

"Nope."

"Well, good. He's missing." Croy turns like he's going back to the car and sees from the corner of his eye how Roy's hooked on the *missing* part.

"Hey, missing from where?"

"I'll take that up with Bella when she calls," Croy says. Reaches into his jacket retrieving one of his cards to hand back to Roy.

"What if I'm Roy or Eddie then?"

"Then I'd tell Roy or Eddie that no one has heard from or had any contact with Ricky since his wife died."

"Betty? In Eustis? What happened to Betty?"

"Suspicious death."

"You sayin' Ricky had something to do with it?"

"I'm not saying anything other than no one's seen him since she died."

"He just got out of prison. But you know all that, I imagine. Doesn't make him a killer, you know."

"No, sir. Just makes him missing."

"You thinkin' someone got him, too?"

"Don't know anything for sure, housekeeper. Have Bella give me a call when she gets in." With that, Croy steps off the porch glancing left and then right as he makes his way back to his car. Not a soul in sight other than three or four turkey vultures circling overhead.

DUST PLUMES TRAIL behind Croy's car as he drives through the woods toward home.

Roy stands hanging on the screen door watching the dust rise above the tree tops a good half mile before it fades. He turns, considers what his next move is. A shower first. Then a peaceful breakfast. After that he'll lock the place up and be on his way. Use this as a vacation place.

After a hot shower and clean clothes, Roy stands at the stove fryin' eggs, a handful of potatoes, and ham. Scrapes it all onto a plate and gets comfortable on the sofa to eat. He hikes his feet up on the coffee table and points the remote at the TV. Was never allowed to eat on the sofa when Bella was alive, but she's not, and he enjoys the news and a little peace and quiet. Peace that's mildly interrupted by an annoying thumping he ignores through breakfast. Loose siding. He'll need to fix it before he goes else the rain finds its way under the wood and rots it to the foundation. Then he'll have termites, then no house at all.

5

eating with zombies

CROY ALWAYS DID like those little trips out of town, trips that give him a chance to cruise through some of the lesser known areas that scrub the underbelly of polite society extinguishing a fever that flares in him every now and then. Connections on the internet whiz him through cyberspace to dark cracks and crevices never cleaned, only explored by those with fetishes. All guys have fetishes of one kind or another, some are into body parts, others more decadent, influenced by bodily functions not talked of around proper holiday dinners.

Croy slid into fascination with transvestite prostitutes about the time of his promotion to patrol lieutenant.

Once back home he'll spend an hour with a scrub brush under a scalding hot shower, alcohol, and disinfectant cleaner he gets in bulk from a hospital supply place—Sani-Kill, deodorizer, virucide, tuberculocidal, fungicide, mildewstat. Not really recommended for personal cleaning, but he feels it'll cover just about anything. Then he's good to go for a couple of months.

HEAVY RAINS DRAW out hidden secrets in a building. Growing mold, percolating sewer leaks, animal infestation in the walls. Croy obsesses over the possibilities as he walks the halls at the P.D. Wonders what's growing in the carpet.

"How'd the interview go?" Detective Arnold asks shuffling from the other end of the hallway. Arnold's ready to pull the pin, to wrinkle away on the beach and die in his sleep in the arms of some redhead hoping to inherit his pension. Only three months left to go.

"I don't think they know where he is," Croy says. Tilts his chin and sniffs the air. Moves close to the wall, sniffs again.

"Really? Why is that?"

"Only one there was Roy. He hasn't got a clue where his brother is."

"You believe him?"

"He was too surprised by the whole thing."

Arnold shrugs and shoves a folder in Croy's hand. "New missing person case."

Croy flips the cover, reads the report. "She owns the gallery on Bay?"

"That's the one."

"Who reported her missing?"

"One of the artists she represents. Had an appointment."

Croy walks four or five more steps and sniffs the wall again. "Does she have anything to do with the gallery on Orange?"

"Don't know, why?"

"No reason.." Croy waves Arnold over close to the wall. "You smell that?"

Arnold hesitates, reluctantly sniffs at the wall. "Nope. Smells like a wall. What do you smell?"

"Stachybotrys."

"What's that?"

"A slimy black mold. Dried, it looks less slimy."

"You don't say? Where's it come from?"

"Water soaked cellulose from leaking roofs or pipes. Probably puffing spores through the building as we speak. Right into the air vents making us all sick."

"How sick?" Arnold's head is cocked in a funny way slightly alarmed.

"*Pulmonary hemosiderosis.*"

"What does that do?"

"Causes severe bleeding in the lungs. One day, you start coughing up blood or get nose bleeds. Next thing you know you're on a ventilator. It's a bad thing, Arnie."

"You're pulling my leg."

"I wouldn't pull anything, Arnie. It's worse than asbestos. Probably have that in the building, too."

"Well, just when you thought it was safe to go back to your desk." Arnold shakes his head, turns, and continues down the hall muttering, "Bad enough we have to dodge bullets and now...*killer mold*."

"Place was locked and her car was in the driveway. That's weird," Croy says out loud. Continues to sniff the walls and read at the same time. Flips pages, sniffs, reads some more. By the time he's back at his desk he's certain mold's growing in the walls and Lydia Stein-Von Gloss didn't leave of her own free will.

"Art."

"What's that?" Arnie asks over his glasses. His desk faces Croy's, so Croy's need to talk to himself is pointless if he wants to keep it close to the vest.

"Art connection to another case. Maybe nothing."

"What connection?"

"Not enough information yet, Arnie," Croy says reading the rest of the file. "It's just a gut feeling."

Arnie's only half listening. He opens all his desk drawers, shoves things aside, closes the drawer. Hikes his brief case onto the desk and rummages through it. "*Damn it!*"

"What did you lose this time, Arnie?"

"Crystals."

"Your mojo beads?"

"Not mojo beads. Crystals. I been saying for months we got a thief in the house."

Croy glances up from his report. "A thief?"

"Hell, yeah. They'll take anything. Damn crystal bandits."

Gathering his reports, Croy wipes his desktop with a disinfectant cloth. Gives a quick spray with linen scented Lysol. "Later, Arnie. Hope you catch your crystal bandit."

DEE DEE HAS high hopes when the doorbell rings. And she's dressed. Sort of. She'd cleaned the house, showered, spritzed her favorite drugstore cologne. A heady musk. Her wet hair is pulled back tight against her head and rolled into a bun, glistening with olive oil. A poor girl's face lift. She's almost giddy answering the door.

On the other side is a woman heavier than Dee Dee, but the similarity in their appearance is uncanny. Dee Dee, only fifty pounds heavier. She's not so thrilled with the surprise.

"Damn girl, what took you so long?"

Dee Dee peers over the woman's shoulder as if expecting the Publisher's Clearinghouse prize check, balloons and all.

"Where'd you come from?"

Marge pushes past her into the living room and gives a long inspection. "Airport. You think I walked my ass all the way here?"

"You didn't let me know you were comin'."

"Yeah, I did. Ever check your answering machine?"

Both women look at the blinking red light on the answering machine next to the recliner.

"Not really."

"That's what I thought. Need to get the hell over that damn dog," Marge announces dragging her rolling bag to the bedroom.

Dee Dee watches the cab driver lift bag after bag out of the trunk and drop them on the sidewalk. "That's a lot of luggage, Marge. For such a short visit."

"Short? Who said *short?*" Marge yells down the hall.

Dee Dee mumbles, "How about going home to wherever the hell home is for you these days?" She waddles down the hall in bare feet on a seek and destroy mission to get Marge out before she settles in. The quicker, the better. The thought of her older sister underfoot on a daily basis won't be good no matter how well intended. Marge will make her disclose personal shit then lecture her about how to improve her life without what she calls, the flea-bitten money pit. Called the dog a flea-bitten money pit the last time they talked and Dee Dee hung up on her. So much for family support.

"Got anything to drink up in here?" Words roar down the hall because Marge's frequently out of breath and she roars to get the words out.

"A little gin under the sink from when you was here last," Dee Dee says.

"And tonic?"

"We'll need to run up to the store then."

"Well, you go and do that."

And that's that. Marge is in the house.

A LOT OF things can be expected to show up on a back porch out in the middle of nowhere, but Roy never dreamed of this one. Spread out on his stomach, Eddie's covered in blood and dirt, passed out on the door mat. Roy can't seem to do anything but stare down at the top of Eddie's bald spot.

Eddie must have sensed Roy standing there because his head pulls up off the mat like a turtle out of its shell and he squints up at Roy through his right eye, the left caked with bloody mud.

"Hey, Roy, how ya doin'?"

"What are you doin', Eddie?"

"I don't know, Roy. Think I must have gotten drunk and pissed someone off. Kicked my ass. Don't feel so good."

Roy steps out onto the porch and helps Eddie sit up. "Don't you remember what happened?"

"My head hurts, Roy."

"Yeah, bet it does."

"You gotta help me clean up before Ma finds out."

"Don't worry none about Bella, Eddie. You got bigger problems."

Roy half carries Eddie into the bathroom, sets him on the crapper, turns on the shower, thinking of what to do. Thinks about taking him out back again and shooting him a second time, but then realizes Bella's gone and there really isn't much point in putting Eddie through that again.

Helping Eddie strip off his clothes, Roy sets him in the tub, mud and blood swirling down the drain. Roy pulls out a jug of liquid laundry detergent from the cabinet and pours it on hunched-over Eddie, the steam swirling thick in the shower until it's hard to breathe.

Eddie moans, "What the hell happened, Roy?"

"Why you askin' me?" Throws a wash rag at Eddie, "Here, wash yourself."

"Weren't we in the backyard? I think—"

Roy adjusts the shower head. "Don't try so hard, Eddie, you'll hurt your brain."

"Ma, Ma got her another one and I, I, I brought her to you. Wasn't that it?"

"Guess so." Roy turns off the shower and hands Eddie a towel.

Eddie sits naked in the tub, steam fading against the fiberglass shower surround. It's like he doesn't want to get out and is happy just sitting there. He pulls the towel around his shoulders hugging his knees.

"It's all kind of fuzzy. We had a good day. I think we had a good day. Ma took care of the girl real quick like and I was thinkin' we'd get to bed early after all. Maybe 'cause Ma wasn't so into it this time, and I'm thinkin' I brought the girl to you, Roy. Isn't that right?"

"Shit, Eddie. What do you want me to say?" Roy can see why Eddie's sitting in the tub and not lying dead in the grave like he's supposed to. Damn bullet just grazed the left side of his forehead, slitting the skin open along the skull just past the ear. No real damage. Just a lot of blood. Bad shot is what that is, Roy thinks.

Eddie slowly looks up at Roy. "You shoot me in the head, Roy?"

"That what you remember?"

"Called me an asshole. I remember that. Then you shot me in the head." Eddie's hand gently creeps along the bullet graze. "I think you did."

"Hell, Eddie. Guess I snapped. Saw you draggin' that poor girl through the woods and you actin' like it's a real bother and you bitchin' like before about your damn gold chain."

"Paid a lot of money for it, Roy! Hard to get the bloody shit out when it dries between the little links like that. And it wasn't my idea to catch 'em and haul 'em back to the house for our damn crazy assed Ma." Eddie pulls out of the tub and sits exhausted on the crapper. "You act like it's all my fault."

"I know it wasn't your fault and I am sorry for tryin' to kill ya, Eddie, but a man can take just so much, ya know?"

"I can understand that." Eddie looks up at Roy, "Please don't shoot me in the head again, okay?"

"Not unless it's a really good reason, Eddie."

Eddie nods like everything's taken care of and he's back whole again. Except for the ugly wound on his head. Bella's gonna drill him about it and if she finds out Roy did it, they'll both go in *the bunker*.

"Ma's gonna put us in *the bunker*, Roy. She's gonna be real mad."

"Well, Eddie, that's the other thing. I sorta shot her, too."

"You shot Ma!" Eddie jumps up off the crapper, "What the hell, Roy! She's gonna get us for sure now."

"I'm goin' out and check, but I'm pretty certain she's not coming back."

"After all that voodoo shit she was into, Roy, she's liable to creep out of the grave and kill us both. Hell, I did. You sure she's *dead*?" Eddie yells disappearing into his room.

Roy's wondering why it's going so smooth, Eddie not being all that upset and he reconsiders the idea of putting him down again. It could be over just that quick, he'd be free, but some voice in the back of his brain impresses how he's gotten a second chance for not really killing Eddie and he might take it as a sign to let things be.

Eddie comes out later fully dressed, fresh blood leaking from his wound. "I'm missin' an earring, Roy. Think you blew it off."

"Not likely. Probably came out when you dragged out of the hole. It's in there somewhere. Come on. Maybe we'll find it now the sun's up."

EDDIE AND ROY stand looking down in the grave. Easy to see where Eddie crawled out. Bella's arm's sticking out, a pretty Fossil watch she'd probably taken from one of her victims glistening in the bright sun.

"How we gonna know she's dead, Roy?" Eddie's got his hand plastered to his wound to keep blood from leaking into his eye.

Roy kneels and carefully checks for Bella's pulse.

"Don't feel nothing. She's dead all right. I'll cover her up better."

"Was gonna fish for my earring. Now I don't care."

Roy tamps down the soft earth with his boot and scatters brush over it. Leans on the shovel and asks Eddie, "You want to say some words?"

"What, like a prayer?"

"Yeah."

"Little late for that, don't you think?"

"Maybe. Think we should say somethin' though."

Eddie shrugs and they lower their heads.

"Dear God, take care of Ma, but my advice is, don't turn your back on her. Amen."

Roy heads back to the house. "Come on, let's get your head taped up and pack you a bag."

Eddie flicks blood off his hand. "Where we going?"

"Think we need to find Ricky. Cop came by said he was missing."

"Thought he's still in prison?"

"Out now. We gotta find him."

"He's gonna kill us when he finds out you killed Ma."

Roy spins on his heel and grabs Eddie by the throat. "You're not gonna tell anyone what happened here, you hear me! Not one word, Eddie. Not one."

Eddie's eyes are wide and bloodshot, the left lightly bruised and swollen from the impact of the bullet. "All right, Roy. Chill! I won't tell anyone."

"Maybe I *should* just shoot you. You always were a little blabbermouth."

"No, no, I will. I'll keep it up, Roy. You say to shut up, I shut up."

Roy can tell from the fear in Eddie's eyes he's got him under control. For now. But it'd be easier dealing with killing him now than in some other town in God-knows-where.

"See to it, Eddie. We gotta find Ricky and find out what's goin' on. Ma would have wanted it that way."

SOUTH ON I-95, Roy's behind the wheel and Eddie's sick and pale behind his forearm in the passenger seat. Hasn't said a word in two hours and for Eddie, that's a bad deal. Blood continues to drain from the side of his head into one of Bella's ancient 1970's Kotex—the necessary added assemblage of elastic belt missing—now held together with masking tape wrapped around Eddie's head. Roy, glancing from the road to Eddie's head, begins to wonder if he'd misread the wound.

"Hey, Eddie, how ya doing, Buddy?"

Eddie remains silent in the semi-fetal position against the car door. Roy pushes Eddie's shoulder. "Wake up."

"My head hurts, man," Eddie mumbles against his arm.

"Yeah, I bet." Roy catches a rest stop sign and glides into the crawl lane behind an eighteen-wheeler. He tucks the Pontiac into a space and cuts the engine, the motor ticking a steady beat under the hood.

"Lean on over here and let me take a look at it." Roy lifts the edge of the Kotex away exposing a swollen bruise steadily bleeding. Looking at it now in sunlight, Roy sees that the bullet entered just under the skin, exited and re-entered again. *No exit.*

"Shit, Eddie, looks like the bullet's still in there."

Eddie re-animates and sits up checking his head in the rearview. "Damn!" Eddie whines, feels around above his ear, "Gotta hole in my head, Roy! That mean the bullet's still in there?"

"Looks like it, but don't panic." Roy sticks the tape back on. "It didn't kill you out right, so you're probably not gonna die."

"How do you know that? You a bullet expert, Roy? I don't remember you going to school and gettin' a fuckin' bullet degree. Shit, I got a hole in my head. How deep do you think it went?"

"Hard to say, Eddie. You'd need an x-ray to tell for sure." Roy pulls the keys and opens the door.

"Where you going?

"Get a drink and see if I can find you some aspirin. Take a nap. You want anything?"

"Water," Eddie says squinting up at him with a swollen left eye.

Roy isn't gone long, and he comes back with a bottled water, canned soda, and a foil pack of Advil and finds Eddie curled against the passenger door again, his jacket pulled over his head to block out the light.

"Take a few of these," he tells Eddie ripping the foil. Eddie shifts, but not really sitting up, and grabs the bottled water, foil pack and retreats back under the jacket.

Roy backs out and heads south again on I-75.

GAINESVILLE IS FULL of pretty college girls and the place is thick with them this time of year. That gets Roy thinking about Bella and her lying in a grave in her own backyard on top of her last pretty moon-stop sacrifice. Roy does feel bad for having killed her, but thinking back he knows it was the only way. But he mourns her in his own way, though not shedding a tear. The second he feels sorry for doing it, he thinks of the hell she put them through and then he's not so sorry after all.

"You should see 'em, Eddie. They're everywhere. In cars, on the sidewalk, stuffed in every store we pass. Get up." Roy thinks of this as a good way to snap Eddie out of his headache funk because nothing gets Eddie snapped to business better than chicks.

Eddie's still fetal in the seat.

Roy pulls the jacket down and right off notices the Kotex is swollen with blood and leaking onto Eddie's shirt. Panic stings Roy's chest and he knows the kid needs real medical attention. Also knows real medical attention means cops. It's the law. Any bullet wound gets reported to the cops. They'd want to know how Eddie got shot, and he could make up a plausible story, but Eddie's a wild card in all this and Roy doesn't trust him not to shoot his mouth off about Bella in a moment of weakness or half sedation.

"Shit, this sucks," Roy says.

Traffic crawls through downtown, congested with free freaking teens away from home for the first time in their lives, living from one keg party to the next. Again, Roy imagines what Bella would have done in a place like this. A killing a week, he thinks. She wouldn't be able to help herself.

Along the miles of strip malls, a vinyl banner catches his eye, advertising: GATOR DRUGS GRAND OPENING—FREE TRAUMATIC WOUND DRESSING.

It's all he needs to see. He hangs a hard right into the parking lot, parks in the fire lane, and helps Eddie out.

It has that *new store* smell—a concoction of industrial adhesives, paint solvents, and popcorn. It's hard to manage Eddie, he's more or less out of it and somewhere in the back of Roy's mind he seems to recollect that drifting in and out of consciousness means a concussion. Can't let him sleep. He pats Eddie's cheek and grabs his chin pointing him in the direction of sorority girls lined in the makeup aisle. "Look here. They're everywhere. Wake up or you'll miss it."

Eddie's eyes, or at least the good one, rolls from the back of his head and tries to focus. "I got a real bad headache, Roy."

"I know, Eddie. Might have a concussion, so stay awake."

"What for?"

"Might not wake up again."

"What else you gonna do to me, Roy?"

"Nothin', Eddie. We can get help here. Just keep your mouth shut and let me do all the talking."

Eddie doesn't say anything and Roy thinks it's because he's more or less out of it anyway which might work out in the long run. Patrons in the store catch sight of them lurching down the aisle and look skittish and confused. Three college girls standing by the make-up counter cover their mouths and laugh, pointing manicured fingers in Eddie's direction.

Guy behind the counter's fat and jolly, sports a beard, has a wicked stainless-steel hook for a left hand—Santa after an ugly sled accident—moonlighting as a pharmacist in the off season. That's Roy's first impression looking up at him, donned in a white lab coat with the name Bert embroidered on the left chest. Roy's hoping he is Santa or at least "Santa like" because he's gonna need all the help he can get.

"Excuse me, but your sign out front says you offer free wound dressing. My brother Eddie here, say hi Eddie, has a bit of a problem on his head. Can you fix him up?"

Old Bert peers over the glasses perched on the end of his nose, first at Roy then Eddie, back to Roy. "What happened to him?"

"You know, it's a long story and we're in kind of a hurry," Roy tries explaining, glances around the place and is suddenly aware that every person in the store has stopped shopping to watch him and Eddie. "If you could just clean him up and put on a real dressing, we'd sure appreciate it."

By then a pharmacist associate—could be from India—has come up because of the strange quiet in the store as if the patrons are animals at a water hole getting wind of a nearby predator lurking in the weeds. Associate's head weaves back and forth studying every inch of Eddie's face, Roy half expecting him to pick up the phone and call the cops.

Bert turns slightly, lifts his hook, some kind of signal to the associate to do something, Roy thinks, not sure what.

"Free with purchase." Old Bert drops that little fact on Roy like a turd.

"That sign true or is it some kind of scam to get people in here so's they'll spend money? Doesn't say with purchase."

It sounds aggressive, Roy realizes it the second the word *purchase* passes his lips, and that makes him aggravated and nervous. Eddie starts to re-animate and his head pops up and focuses on blurry Bert.

"Dude, it's Santa." Eddie sounds a little drunk even though he hasn't had a drop in three days and that can't be good. Bullet's probably wobbling around in his brain shorting things out, Roy thinks.

"Says with purchase! Look underneath the big words. And we don't treat wounds. We offer the supplies for them, heavy gauze, tape, Betadine. We're not doctors. Your brother looks like he might need to go to the emergency room.

Hospital's not far," Bert squints, points his hook towards the door and a little to the right.

Roy sweeps a pack of gum from its box and slaps it on the counter. "We'll take it. And you're right. I'll take him to the hospital. So, can I have the free stuff?"

"He shot me in the head," Eddie says. Smiles when he says it and that confuses the hell out of the pharmacist. Not like it's the first time some damn idiot's dragged a friend into a drug store with a suspicious story. This is, after all, a college town and kids do stupid things.

Bert's right eyebrow arches in that, *I don't believe a word of it, but I don't want to get involved* look. Makes Roy happy because he's sure any minute the dude from India's going for the phone, and at that exact moment, that's just what happens. His dark little hand is creeping for the phone and Roy can already imagine the conversation.

"*Can I get it NOW!*" Roy yells. Eddie's getting harder to hold up and he's praying he can get him back to the car before he passes out on the new terrazzo floor, and they call EMS and the cops, and then the questions, *interrogation*, and he's sure Eddie will spill his guts just to sleep.

"That'll be a dollar seven," Bert says.

Roy pulls two bucks from his rear pocket and slaps it on the counter. "Keep the change."

India guy backs away from the phone and collects a bag with GATOR DRUG logo in orange against the crisp white paper and hands one over to Roy.

"Thanks. Have a great day," Roy says, hiking Eddie up for a better grip and turning for the door. By now, everyone in the store has grouped behind them. Makes Roy think of the zombies in the *Dawn of the Dead* movie. He pushes his way through the small crowd and shoves Eddie in the car, slams the door.

Roy's not wasting time getting out of town in case ol' Bert decides maybe he should call the cops because he suddenly remembered the injured guy said he was shot in the head, and Roy prays no one thought enough to take down the tag number. Once he finds Ricky, he won't have to deal with all this on his own, and at eighty miles an hour southbound, Roy rolls the window down and screams. Just to clear his head.

6

probable cause of mongrels

IN THE LATE afternoon when the scrub oaks at the woods line cast long shadows across the backyard, Marge drags the lawn chair to where sun meets shadow to sit and drink. She's developing a nice back yard routine, but it's only in the last couple of days she's noticed what she thinks are trolls.

Marge isn't sure if they noticed her first, or her them, but each afternoon she brings out a large box of animal crackers, a large gin and tonic—more gin than tonic—and gets comfortable in the lawnchair with frayed webbing splitting at the rivets and waits.

She'd come across the idea of feeding them animal crackers when she noticed their love of gin and tonic, because any time she left her drink unattended in the grass by the chair, the glass would be empty upon her return, but offering them booze didn't seem a good idea because of the lack of information on the negative effects of booze on trolls such as how much was too much—an ounce, half ounce—and she had no way to evaluate how much each troll consumed or if just one or two trolls did all the drinking.

Searching the Internet doesn't offer much in the way of information on the habits of trolls, so Marge decides she'll pioneer a study while sitting in the lawn chair drinking her gin and tonic and slinging animal crackers, hoping to gain an accurate count of the size of the colony. She calls it a colony, not a herd, or a covey, or a pack, because pack sounds aggressive and she doesn't feel they're aggressive, nor are they a cluster, or a pod, or group because group sounds disorganized and unintentional, like folks gathered at a crash site or fist fight, and she feels trolls know exactly how to organize even though she's never seen one up close. Only the eyes, a slight discoloration in the foliage when the scrub oak shadows grow long enough, but after that, she can't see a damn thing.

Every morning when she investigates the woods line where she knows she's slung the animal crackers (*at least a dozen*) she discovers they've been eaten, sure proof of the existence of trolls.

While walking through Dime Discount hunting a fresh lawnchair with low mileage and a new box of animal crackers *(two for five dollars)* Marge comes across a row of concrete gnomes lined up like little soldiers in the garden section and is stunned to see that somehow Dime Discount has found a way to capture trolls and exploit them for profit. Nowhere on the Internet has she read how to capture trolls and wonders if the colonies in Dee Dee's backyard are escapees desperate for a hideout, or just random trolls with no knowledge of the exploitation of their kind.

Knowing Dime Discount and how it churns out massive quantities of price slashed merchandise, she concludes that, one, either trolls are as available as plastic foliage, or two, they are a one-shot purchase while supplies last.

Does that make her trolls more or less valuable, if she were in the market to sell them? And does she need a permit to even capture them in the first place? What government department does that fall under? County or state? She remembers you have to have a permit from the State Department of Game and Fish to capture and exploit alligator, but what does troll fall under? Is it classified as exotic or protected? Is there a limit one could bag in a season? What's a season? Two weeks, a month? Do you have to throw back the small ones? Can you determine the age of a troll, and can you keep the males and not the females?

Marge examines the gnomes carefully and up close, takes one off the shelf and tries to ascertain whether male or female. She never thought to do that to the one sitting in Dee Dee's backyard. Can't tell now, either. Each one has a hole in the bottom as if their genitalia have been removed. She wonders if maybe Dime Discount is selling them illegally or if the genitalia have been removed as a way to preserve them for sale and calling them Gnomes—neutered trolls with better dental coverage.

Going up to an associate and asking will prove fruitless because if they are in fact illegal, they certainly aren't going to admit it, and if they are legal, why should they help her in making a profit? They might, in fact, assume, *God forbid*, she's an advocate who'll start picketing the store in protest of the exploitation of trolls as those in the past had done for low wage and no health care.

Marge isn't sure where she stands on the matter. The profit would be good, but what would she really be gaining? And she really doesn't even have the energy to trap and bag trolls, perhaps by leaving animal crackers in a squirrel trap, hoping someone would take them off her hands. Then she'd feel bad for them and she thinks of being in the backyard in the long shadows with her gin and tonic and how the trolls make her feel every evening in the calm dusk just before the fireflies come out.

With animal crackers in hand and the new lawnchair under her arm, Marge smiles at the associate who checks her out, making a mental note to stop by the liquor store for more gin and tonic because clearly some of the trolls like to drink and it just seems mean to cut them off now.

BACK AT THE house, Marge lumbers in toting her booze, crackers, a spiral cut ham, fresh collard greens, ready-made potato salad, and hot sauce. One good look in Dee Dee's fridge and she saw all she needed to. Nothing. Girl's surviving on nothing. No real food in the house and Marge wonders how long it's really been going on. Not like Dee is gonna confide the truth. Been that way since childhood and from the prescriptions in the medicine cabinet there's more to the missing dog than she's been lead to believe. A quick jump on the Internet has at least given her an idea of how bad.

Marge finds her sister in the recliner gazing out the window, lost in a world of her own. It's a sad, lonely expression on a girl who used to be the bright light of the party. Deep down she's scared for Dee. Hasn't volunteered a full conversation since she got here.

"Something going on out there?" Marge huffs.

Dee Dee acts like she doesn't even hear her, but in a small voice says, "You suppose it'll always be this way?"

"What way?"

"One endless day after the other until I die."

"Why you wanna go die for?" Marge moves into the room setting the ham on the coffee table.

"Worst things than dying," says Dee Dee.

"Like what?"

"People thinking I'm crazy. Too afraid to talk to me. Whispering behind my back and I can hear what they saying. I'm not crazy, Marge."

Marge sits on the end of the sofa, "Girl, I didn't say you were. Look here, you gotta get a hold of yourself. I don't know what the hell's been going on, but I'm here now. Whatever's bothering you, we'll get it taken care of."

"I didn't tell you everything, Marge. They threw me in jail, and before that, the nut house."

"All over the dog?"

"No. Over them *dead* people."

"Dead people! Girl, you snap and kill someone, Dee?"

"Me? Hell no, not me. He did!" She points to the west wall as if that'll clear it all up for Marge.

"Who's *He?*"

"Asshole Joe Salas. Wrapped the head up just like that ham, like he was gonna vacuum seal it."

Marge looks at the ham. Looks back at Dee.

She's lost her. Dee Dee hears the way it sounds out loud and thinks if Marge said these things, she wouldn't believe it, either.

"That why you taking all them drugs?"

"Don't help. I know what I seen. And if I didn't, it means I'm crazy."

"I'm getting us a drink. You stay here. And I don't think you're crazy." The words came out, but in Marge's head she thinks Dee Dee's totally lost it.

"Don't you worry none. From here on out, I'm makin' you my special project, and ol' Marge here always gets what she wants girlfriend. Don't you go and give it another thought."

For the first time in months, Dee Dee feels she has someone to count on.

found and lost

JOE, HALF PANICKED, darts into one store after another, searching for Pop, who's lost, adrift in damned South Beach of all places, and how does an eighty-year-old guy with a bad hip disappear in a place he's never been? At least Joe doesn't think he's been, Pop would have said, Joe's sure of it, but Pop's full of secrets. Joe thinks he is, a little worried now because of Pop's slip-ups and his flashbacks to Korea when he tried to save the life of poor Fred or Frank Something (*Not in this store either*) screaming for a medic, and the trooper looking at him funny, but thank God didn't ask. Maybe he's in a bar, it's near cocktail hour. Shit, he'll never find him.

Between shops are lounges, not bars because there are no bars in South Beach, they're clubs, invitation only, not the dank pissholes he grew up with, full of smoke and the smell of stale beer. Makes him think of the shithole he found Ricky Vega in and their fist fight in the back parking lot. Reminds him of Ricky telling him all about little Jamie and suddenly the anger swells on top of the fear of Pop's—

Halfway past the antique shop, Joe spots Pop standing at the checkout counter. For the first minute or two Pop looks at him like he's a stranger, no one at all. Pop leans on his walkin' stick, grinning, four or five lace doilies in his hand.

"Pop, you know how bad you scared me?" Yeah, he says it like that, like to a five-year-old who's wandered off. Then it dawns on him Pop doesn't know who the hell he is. That makes three. Three times Pop's mind has drifted off and left his old husk of a body behind to fend for itself. For a moment the old guy withdraws and steps back fearful, and then like a light bulb has switched on, Pop smiles in recognition and holds up his doilies.

"For Mom. She loves these things. Even got one in green. Her favorite color, you know. I know she's got the damn things all over the house, but they make her happy. Just a little something," he says flipping them over and inspecting the needlework.

Joe doesn't know how to answer. "Whatcha buying those for?"

"She'll get all excited pulling them out of the bag. You watch."

Joe pulls at Pop's arm, tries lifting the doilies from his hand.

"What are you doing? These are mine. Get your own."

"Pop, put 'em down and let's go."

"Don't do that. I'm getting her these."

"Gotta go, Pop."

"You go. I'm getting these."

"Pop, Mom's gone. She's been gone over two years."

"Where'd she go?"

"Died. In the hospital, remember?"

Joe feels it the second the words slip from his lips, sees the trauma in Pop's eyes as if it's the first time the old guy's heard the news. "Come on, we gotta go."

"That's a damn lie. Who are you? I don't know you!"

Shoppers stop. Turn. Watch. Joe can feel their eyes roll all over him, judging, speculating his treatment of an old guy who just wants to buy something nice for his wife.

"Is there a problem here?" Sales clerk asks from behind the counter concerned enough she's watching Pop real close, taking cues from him whether the guy harassing him is a stranger or not. If Pop was a little kid, she'd be reaching for the phone right now, but doesn't remember hearing anything about strangers snatching old folks.

"I'm his son. He's just a little confused," Joe explains.

"No, you're not! My boy's only twelve. I don't know this fella." Pop staggers back a step or two, his walkin' stick suddenly rising in front of him.

"No, really, he's my father. He's having some sort of episode. Come on, Pop, I gotta take you back to the hotel."

"Can you prove he's your father?" Clerk asks.

Now four or five people have gained an interest in the story, not like they're getting out quick until this gets resolved anyway and some are nodding heads in agreement like it's a good idea to find out who this guy is.

"How do I do that? DNA?"

She's unimpressed by his being flippant, and it really sours her to him. She squints and says, "I.D. will do just fine. That is if you have I.D. Do you?"

Joe pulls his wallet, slides out his driver's license, and hands it over.

Clerk reads, looks at Joe, reads some more, looks up. Hands it back.

"What about you, sir. Can I see your driver's license, please?"

Pop's got the deer in the headlights look, not moving at all until his hand reaches into his wallet searching for a driver's license he hasn't got anymore. He pulls out two twenties and hands them to the clerk.

"Any I.D.?" she asks again. The two twenties sit in her palm as if a bird's shit in it and she is still, *in her most caring way*, waiting for I.D.

"Doesn't have D.L. anymore. Lost it this year. Long story," Joe tells her.

"Drove right through a fruit stand. Twice." Pop says. It rekindles some kind of memory and Pop begins to fade back in.

"Only once, Pop. Julio did it the last time, remember?"

"Sissy boy, that one. But liquor him up and put him behind the wheel and he'll get you somewhere. Not sure where, but he'll get you there."

"Do you know this gentleman, sir?"

"That's Jo Jo. Why?"

"Then he isn't a stranger?"

"Only when he wants to be, but no, he's mine." Pop steps forward to leave the store.

"Sir, do you still want those?" the clerk asks, the twenties still in her palm.

"No, he won't be needin' those," Joe tells her and trades the doilies for the twenties. Doesn't waste time hustling Pop back to the hotel.

THERE'S SOMETHING ABOUT sitting bare-assed in a webbed lawn chair, feeding animal crackers to trolls. And the gin and tonic. Of course, the gin and tonic. Marge fishes out another handful of price-slashed Dime Discount crackers and pelts them, one by one, at the woods line. Maybe if she hooked up a camera out here she'd get proof. Set it here by the chair; aim it at the corner, right about there. She uses her empty glass as a makeshift camera lens, but the focus isn't so good looking through the fat end of a cheap glass.

And what about that little bomb Dee Dee dropped on her? Killer neighbors. No wonder Dee's on medication. Poor girl. Too much time on her hands. "Hey Dee, got any polish?" Her voice echoes off the hot stucco wall.

Sliding glass door opens. Dee Dee's head pops through. "I hear you screaming, but I don't know what you're saying."

"Got any polish?"

"What kind?"

"For these." Marge lifts her foot flaunting her bare toes.

"What color?"

"Surprise me. And could you get me another drink?"

Dee Dee's head disappears and pops back out again. "And why you keep throwing perfectly good cookies out at them woods?"

"Feeding the trolls."

"The what?"

"Those things out there."

"What things?"

Marge points her empty glass to the woods line then holds it over her head for a refill.

"Girl, those are squirrels."

"I know what a damn squirrel is. You ever wonder where gnomes come from?"

Marge massages her foot on the pointy end of Dee Dee's creepy concrete garden gnome's hat.

"Got it at Big Save."

"No, I mean where did they come from?"

"You mean are they real? Hell if I know." Dee Dee plucks the glass from Marge's hand, "Girl, you're gonna burn those." She gestures at Marge's flaccid boobs with the glass.

"You have them in the yard."

"Boobs?"

"Trolls."

"I do not."

"Do too. Right there in the corner."

"You sure you want another drink?"

"They done eat up the crackers. I looked 'em up on the Internet."

"What it say?"

"Not a lot. But you got 'em."

Dee Dee disappears inside. Marge chucks another cracker to the woods and squeezes out of the chair, her ass now cross striped red from the webbing. "Yeah, I know you're out there. I'm watching ya," Marge says opening the slider.

FOR SOME INVESTIGATORS, it all falls back to the gut, the deep probe writhing inside, pushing, insisting that no matter the lack of evidence, something's there waiting to be discovered. For Croy, despite his flaws and peculiarities, has learned to trust his gut. No matter what.

Lydia's things are just as she left them. But not voluntarily. Croy's gut tells him that the instant he steps over the threshold of her gallery. And he can't prove it. At the moment that doesn't even matter. What does matter is she's not kept her pattern and not told a soul, not her business clients from whom she makes her living, not her rivals, not even her friends. He's spent the better part of a day in interviews, phone calls, computer follow-ups. Nothing ekes a clue. It's happened before, and Croy knows sometimes you just have to stand still and let it come to you.

He stands in front of Lydia's solid *Rosewood Partner's* desk and briefly closes his eyes, listens, smells the room around him. Waits. On Lydia's desk her check book's open, a large professional leather bound with neatly written stubs filled out in beautiful script next to where the check used to be. All but the last. Snapping on a pair of latex gloves, he carefully lifts the page to the one behind it, tilts the book to catch the light through the window. Methodically flips page after page reading the stubs, tracking what and whom she spent her money on, when a familiar name surfaces. *Joe Salas.*

A check written every week for fifteen months. And they ended four months ago. Croy sits in her *Karpen Art Nouveau* mahogany arm chair, opens her desk drawer, pulls out paperwork, sifts through them one by one. Opens the small top drawer and retrieves a folder. Inside he finds the draft of a letter written to the committee of the Art Basel Miami, special attention to Ferguson Novello.

Dear Sirs,

It is my understanding that Joseph Salas has been nominated for a showing at Art Basel Miami, and it is great concern that I write to inform you of this misguided selection. Mr. Salas, who was in my employment, had to be terminated for his unprofessional and disruptive behavior during the gallery showing of Ferguson Novello which resulted in the defamation of Mr. Novello's fine name and the loss of personal revenue. It is my hope that my intervening in this matter will spare the fine reputation of both the committee and Art Basel Miami. Yours truly, Lydia Stein Von Gloss.

The little hairs stand erect on the back of Croy's arm as he rubs his thumb and forefinger together to keep pace with his brain chugging along as it pieces together what his gut already suspects. He stands up, pulls a mini-Maglite from his inside jacket and scans the floor—discovers a narrow scratch along the otherwise perfect mahogany hardwood. He crouches on his hands and knees noticing a purple wax-like substance. Sniffs. He stands up, carefully placing a chair over it. Calls crime scene. No, she didn't leave on her own and he just might have found proof.

TRAFFIC THINS OUT, a far cry from the hormone polluted streets of Gainesville, and any other time Roy would have loved to duck into the clubs and frat parties, but here he is with Eddie curled against the passenger door, mumbling from delirium or blood loss or concussion—God, could this get any worse? It dawns on him he doesn't have a clue where to go once he hits the Eustis city limits, and at some point, he needs to pull over and clean Eddie up.

Roy slits the bottom of the gum package with his thumb and tilts it to his mouth, the hard-coated gum clinking on his teeth, an old familiar memory of childhood. One of the few good ones.

Driving in silence with nothing but the wind blowing through the crack in the window, Roy resents going back in reflection. Nothing's gonna be the same again and there isn't any going back to change it. Not sure he would if given a second chance because he's smart enough to know he can't change other people. Couldn't change Bella no matter what he threatened her with, and even if he wasn't around, she'd have killed those girls anyway. Dragging him, Ricky, and little

Eddie into the middle of it wasn't what a mother's love is supposed to be. He realizes all the things he probably won't ever get to do. The trip to Vegas is probably off, as well as meeting some nice woman not in menopause—thinks the government ought to be investigating that. Who knows how many women out there perform strange deadly rituals during the full moon. He can't imagine his mother being the only one.

Eddie moans from under his jacket and Roy punches him in the shoulder.

"Wake up! Didn't I tell you if you fell asleep you might not wake up!"

Roy's not certain Eddie has a concussion, and the possibility of something worse makes his stomach twist like when he had to dig the holes for the girls, but how would he get rid of Eddie if he died now?

Miles and miles of pine and scrub land as far as the eye can see and he could just pull over and drag him deep into the woods. With his luck, some damn nosey would pull up behind offering help and there he'd be, Eddie limp in the front seat, or worse, over his shoulder, caught in the act. Shit, he'd have to kill them, too. And what if there was more than one person in the car?

Already, the scenario is getting out of control and all thanks to a bad shoot. Eddie would have been better off dead, but so far he's hanging in and if he makes it to Eustis, then he'll have a chance at a plan.

"Wake up, damn it. You don't get to die in the car!" Roy pulls the jacket off Eddie who responds like a vampire caught in sunlight, but it wakes him up. Glancing over, Roy can't help feeling how pathetic Eddie looks, half his face swollen and Bella's blood-soaked Kotex stuck to the wound without the help of masking tape anymore. Going to be ugly getting it off this time, but at least it's a sign the bleeding's stopped. Better not to touch it until they get settled somewhere safe. *Just in case.*

Never gonna have a family, he thinks, God, what if it's in the blood? What if killing is passed down from generation to generation? What if months or years down the road he wakes up with a Bella craving? What if that voodoo shit stayed in the family and didn't die with her? What did that mean for him and Eddie? What if Eddie's right and somehow, she crawled out of the grave, bitter and more pissed than he'd ever seen her and she took vengeance—could be by spirit, a ghost tripping down the highway after them, waiting for the perfect moment. God, he needs sleep, but keeping Eddie alive is more important.

"How you doing, buddy?"

"My head still hurts, Roy."

"I know, Eddie. We're almost there."

ROY ISN'T SURE when the needle on the gas gauge sunk past the red line. Must have done it after dark. Gotta be going on fumes and he can't chance running out of gas in the middle of nowhere on a road patrolled by bitter troopers holding grudges.

Eddie's started singing from under his jacket, a quiet somewhat muffled version of *Little Bittie Gals blues* they used to listen to when their old man was still at home. Old man played that damn Joe Turner forty-five night and day until Bella finally snapped and took it, and the player, and heaved it out the front door. Hell of a fight that night and the old man didn't come out on top. Disappeared shortly after that, and Bella seemed okay with it. He and Eddie only asked his where-a-bouts once, and after that it became one of many family issues never mentioned in front of her.

CITGO sign beams through the Pontiac's cruddy windshield and Roy's thrilled to see it, if for nothing else than to get away from Eddie's singing. Shithead always thought he could sing, but truth be told, he sucks.

"Gettin' gas, Eddie. Need anything?"

Eddie sings right on.

Roy's the only one at the pump, and from here he can see there's only one clerk in the store. Shoving the nozzle in the tank, he relishes the fresh air, enjoys the gas fumes. With the tank filled, Roy goes into the store, nods at the old lady clerk and heads for the coolers in the back. He's not in there more than a minute or two and hasn't even made his selection of soda yet when Eddie comes through the door and stops. Roy sees him from the corner of his eye, about the same time the clerk does. Eddie's standing with the Kotex hanging from the bullet wound looking pale and unsteady on his feet but determined to do…Roy's not sure what, sweeps a Gatorade out of the cooler and hustles back to the front.

"You need to get back to the car, Eddie." Roy sees the shock on the clerk's face and a list of things spin through his head.

"Is he all right?" the clerk asks, pulls her glasses, hanging by a chain, up to her nose as if she'll see better trying to see far a way with reading glasses. Lets them drop back to her chest. "What happened to him?"

Roy's hoping to stall the whole inquisition and doesn't say much other than grunt while shaking his head and reaching into his back pocket for his wallet. Gone! Checks his other pocket, pats his chest even though he's never carried his wallet in his shirt, but it's been an odd couple a days. *Must have left it at the pharmacy!* Roy realizes he doesn't have any money for gas or the Gatorade and she's gonna call the cops and he's gotta think of something fast.

"Umm, I think I've lost my wallet and I'm real sorry. What do you all do in these kind of cases? I sweep the store or fill the cooler?"

Old Lady Clerk is still staring at Eddie, her hand over her heart as if it's beating too fast, and her other hand slowly lifts to a point towards the thing on Eddie's head.

"Is that…a sanitary napkin on that young man's head?"

"Yes, Ma'am it is. We were in a really bad car accident and our Ma is being rushed to the hospital as we speak, but I ran out of gas and now we can't get to the hospital. They said she might not make it." Looks her straight in the eye when he says it.

"Why didn't they take *him?*"

"Didn't have enough room and Eddie here said he could make it in the car. They could get there faster without him."

Clerk leans to the plate glass window and squints at the Pontiac at pump number three. "Car doesn't look damaged."

"No Ma'am, it wasn't. It was a pedestrian thing. We'd stopped on the side of the road so's Ma could get in the back to sleep, bad arthritis in her knees, and her and Eddie were switching places and some asshole comes by and hits 'em both. Didn't even stop, can you believe that? Just glanced Eddie here, but Ma, she got the worst of it. They said she might not make it and Eddie and I have to get there before she passes. We'd never forgive ourselves if she passed without us sayin' our good-byes to her."

Eddie's as confused as the clerk, but he doesn't say anything. Has it together enough to nod in agreement when she looks back at him.

"You *poor* boys. And you're a good ways from the hospital out here." She slips her glasses back on her face, and clears number three pump. "You boys go ahead and get to your Mama. Much as these damn oil companies screw us, I don't think they'll miss a couple of gallons. Here, take the Gatorade for the young man there."

Roy can't believe it, but he doesn't stand around. He grabs up the Gatorade and steers Eddie to the car before she changes her mind.

Back on the highway, Eddie reaches in his back pocket and hands over Roy's wallet. "You left it in the seat. Came in to give it to you."

"Why didn't you say so?"

"Got caught up in the story and by the time I figured out you'd made it all up, she'd given you the gas and we were out the door."

"Shit, Eddie, we've screwed CITGO."

"Put it on the list, Roy," Eddie says crawling back under his jacket.

8

neon g-strings

A GOOD NIGHT'S sleep, on Pop's end at least, seems to have stabilized his brain function. All morning Joe picks his memory, quizzing for the Jeopardy jackpot of past facts and anecdotes, and if he remembers where he just laid his walkin' stick. Passes them all. And Joe's not sure about the doily incident. Pop's elusive about that whole thing as if he might have known what he was doing but been too embarrassed to admit he missed his wife so much he was buying her stuff. Maybe it was just a brain fart. He's an old guy and things are bound to hitch and squeak now and then. At least that's what Joe tells himself.

"Hope you're all rested up, Pop. Got a long day. They say these folks play all night long."

"Gonna meet any celebrities?" Pop's stopped greasing his hair and looks at Joe hopeful he has the hook-ups to meet celebrities.

"Maybe. It's a big deal down here. Have one in Switzerland, too. All the bigwigs in the art world come here."

"Who's it gonna be?"

"I don't know, Pop. They didn't tell me. Could be anyone. We'll just have to keep our eyes peeled."

"I can do that. You bet." Pop turns back to the mirror and his hand trembles smoothing down hair.

"Ready for a breakfast?"

"Always. Think they got prunes?" Pop smiles when he says it.

Joe smiles back and ushers him through the hotel room door.

"Big fancy room. Like celebrities' use, don't you think there, JoJo?"

"Yeah, it's fancy all right. Maybe the waiter can find you prunes. Wouldn't want you gettin' all backed up or anything," Joe says hitting the button on the large copper elevator.

"Got that right." Pop backs into the elevator behind Joe shared with several other people waiting to go down. "Got the gas so bad once, I had to keep trying to outrun it. Hard to do with a bum hip. Think I ran the dog off. It's bad if you can run the dog off 'cause everyone knows dog farts are the worst."

A couple of people bow their heads and smile.

Joe notices hairs on Pop's head have gone astray and he gently pats them back down. "Dog farts are the worst, Pop."

Convention center's a maze of rooms, hallways, tents, odd construction built to enhance the art inside. Joe and Pop stand in amazement at such a thing. Julio and Sadie appear from around the corner, programs at the ready, Sadie checking her watch. Julio seems to have recovered from his harrowing experience on the turnpike and walks with his head held just a bit higher in a bright pink shirt and matching pants, hair slicked back and tied in a small ponytail. He glances around the room like a celebrity in hopes of being recognized and pressured for an autograph from his fifteen minutes of fame on prime-time news.

"Ooo chew loos so fresh this morning. Don they loo fresh, Miss Sadie?"

"Perfect. Joe, that jacket I sent to your room looks divine on you. I hope you don't mind my imposing."

"No. It'll do. Not much need for dress clothes cleanin' galleries."

"Well those days are over, Joe. I don't think you'll need to worry about menial cleaning jobs again," she says lifting her foot and wiping dust from her Monolo Blahniks. "And from the buzz I hear, you're well on your way to being an overnight success. How does that sound?"

"Sounds good to me," Pop says. The hairs on his head have sprung back up and Julio, standing behind him, points it out to Joe without Pop noticing.

"What happens now?"

Julio, distracted by the wayward hair, attempts to touch it, jerks his hand away and tries again.

"We wait. I have meetings to attend, but you can visit the exhibits and I'll meet you at one for lunch." Sadie tries to ignore Julio's obsession over Pop's wayward hair. Tries ignoring most of the things he does. At least tries not to laugh out loud.

"Forty thousand art lovers and professionals from around the world come to this event. There are 190 galleries from twenty-four countries and works by over fifteen hundred artists both renowned, established and," she says laying her hand out to Joe, "cutting edge newcomers."

"You don't say!" Pop's impressed, turns and catches Julio with his hand in the air at the top of his head.

"Ooo hell, stop mister Salas. I can stan it no lonker. Stan still." Julio licks his fingers and carefully smoothes down the hair. "See? Very nice."

"I've got to run, but your exhibit will be in Art Nova. It's for galleries presenting new works created in the current or last two years." Hands Joe a copy of the program and turns to a map of the exhibit and points. "We're here, and I'll meet you all here," she says. "Have fun. Julio, are you coming?"

"*I wish,*" he tells her falling in behind her. Flips his hand back in a wave.

It takes most of the morning just to visit *part* of the exhibits. Joe and Pop take their time wandering from one display to the next, at times both Pop and Joe tilting their heads at the same time trying to figure out what they're looking at.

"What the hell is that?"

"Says naked girl in room," Joe informs.

"That art?"

"Is to somebody, Pop."

"Weird is what that is."

"It's a shelf full of boxes. I got 'em at home. Bring it next time." Pop steps up and pokes a box with his walkin' stick. "Think I got this box, too. Nothin' in this room, JoJo."

"It's the sticks comin' out of the wall, Pop."

"They call this stuff art?"

"Is to someone."

"Maybe it's a heat lamp. Expecting cold, I guess," Pop mutters. "Naked girl lying on a bed. She needs to eat. Be art if it was real."

Joe misses the gleam in Pop's eye as he lingers a moment.

"Dudes with afros. Think I met that guy in the sixties in west Philly where your Aunt Lou lives."

"Aunt Lou doesn't live in Philly, Pop."

"Sure she does. Sent you up there, remember?"

"You didn't send me to Aunt Lou's."

"Where'd you go, then?"

"Uncle Sid's."

"What's that called?"

"Abstract, Pop."

"Abstract alright. They like nudies down here, don't they?"

"Guess so, Pop."

"Sid died, you know. Was married to Thelma."

"His first wife. He remarried pretty quick after." Joe looks inside a red tube with a small blue light in the bottom.

"That right? Who'd he marry?" Pop peers in the tube.

"Don't remember her name. Didn't Ma tell ya?"

"Why don't I remember that?"

"It was Mom's side of the family," Joe says. "You always hated 'em."

"Not all. Most. Weird group of people."

"Then why'd you send me up to 'em?"

"Thought I sent you to Aunt Lou."

"Could a sent me to Uzbekistan for all you knew."

"Ubeck what?"

"Never mind, Pop. In the past. Leave it there."

"Car looks like my Buick after the accident. See there, I could've had two exhibits."

"Let's go see what they got outside, Pop. Almost lunch time."

Outside, the palms sway in the warm Miami sun, ocean waves roll on shore. Seagulls drift above hoping to steal pate' and finger sandwiches from wandering spectators. Under a cluster of palms, an exhibit catches Joe's eye. A hole dug in the ground and inside what appears to be skeletal remains. "Fabricated. Says so on the artist marker. Wouldn't want folks thinking it was a real dead guy," Pop says standing next to Joe staring down in the hole. They briefly glance at each other and leave.

ANY OTHER NIGHT Joe knew exactly where Pop would be, which, more than likely was in bed. Was every night since he moved in with the exception of the VA hospital nights—and he only turned his back for a second to answer some damn question about his artwork—maybe Julio will know. Second time in thirty-six hours the old geezer's disappeared, but now it's close to midnight. Would he go back to the hotel without him? Joe's torn. Search for Pop or work the buyers. It's only the most exclusive art event in the country.

Some Argentinean, slick back hair, expensive suit, three comrades lurking close by, could be armed, is real interested in the multi-colored "*Ricky*" piece.

"It's so life like, who posed for you?"

Okay, he isn't about to give the guy details, just says "random volunteers," as he scans the crowd for the tuft of wayward hair that's become Pop's signature tonight. Joe catches sight of Sadie, gives her a panicked head signal and she's bright enough to catch on, not sure of what, but introduces herself to the Argentinean while Joe slips away for an all-out search.

An hour into it through every exhibit on the place, Joe hits the hotel and finds the room just as he left it. Pop's loose in South Beach again in the dead of night amongst God-knows-what.

Joe doesn't remember leaving the hotel or how many blocks he'd gone, but man, the art deco district's a lot different after dark. Wall to wall geometric forms in brilliant neon of pink, blue, pale green, yellow, orange, glass block, people he's not sure are male or female, bouncers posted outside of clubs—not bars, *invitation only*—and women he'd only seen in porno mags. After about another hour of it, Joe's seriously considering calling the cops when a familiar voice echoes from what Pop calls a *cabaret*. No bouncer at the door—a slummy little hideaway tucked back off the street in the shadows of expensive remodeled art deco buildings slinging color to the warm Miami night sky.

Inside, a massive bar, round center stage, and Pop up front tucking fives in the G-string of some exotic stripper humping a pole to heavy metal. Can't be, but the familiar walkin' stick's propped between his legs and he doesn't seem bothered so much by his bad hip anymore. Seems far more absorbed in getting the five in the G-string. Stripper doesn't seem to mind his fumbling attempts, if they really are, and how dangerous can an eighty-year-old guy be? Joe can hardly believe it. Old man must have slipped a gear again; what decade was he in this time?

Joe steps up, glancing at the brunette stripper twirling the thin strands of hair on Pop's head around her finger, and for a good five minutes Joe can't get his mouth open to say anything. He pulls on Pop's shoulder to get his attention, getting a whiff of the sweaty stripper and Pop's soured *Old Spice*.

"Pop, what are you doing?"

Pop swings around—swivel chairs more convenient for this sort of place—smiling a cheesy grin. "JoJo, have a seat. Meet Starlight. She's a celebrity. See? Says so on the poster out front."

"I bet she is, Pop. What are doing in a titty bar?"

"What, you never been in one? And you're how old? Well, sit your ass down. You're in for a treat." Pop pulls another five from his wallet to give to Starlight-or-Star Bright, doesn't really remember which.

The thought of spending hours in a sleazy strip joint with his father makes Joe's stomach ache. It's just wrong on so many levels. "We gotta go. It's late."

"Can't yet. She doesn't get off for another hour. Got a date."

"Pop, it's almost one in the morning. Way past your bed time."

Pop gives Joe a look. "I'm a grown man and if I want to blow money in a titty bar on a nice young lady like Star Bright here, then I will. Don't need a babysitter and if you're tired then go back to the Hotel. I'll see you tomorrow."

"Can't leave you alone in here, Pop. Too dangerous. You don't know anything about these people."

"So you think! Starlight here says she's a single mom tryin' to put food on the table. Sorry if her way of makin' a livin' don't suit you."

"It's not that, Pop. There's crime out here in a big city. You could get hurt. I got to get back to the show."

Pop raises his walkin' stick in the air, points the rubber tip at Joe. Amazing how steady it rests in his hand, might have something to do with the empty whiskey glass in front of him and Joe wonders how many times Pop's emptied it.

"If you think I can't care for myself, boy, you got another thing comin'. Mind your own damn business. Kill another neighbor!"

"Pop!"

"Oh, right. Wasn't a neighbor." Turns back to the stage, another five in hand, "Well, wherever you get 'em."

"Can't just leave you like this."

Pop swivels around again, his finger hooked in the G-string "Look, if you want, we can double date. There's a real nice gal in the back, what's her name, honey?" Pop now has his other hand on Starlight's ass and Joe wants to hurl, gets a good glimpse of her *Hello Kitty* tramp stamp just above her butt crack. She bends down to Pop's ear, whispers, and swings back up on the pole.

"Rita! That's right. And you see that? See what she just did? Real athletes these girls. That takes practice, JoJo."

Joe thinks about what's hiding in a place like this. Jealous boy friends, pimps, drug dealers and how Pop can't possibly know this girl's true-life story. She'd probably tell him anything to drain the last dime from his wallet or ATM card.

He pats the old man on the shoulder and tells him he'll be back, praying Pop doesn't bring Starlight-or-Star Bright home as his new *step mommy*.

Pop briefly raises his hand. He's too fascinated at how Starlight can maneuver around that pole upside down with both legs straight up in the air like that. Yep, a real athlete.

JOE'S SURPRISED TO see how many people are still at the exhibit. He finds Sadie—now pissed Sadie—who shoots him a scowl his Mom used when he drifted home late.

"Where have you been? I've got the multicolor sold."

"Pop disappeared."

"Oh, no. Have you called the police?"

"No. I found him, but can't get him out of the titty bar. He's attached to some damn stripper and won't leave. Know where Julio is?"

"At the reception area, I think. What do you want with Julio?"

"He lived here. Thought maybe he could talk sense into him or at least tell me he's gonna be okay in there."

Sadie bows her head in deep thought. "Check the lounge."

Joe turns to leave then turns back, "What'd you get for the multicolor?"

"A hundred and thirty-five thousand."

"Dollars?"

"Think I was kidding? I think the fish have sold and there's a bidding war on the gold woman."

JULIO'S LOUNGING IN a dark corner back booth with three other people, two guys and a gal—looks to be a date thing— one guy and gal making out, Julio and the other guy making out. Julio's just a little drunk. Joe's heart sinks thinking Julio won't want to help him, and even if he did, what kind of condition is he in to do it?

As Julio tilts his head, Joe notices the graceful swan- like curves of his neck, definition in the chin and high cheek bones softened by candle light. A he-she mix Joe imagines printed on rice paper.

"Mister Salas, how are chew?"

"Can I talk to you? In private?"

Julio kisses his date and crawls out of the booth, slides his arm around Joe's shoulder. "Wha can I do for chew, Mister Salas?"

"Pop's in a strip joint downtown and I can't get him to leave. Don't trust him by himself. He's not himself." Joe tilts his head quickly and Julio gets the jist of it. "Can you run down there with me to get him out before he does something stupid?"

"Chew wan me?"

"You know the area."

Julio's so overwhelmed being asked he's almost in tears. He flaps his hand at his face, turns on his heel and bids his friends farewell.

9

gangland hospitality

TURNS OUT IT'S a bad idea dragging Julio along. Sober, he's manageable, but drunk, it's impossible to understand anything he's sobbing about in his drooling, slurring, Cuban accent. Joe pulls him along, his shoulder now snot soggy, and he wonders if he can take Julio back to the hotel before Pop gets whisked off by Starlight-or-Star Bright?

"Shut up! I don't even know what you're cryin' about and don't care!"

"Ooo Miser Salas, I so sorry. I zip it," Julio sniffs through the back of his hand. Glances at Joe and starts crying again.

"You gonna be able to help me or not?"

"*Yessss,*" he whines.

"What's wrong with you?"

"Chew no understan."

"Give it a shot," Joe says then mumbles, "And stop whining."

Julio stops on the sidewalk, sways, pulls up his shirt, *"Chew see!"*

Hard to focus in the blue neon from the art deco building next to them, Julio's torso a sleek blemish-free highway shaded in pale blue with a strip of yellow from another building nearby. Joe tries real hard, says, "Not really. What am I lookin' for?"

"This! This righ here!" Points to a two-inch keloid scaling his side. Pulls the shirt off and slings it to the street. "I was fifteen, God bless me, when Rico stab me. Righ here."

"Not a stab. Looks like a cut. What did he use?"

"These really men looking file," Julio gives a slicing motion and stumbles.

"What kind of file?" Joe pulls him out of the street, sweeps Julio's shirt off the pavement. Handing it over, Joe can see the evasiveness to his question, like Julio doesn't want to answer because Joe won't like the answer.

"File, Julio? What kind of file?"

Julio glances at his hands, spreads his fingers, "Feener nail file. But it hurt, Miser Salas."

"Why you crying about it now?"

"I don know. It lay on my mind when I drin too much. And—"

"Any other time I'd love to hear it, but right now I'm tryin' to keep Pop out a jail."

Another wasted five minutes and they'd have missed him. Pop's limping out the door with Starlight-Whatever on his arm, gum smacking in a big *I got me a sucker!* grin. They don't even notice Joe and Julio until Joe yells, "Pop, where you going?"

"Told you already. You losing your memory?" Squeezes Starlight's ass.

"You takin' her home?"

"Nope. She's taking me home. Whatcha think of that?" Winks when he says it.

"Can't let you do that, Pop. You need to come back to the hotel."

"Yes, Miser Salas. We all miss chew."

"That the best you can come up with?" Joe scolds.

Julio shrugs defeat.

"How about you bring Starlight back to our hotel?"

Joe figures that'll at least get him back to the safe zone where he can keep an eye on him. Tries not to think what she and Pop will be doing there. What can an eighty-year-old guy do, anyway? "Excuse me a second," Joe says pulling Pop aside.

"Think this is a good idea, you not being a spring chicken and all?"

Pop leans in, "She's got the hook-ups."

"Hook-up to what?"

"*Viagree!* Guaranteed. Said it works every time."

"God, Pop. I didn't want to know that."

"Yes you did. Let's go. Gotta get her back by daybreak. Turns into a punkin'.'"

At least they get headed in the right direction, but halfway down the alley Joe notices three, maybe four hooded forms loitering by the sidewalk—dark clothes, hands crammed in pockets, pack-stalking like hyenas hunting an easy kill.

"Who's got cash?" Joe says sizing them up. Thinks throwing a wad of cash at them might buy time.

"Tha no can be good," Julio says in a more sober tone.

"Any other way out?"

"With Miser Limpy here? I no thin so. Wha chew gonna do?"

"Me? You live here. What do you recommend?"

"*Run.*"

"Okay. We'll go inside and out the back. Maybe they're just waiting on someone." Joe turns around for Pop and sees he's standing alone with his walkin' stick and nothing visible of Starlight except her Hello Kitty tramp stamp disappearing back in the bar. Door slams shut. Locks.

"Tha no so good," Julio says. Steps behind Joe, pensive.

Joe turns Pop around and pushes him towards the bar, doesn't care the old guy's bitching about his runaway date. Blames Joe. Joe doesn't think Pop's clued in on the problem yet. "Sorry, Pop. Gotta go. *Now.*"

Joe beats on the door and suddenly the lights go out. And it probably only took those few seconds for the homies to slip in behind and trap them. Joe's heart's pounding and his brain's trying to capture an idea to get out of what he thinks is coming next.

A semi-automatic drifts among them as if floating in air. Joe can't tell which one actually has it. Julio swoons against the pink stucco wall.

Joe hears one of them mumble "money," "blast your brains." Julio screams in his high female octave. Pop swings the walkin' stick and whacks someone in the dark. He's suddenly going down, the walkin' stick useless under the weight of him. Joe doesn't know why Pop's down, didn't hear a shot.

"I got money!" Joe yells, torn whether to help Pop or watch the gun.

The hood team switches places, merges, separates— hard for Joe to see Pop's condition between shifting shadows. Julio reaches for Pop, takes a fist to the mouth and goes down. Joe jumps, and the gun, now flipped on its side, sprouts inches from his nose. He inhales gun oil and cologne, doesn't think he can fight all three of them. "Let me get my wallet," he begs. Slowly reaches back to pull it out.

Deep within the hood, Joe can see eyes surrounded in chocolate hues from dark to milk, haloed by orange neon from the building across the street. There's nothing in the eyes but edgy rage and Joe knows they've no intention of letting them leave alive.

"Go G," one says.

There's movement, confusion, not enough light. One of the homies gets slammed to the wall. A flash of light as the gun goes off. Bullet ricochets.

Joe uses his leg to sweep the gunman off his feet and the gun blasts five more rounds into the locked bar door. Joe grabs Pop's walkin' stick and blindly knocks the gun from homie's hand as if he's going for a home run.

More confusion, pushing, shoving, and Joe's over the guy's body beating his brains out. Doesn't realize he's spitting obscenities with every strike.

Joe stops, heaving air, trying to crawl out of his rage. Julio and Pop are on their feet huddled together wide-eyed against the wall.

"Chew alrigh, Miser Salas?" Julio whispers.

"Yeah, yeah, I'm okay. Just gotta catch my breath." Joe looks around, "Where are the other two?"

"They leaf. One chew star beatin on him, they run."

"Good. That's good," Joe says breathless. "Come on, we gotta go." Hands the walkin' stick back to Pop. "You hurt?"

Pop shakes his head, shuffles behind.

Julio sprints up to Joe's ear, "You thin he dead, Miser Salas?"

"Don't know. Don't care."

"Shoo we call the police?"

"And say what?"

"It no chew fault," Julio says, has his arm around Pop to keep him steady.

"Everything's my fault, Julio."

10

how to drown a jerk

PAPERWORK'S NOT A *PAPERWORK'S NOT A* cop's favorite thing. It ranks somewhere with revolving domestics and scrubbing drunk vomit from the back floorboard of the patrol car. Croy's the exception. He revels in paperwork. Got hooked on the heady alcohol of fresh Ditto worksheets in elementary school. He especially loves opening a new book, running his fingers over virgin print, listening for the subtle crackle of the binding when pulled opened for the first time and flipping the pages close to his face smelling the flutter that wafts that "new book" fragrance to his nose. Then there's the pristine report sheets waiting for the marriage of pen to paper, neatly stacked on the corner of his desk.

Used reports comfort like old friends. Stories thread through the narratives revealing secret lives. Cold traumas in print. In his mind they become daytime soaps—reality manifested on paper.

Report number one: Middle aged Hispanic female dies at the hand of unknown suspect.

Report number two: Missing white male, prime suspect of report number one.

Report number three: Missing elderly white female. Suspected foul play.

Croy slides photos to each report from their folders and places them in his leather brief.

Arnold blows through the door, "You borrow my car?" He's not frantic yet, but close.

"No, wasn't me, Arnie." Croy wipes down his desk. Gives it shot of Lysol.

"Know if anyone else borrowed it?"

"Not that they told me."

"Shit. Think it's been stolen. You know the paperwork they're going to make me fill out?" Taps his fingers on his belt. "They're gonna give me days off."

"They probably will," Croy says reading through a file.

"What moron steals a cop car?"

Croy looks up and considers. "Me. If I was going to steal a car. If I had a choice."

"What?"

"Well think of all the cool things in them."

"Like what?"

"Department issue. You know. Vests, shotguns."

"I don't keep that stuff in the car."

"Where do you keep it?"

"Home. In case the car gets stolen."

"Are you that certain no one will break into your place, Arnie?"

"Not the way I keep house. They'll never find it."

"Can you find it?"

"Not really. I mean if I had to, I could. Not stuff I use anyway. When's the last time you used yours?"

"Three days ago on that warrant arrest on Grove Street."

"Shut up."

"You asked. What if you roll up on a bank robbery?"

"*Bank! That's it!* I left the car at the bank."

"Then how did you get back here?"

"It's a nice day. It's only six blocks away, so I walked."

"Want me to take you to the bank, don't you?"

"That'd be nice."

"Take a ride with me? Got an interview I don't want to do alone."

"Bad people?"

"No. Some woman who thinks we're going steady."

"Really? What's she like?"

"I'll let it be a surprise."

IT ONLY BLED a little when Roy pulled the Kotex from Eddie's head, the edges dried and crusting, and Roy's not sure he's seeing pus in there. Heard brain infections can be painful enough to cause insanity, the kind of pain to send a guy to the basement to cut his own head off with the Skil Saw. That story drifted around J and J's automotive when he was getting a new transmission dropped into the Suburban, back when the boys were debating on the logistics of one even being able to commit a suicide like that without help. He didn't really believe you could kill yourself that way, but hell, Eddie's still alive with a bullet in his head. He's been grinding his teeth for over an hour now.

"You gotta stop that, Eddie."

Roy squirts Betadine on the bullet hole, turns it all a graphic translucent brown trailing down the side of Eddie's face and into his ear, but doesn't appear to hurt. Blotting his cheek, Roy watches Eddie's good eye flutter as if coming out of a dream. Still nothing verbal.

Unwrapping the gauze pad and tape purchased in Gainesville, he squeezes more betadine on the gauze and pastes it to Eddie's head wound. Feels spongy like there's stuff in there ready to blow. Grosses Roy out the way it gives under his finger tips. A few strips of tape and Eddie's all fixed up, at least best as Roy can do. He wads up the pad and wrappers and chucks them into the garbage.

Motel room harbors the ghost of rancid cigarette smoke fused in the rubber-backed curtains stretching across the plate glass windows that overlook the parking lot—haunts of past depressions, lonely break-ups, stolen affairs, folks looking for second chances on their last dollar. The ancient air conditioner blows wet rotted filter to the floor, but air's cold—Roy's hoping the water'll be hot because Eddie stinks.

"I'll run you a bath, Eddie. Crawl outa that stuff."

Roy turns on the bathroom light pleased the place is clean, but needs renovation. He draws Eddie's bath, pours in complimentary bath bubbles—a tropical fruity blend—and checks his face in the mirror. Needs a shave. A bath of his own wouldn't hurt so much, either.

"Come on, Eddie, water's ready. Nice and hot. Just the way you like it. And no one's gonna bellyache about you being in too long. No one at all."

Eddie's sitting on the edge of the bed, tilted a little to the right, chin to chest as if he's fallen asleep like that. Roy watches him, waits for the rise and fall of his chest, maybe for nothing more than a twitch. Heard people can die upright in weird positions like that and he's not past wondering if that's just what Eddie's done.

"Hey, Eddie! You all right?"

An exaggerated exhale on Eddie's part gives Roy relief. He's gonna have to undress and drop him in the tub. In this cleaner environment, Roy smells just how bad Eddie stinks. Stripped naked, Roy hikes his brother to his feet and helps him into the tub. Eddie seems relieved.

"Gotta go out and get ice. There's a snack machine in the hall so I'll bring us somethin' back."

Eddie slides deeper in the foam, nothing but his head showing, and as if severed from the body, it floats.

Small motor lodges don't offer much in the way of hallways, just covered porticos to keep off the drizzle, not much protection in a heavy downpour. Both the ice and snack machine are huddled against the wall weathering the heat and another sudden Florida thunderstorm and Roy squeezes against them, his back to the wind trying to stay dry.

Back in the room, Roy slings the bags of chips and Snickers to the table, grabs the phone and dials a number, but the recording on the other end says service has been discontinued. Bad deal, Roy thinks. Ricky would never let his phone get disconnected. Maybe something bad did happen. Suddenly Roy thinks of Eddie and realizes he hasn't heard him splashing around in there, or God forbid, singing. That can't be good.

"Hey, Eddie, you okay?" No sound back but the low roar of the air conditioner.

Roy pops his head in, but Eddie's gone. Roy's eyes skitter around the room as if Eddie will magically appear, as if he'd somehow passed and missed him. There's nowhere to hide in a space this small, but Roy checks the closet anyway. Three hangers. Two dead cockroaches on their backs. Roy's wondering if Eddie slipped out while he was getting ice. Man, this is—

Roy glances over his shoulder and bolts for the tub, reaches in and yanks Eddie's head out of the water. He's limp and turning a weird shade of blue. *"Eddie!"*

Roy drags him out of the tub onto the cold tile floor, listens for the rise and fall of his chest. Nothing.

"This is gonna hurt, Eddie," Roy says punching him in the chest with his fist. Learned it on TV. If someone's not breathing, punch them in the chest. They'll come right back.

"Shit, Eddie, don't die on me here. You had all that time back home to do it. Don't damn die on me here." Roy punches again, mumbles, "I'll never explain this right. They'll think I killed you."

Suddenly Roy remembers you had to do mouth to mouth to get them to breath and reenacts an episode of *ER*. He pinches Eddie's nose shut and blows air in his mouth getting a little light-headed. Eddie's chest jerks. He coughs, clutches his chest. Coughs again. Blue coloring begins to fade to pink.

"Damn, Eddie, what are you doin'?" Roy pulls a towel from the rack and rubs foam from Eddie's nose. "You okay, buddy?"

"Think I fell asleep. I was dreamin' about when we were kids and playin' round the garage." Coughs, "You pushed that kid off the roof and we thought you killed him. It was great."

"What the hell are you talking about?" Eddie's shivering in Roy's arms and Roy drapes the towel over him. Strokes Eddie's head and thinking he's hallucinating from some brain infection.

"Naw, you remember. Dumb fuck dared you and you slung him right off the top." Eddie wipes his nose with the corner of the towel. "Forgot about the tools at the bottom, though."

"Sure you didn't just dream all that?"

"I'd forgotten it. I remembered that kid screamin' and runnin' out."

"I pushed him? That how you remember it?"

"I remembered Ma taking the strap after you. Then took it after dumb fuck for fallin' in the first place and for gettin' blood all over her clean floor." Eddie curls up tight against Roy. Shivers seem worse.

"Wasn't me who pushed him, Eddie."

"It wa, wa, was."

"No, Eddie. You pushed him off the roof. Laughed about it the whole way down."

Eddie's quiet but still shivering. There's a rasping deep in his chest Roy can hear every time Eddie takes a breath.

"But Ma be, be, beat your ass."

"Yeah, 'cause she blamed me for lettin' ya. You were her favorite."

"Then why'd she put me in the bunker?"

"She was messed up, Eddie."

"Shoo, shoo, shouldn't talk about her like that, Roy," Eddie stutters. "She had a hard life."

"I don't know what she had except demons. Might explain the way you are."

"What does?"

"Drinkin' and shit while she was pregnant with you."

"Lucky I didn't get some defect like harelip or drunken baby disease."

"Right, because killin' innocent girls isn't like having a real defect," Roy says sarcastically. Realizes sarcasm is wasted on Eddie.

"You don't know that. You don't know nothin'."

"I know we had a hard life livin' with her. Our daddies had it even harder. But she liked your daddy best. Think he really tried puttin' up with her black moods. But she ate him like a spider."

"That's messed up, Roy."

"She was messed up. Maybe we are, too."

antibacterial cookies

NOT THAT HE minded Arnie in the passenger seat, it wasn't his personal car, department issue, but still, driving around with a chronic chain smoker polluting the fabric with nicotine and tar—wasn't such a good idea having him ride along. He should've just met him over there.

Croy wrinkles his nose, doesn't dare wipe it with his hand and wonders if he's got enough hand cleaner. Can't remember when he replaced it or how much is left. He subtly slips his hand into his interior jacket pocket feeling for the small plastic bottle, carefully lifts it with his finger tips trying to judge the volume of fluid.

Arnie coughs at the windshield, reaches in for his smokes and smacks the pack against his hand to flush a cig forward.

"Let's not do that, Arnie."

"You gonna make me wait 'till we get there? You're not one of those cigarette Nazis, are you?"

"Yeah, Arnie. You strike a match and I'll pull my gun and shoot you right here at the red light. Then I'll roll your body out to the street and drive off. Do the interview without you. And when command staff asks why I did it I'll say to save them a hell of a lot of money. No pension, no disability because of lung cancer or emphysema, just a nice quiet funeral with a bagpipe. Does McPherson still play?"

Arnie stares at the cigarette between his fingers. "They have medication for what you have."

"I'm just saying, Arnie. You smoke on top of all the black mold you inhale everyday at the PD and it's a disaster waiting in the wings."

"The wings of what?"

"I mean just when you're free and clear, having a great time on some beach in Mexico, it is still Mexico isn't it? I'm telling you, you'll start coughing blood and be dead in three months. Coroner will say, 'This guy's lungs are shit. Smoker. Mold breather. The two together…better if he'd jumped off a building. Would have saved him all that pain.' Then there's always radon. Odorless gas. Second leading cause of cancer in the country, Arnie."

"You need a girlfriend, Croy. Some damn distraction."

Croy parks the Ford on the street in front of Dee Dee's house, dreads ringing the bell. Hopes she takes a quick shine to Arnie.

"What's the deal?" Arnie asks slipping the cig back in the pack. Thinks he might sneak a smoke after the interview. If nothing else, slip into the bathroom and puff away under the exhaust vent.

"Patrol's taken four or five reports with this woman. Arrested her, had her Baker Acted. I think she knows something."

"What's her issue?"

"Not what. Who. Her neighbor Joe Salas." Croy gets out of the car, waits for Arnie to close the passenger door then leans back in and sniffs.

"This have anything to do with the missing person's files?"

"Gut tells me it does. I interviewed the guy a couple of weeks ago. He knows something. Anyway, I'm going to show Miss Turner some photos and see if it sparks a memory," Croy says stopping at the mailbox. Opens it and peers in. Closes it.

"Then you don't think she's a whack job?"

"Doesn't matter what I think. Just because she's a whack job doesn't mean she lies about everything. If she's telling the truth we at least owe her an apology." Croy presses the door bell, wonders if he can swing by the pharmacy and pick up a small can of Lysol for the car to lessen the time he has to ride with the tar and nicotine.

Croy rings the doorbell several times and gets no answer. They turn back to the car when he hears laughing coming from the back yard. He and Arnie find their way back through unruly hibiscus to the back fence. Pounding on the wooden gate, the metal hardware clanking echoes in the side yard, the gate swings open and Dee Dee's standing with nothing but a beach towel wrapped around her waist.

Arnie's eyes swell saucer-like at the huge breasts nestled against her rib cage glistening with coco oil like great loaves of buttered brown bread. Croy turns and stares at Arnie.

"Detective, Croy! You came back. And you brought a friend. How did you know? Did you call and talk to Marge?"

Dee Dee grabs Croy's arm and drags him into the back yard. *Great, something else to wipe down with hand cleaner.*

"Come on back. Already started the party. And what's your name, honey?" She aims the question at Arnie whose eyes watch with fascination the way Dee Dee's boobs keep time with her steps. Croy elbows Arnie in the side, almost drops the files under his arm.

"Arnold. Detective Arnold. But you can call me Arnie."

"This here is Marge," Dee Dee says walking behind Marge's lawn chair to the sliding glass doors. Marge is stretched out naked on the recliner, gin and tonic in one hand and a wet wash cloth draped over her face. She fishes an animal cracker out of the box and throws it blindly in the yard with others. Raises her glass.

"You know, I think we'll come back later. I'll call next time," Croy says. Arnie looks deflated, just shy of depressed.

"No, no!" Dee Dee squeals, "Come on back in the kitchen and I'll grab a robe." She pulls the towel up. "I forgot you're all the shy type."

Arnie perks up, "Shy? We're not, at least I'm not…I'm fine with it."

Croy jabs Arnie in the side again. "We'd appreciate that."

Left alone in the kitchen, Croy takes note of the mini bar set up by the sink, a half bottle of gin, bottle of tonic, tray of half melted ice cubes, butchered limes. On the table, a large box of Cheez-Its, bags of chips, cookies, a half-eaten ham gnawed to the bone.

"Now, what brings you here? Not stupid enough to think it's me."

She's wearing the bear pelt again, but at least it's cinched up covering everything.

"I brought a few photos I'd like to show you, see if you recognize anyone."

"And who they be?" she says sitting at the table, shoving empty animal cracker boxes aside.

"You just look and tell me if you've seen them."

"Oh, we're going to play it that way, are we?" Winks and holds out her thick hand.

Croy hands her the photo from file number three. Dee Dee holds it a distance away studying. "Woman in the shed. But she wasn't dead like them others." Says it in an authoritative voice.

Croy knows she's telling the truth, or at least she believes it's the truth. "How about this one," he says handing over photo number two.

"Can't be one hundred percent positive, but shrink wrap his head and this could be the guy I saw on the bench. His head anyway," she says handing it back.

"That's okay, Miss Turner. Take your time. How about this one?"

"Yeah, seen her several times."

"Where?"

"With that asshole Salas. Think she was his girl."

"Why do you think she was his girl?"

"Only one he ever brought over. Not what you'd call a ladies' man."

"What makes you say that?"

"You ever seen him? Creepy. Never liked him. Ever since he moved in with his father. Always bitching about my dog. 'Till he kilt it." Just saying it out loud drops a dark mood on the kitchen. "So, where's the other guy?"

"Excuse me?"

"The other one. The one he dragged in during the hurricane?" She asks.

"Ever see the guy before that day?"

"No. Never."

"How did he look?"

"He looked *dead.*"

"I mean, what did he look like?"

"Well," she says pulling a box of Keebler chocolate covered grahams to her, "from what I remember," she pulls out a cookie, stuffs it in her mouth, and chews thoughtfully, "and mind you it was in the middle of a hurricane now," chews on, "bigger guy than Joe. Had a hard time dragging him around to the back of the yard. Guess you don't realize how heavy a person is until you have to carry their dead ass a few hundred feet in a storm. Muddy down here after a rain, too." She pulls another cookie from the pack. Stops short of biting it. "You know, it was what he was wearing. Like what those doctors wear. White coat with matching pants." Hands Croy a cookie.

"Like a lab coat?"

"Yeah, somethin' like that."

"You said white?" Croy pretends to nibble the edge waiting for her answer.

"White."

"How old you think he was?"

"Thirties, maybe. Never got a good look up close 'cause Joe, he heard me scream, like I said before."

"Are you certain he was dead and not just drunk?"

Dee Dee stops chewing. Croy can see she's revisiting the event.

"Asshole Salas was talking in the shed." Giggles. "To his self if you ask me. Guess the guy could have been alive, but he looked *dead*."

"Did you happen to hear anything he said?"

"No, but he talked like me and you are, you know?"

"Ever see the guy after that?"

"Hell no. Another cookie?" She holds one out, the chocolate melting between her fingers.

"No thank you. Still working on this one. Well, thank you for your time. If I have any more questions I'll give you a call. Thanks for the hospitality, Miss Turner."

"Call me Dee Dee. You fellas have time for a drink? Or stay for supper!" She's on her feet clutching her hands together hopefully. "Marge, she can do some cookin' now."

"I'm sure. We have to get back, still on the clock." Croy taps his watch.

"Do whatcha want," she says going for the sliding glass doors. "We're here mostly any time. Hell, just drop by."

Croy's feeling that trapped sensation again. He can see Arnie outside sitting on the edge of a lawn chair next to Marge, deep in conversation, all eyes and yellow smoker's teeth. While Dee Dee's back is turned, Croy drops the cookie back in the package.

Dee Dee yells out the door, "Marge! Get up! They're leaving!"

"You make my damn drink, yet?" Marge yells back.

"In a minute," Dee Dee smiles quickly at Croy. "Sure wish you'd stay for supper."

Arnie's giving Marge a drag off of his cigarette, holds it to her lips, pulls his gaze from Marge long enough to catch Croy's eye.

Hopeful. That's what Croy sees on Arnie's face. Like he's expecting him to say, 'Sure, we'll stay and party.' Not in his lifetime. "We have to get back to the case, but you ladies have a nice night." Croy avoids looking at Marge and makes a quick getaway to the gate. Arnie trails behind like a kid that had to dump his ice cream cone.

"Wouldn't hurt to stay a little longer. Not everyone's as obsessed as you, Croy. Some of us have needs. Like companionship and…"

"Don't say and the love of a good woman."

"Not since you've already said it," Arnie says crawling into the car. "She has trolls."

"You mean crabs?"

"No, trolls."

"What?"

"Says they live in the woods out there. She's trying to get a picture of it. Feeds them cookies."

"What is *it*?"

"Hell if I know. She was kind of vague now that I think about it and I wasn't really paying attention to tell the truth."

"I noticed that."

"Not like I get to sit with a naked woman everyday, you know."

"Got that, too. You two going to be an item now?"

"Not my type. Too many issues from what little conversation we did have. Told me all about her whacko sister, but sounds like it runs in the family."

"So, she's the sane one, feeding crackers to imaginary trolls?"

"Exactly. I don't need the drama. I've had thirty years of drama."

AT THE PD, Croy considers wearing one of those paper masks, the kind with the rubber band head strap and plastic fitable nose piece. Might need an upgrade to a TC-21C particle respirator those guys use when detoxing a remodel from lead or asbestos, so he takes shallow breaths to avoid inhaling all those poisonous spores that turn your lungs to applesauce. ADMIN will give him shit about wearing it, go off on some tangent about scaring the other employees until the whole building's evacuated—personal choice of course—then the EPA will get involved and send in Haz-Mat inspectors to take metered tests that'll show high particulates of stachybotrys and insist on containment with heavy plastic sheeting sealed with duct tape, and rip out all the interior walls and insulation, then go for the air vent system. They'll have to install air purifiers for thousands of dollars on top of the hundreds of thousands spent on clean up—higher with delays and cost over runs—and what about the leak that caused it in the first place? New roof or maybe rip out the plumbing. Might give him days off for instigating trouble. He could just be wrong about the whole thing.

"Arnie, can you pull all the missing persons fliers within a two-hundred-mile radius?"

"What for?"

"Looking for someone. Maybe in the medical field."

"I can do that. I am the wizard of the keyboard, you know."

"You are the wizard, Arnie. Wouldn't have anyone else do it."

Cheesy, but it gets Arnie's mind off his *coitus interruptus*. Who knew there'd be two women? Arnie was going for it, no question.

Croy slips into the bathroom and turns on the hot water. *Hot* water. Lathers five or six squirts of anti-bacterial hand soap in his palm and scrubs hard because he's picked up foreign germs while at Dee Dee's place. He had to touch the doorbell. The gate. The cookie contaminated with her sweaty fingerprints. Gooey melted germs imbedded in the chocolate. He didn't sit. Glad he didn't sit. They don't wear underwear. Ass germs. Bare feet all over the house. Feet sweat. Dirt. Old dog germs. Probably scooted on its ass across the carpet leaving fecal matter embedded in the fabric where anyone could pick it up. On bare feet.

Croy scrubs harder, tucks his hands under the scalding hot water until they turn red. He pulls a paper towel from the canister, notices a gun on top of the next sink over. It's Arnie's. Arnie who probably hasn't a clue it's missing. And it's not the first time.

Croy goes back to the squad room slathering on antibacterial hand sanitizer. Arnie's at his computer and documents are pushing out of the printer.

"So far, got a bunch of missing women, but none around here. None of them work in the medical field, either," Arnie says sliding on his rollie chair to the printer."

"Looking for a man. But I'll take what you've got. Know where your gun is, Arnie?"

"Always know where my gun is. What kind of a question is that? This a test?"

"You better hope not. Well, do you?"

Arnie looks down at his empty holster. "Shit." Quickly inventories his work station, drawers. Briefcase. Croy's enjoying his enthusiastic panic.

"God, now I'm really gonna get days off. Might get fired. And the car's still at the bank."

"Check the bathroom. And I'll drop you at your car before I go home."

"Thanks," Arnie says bolting from his desk to the door. "You're an okay guy, Croy. Even if you are a freak."

"Thanks, Arnie. Love you, too."

Croy collects the thirty missing person's fliers, sits at his desk and reads them one by one.

"Arnie, take a look at these. What do you see?" Croy hands the fliers over as Arnie shoves his gun in his holster. Spreads the fliers across his desk and studies, separates three from the stack. "So, what do you think?"

"I think this blue Suburban is a suspect vehicle. Even though it wasn't seen in every case, it's around enough to warrant a close look. Too bad no one got a tag."

"Maybe it didn't have one."

"Most of these girls are likely runaways. Some missing since, what, over twenty years ago? It is close to a college town."

"I think I've seen that Suburban. At least one that matches the description."

"Oh, yeah?"

"Just a few days ago in the same area."

"But the girls are missing from different jurisdictions. Think anyone's noticed the big picture?"

"No one was looking for a big picture. We just happen to catch it by accident."

Printer pukes another document. Croy pulls it out and reads.

"Another one?"

"Maybe *the* one."

"What is it?"

"Missing male nursing assistant from the VA in north Florida. He went missing after the hurricane. He's wanted for questioning about the suspicious deaths of elderly patients."

"What's it got to do with this case?"

"Oh, I forgot. You weren't really there for the interview part. You were drooling over the gal throwing food in the yard."

"Kept her out of your hair. Just think of how bad it would have been if I wasn't there to distract her."

"Right. You were doing me a favor. Anyway, Miss Turner said the first guy she saw Joe Salas drag into the shed—and that would be during the hurricane—was a male wearing white scrubs. I think it was Mr. Keys here."

"Whoa. Why would some male nurse be killed here if he lived hours away?"

"That's why they call us detectives, Arnie. To find the little cogs that fit in the wheels that make the case go round and round."

"You're a frickin' genius, Croy."

"Are there anymore dark green folders?"

Arnie swivels around, opens a drawer. "Yellow." Hands two folders to Croy.

Croy doesn't touch them. They lay limp in Arnie's hand.

"What?"

"Wrong color."

"It's a folder!"

"I know that, but it's not a dark green folder."

Arnie swivels back, fingers through the cabinet and retrieves a single dark green folder. Hands it over.

Croy scowls at it. "The corner's bent."

"So, what?"

"Is that the last one?"

"Yep, the very last."

"We'll stop by *Office Depot* on the way out."

"You can't use it because the corner is bent?"

"It's damaged."

"How bad is this thing you have?"

"There are just things that have to be a certain way."

"You are messed up."

"At least I know where my car and gun are. Come on. Let's go get it before the captain finds out."

12

languid nightmares

MARGE, MARGERY, MAGGIE, Maggie May. Isn't that a song? *Rod Stewart*, hot Rod, stiff Rod, sing me a song Rod, whisper in Marge's ear Rod. The list marches through Marge's brain, her sun-roasted brain, floating in its cerebrospinal fluid nestled in its safe Dura mater, Arachnoid, Pia mater—the soft blanket of sanity. She's happy in this world, sucking co-dependence for the right to be dependent.

Marge, her real name unless Mother lied because Mother does lie, quickly and without remorse, lied to Dee the most so Dee never had the self-worth to look a man in the eye without fever, without desperation, without hunger until she shrank from society and took up with that black weakling baring needle sharp teeth, a real dog she still mourns months after its escape. Marge believes it escaped, wasn't taken, wasn't killed as Dee had screamed over the phone. It couldn't take it anymore, she suffocated it, spoke baby talk until it went mad, couldn't stand life being her man. It wanted to be a dog, to slip away and chase cars, to knock over garbage cans and eat rot, to hump anything until exhausted on the lawn.

It got away, left her, just like their father, left them with a mother that lies, but Dee's still here rambling around in this block stucco house hoping she'll get a call that her man's been found, and she'll squeal and cry and forget her pills, decide she doesn't need them now. What would dog say if he had the voice? Would he stay quiet on the phone, breathe a heavy silence? Would she be grateful for nothing more than to hear him breathe? Would he try to explain how his life had changed and that coming back just wasn't good for him? And would he say, 'wasn't good for her, either'?

For over thirty years she's picked up the remnants of Dee's lost hopes and tried to forget her own, but unlike Dee, she wanders from cruise ship to casino to spa to clubhouse as if staying too long will force her to examine her own betrayals, and now she's lying naked on this lawn chair in Dee's backyard roasting in autumn sun, her face covered with a wet pink terry washcloth to keep off the heat, to hide because she can't flee, she can't leave Dee alone in this house with the thoughts of that bastard dog, that bastard who left her without remorse. Is it time to buy more gin?

The skin on her breasts feels tight and dry as her dreams, and from under the cloth now hot and steamy and dried at the edges, she can hear fluttering close by, not small and wistful, but heavy and rhythmical. With her thumb and forefinger, Marge gently lifts one corner of the cloth and peers up and a little to the right.

She counts five vultures stalking her from the fence line—from an angle that only one eye can capture—cold fear blooming despite the heat of the sun, and she's exposed, vulnerable, and a little too drunk. She squints to block out the sight of them in case it's just the gin. Too much gin and sun, too much free reign of her brain to bound into dark spaces and roust evils that have plagued her since childhood.

Only the right eye's allowed to venture, as if the left is incompetent, as if the gin has control of the left side and not the right. Is it a stroke, has her brain bled, has it turned against her, has she finally met hell while lying naked in the sun? Are they angels of death, guards come to escort her back? Would they vaporize if she sat up? What if she yelled and clapped her hands?

It's as if she's just as they like it, prone and dying. They watch with a bitter eye, spread their wings as if an invitation to be comforted. An offer, a choice to disappear, to vanish, and for a moment she allows the possibility.

A sixth, glides just above the roofline and lands less than ten feet from her chair. Dusky black, hump backed, it waddles awkwardly through the thick overgrown St. Augustine picking at animal crackers like a good dog.

The cloth, now stiffened from the heat, falls to her chest. Her heart pounds, pressing rivulets of sweat into her clavicles. And her brain's like a convict jumping the razor wire, shredded and bleeding, desperate for the field, for the highway, for the lone traveler to stop and pick up a stranger.

A seventh vulture glides to the ground next to the sixth, followed by two on the fence line. Two more take their place. They've surrounded her on three sides, hissing and groaning to each other in secret code like the hand signals of a dangerous gang that's found a mark, a victim to feed to the new inductees, the initiation rites of passage.

Marge whimpers. Her bottom lip quivers like her breasts, knuckles tight, clutch the side of the aluminum recliner. The webs dig into the tender flesh of her fingers. If she shuts her eyes, will they be gone when she opens them?

The sliding glass door draws open. Dee Dee, writing list on pad, steps onto the patio. "Going to the store. Whatcha want for sup—" Blood drains from her face. The pad and pen hit the concrete. "*Dear, God.*"

"YOUR BUDDIES ARE still hangin' out." Pop shuffles from the back door to the sink checking the window. "Just a couple on the pine down back. Like they're expectin' dinner. Why don't you pitch this stuff out back for 'em?"

Joe, pulling suitcases in through the front door, only hears the last sentence of whatever Pop's been saying. Slings Pop's suitcase on the bed for him and shoves his own bag across the hardwood through the doorway of his bedroom.

"What stuff?"

Pop's stooped in front of the open refrigerator shoving things around. Pulls a couple of plastic wrapped (not sure what it started out as) bags of, thinks it was lunch meat. "Got bags of meat." Turns to the living room, "Think they'll eat it? Look hungry out there."

Joe steps in. "Haven't heard a word you said, old man. Who eats what?"

"This meat. For the birds, there."

"What birds?" Joe asks looking out the back door. "Birds don't eat meat, Pop."

Not a second passes before they hear a blood-curdling scream from over Dee Dee's place.

"Those birds do," Pop says stacking bags on the counter. "Been gone awhile. Maybe they got used to eatin' around here. Feed any wild animal and they're just like people. Stick around if someone'll feed 'em. Not stupid, those ones."

Joe can see a great drift of black feathers cascade into the trees at the woods line, vultures spooked by Dee Dee and Marge's shrieking, then a brief glimpse of lawn chair sailing through the air. A hellacious fight the whole neighborhood can hear ensues between Marge and Dee Dee, accusations about the damn crackers luring the birds down and Marge's visit needing to come to an abrupt end. Joe hears Dee Dee's sliding glass door slam violently. Three or four vultures land on the Drake Elm by the shed and bicker for room.

"Shit."

"What's that?"

"They're all over Dee Dee's place."

"She feeding 'em, too?"

"Not so much."

"Why you suppose they're over there?"

"Wouldn't know, Pop. She doesn't confide in me these days."

"Yeah, well I don't guess she'd want to. Maybe if you stop callin' the cops on her, she'll settle some."

"I didn't call the cops, she did. Remember?"

"If you say so. I'd be pissed too if you had my ass thrown in jail. Why don't you sling these out for 'em?" Pop gathers the spoiled rejects from the fridge and holds them out for Joe.

"Don't think so. They need to move on," he says going back to his room.

Pop stands at the back door and watches the birds preen for a good ten minutes. He unwraps the meat and tosses the contents into the back yard. Nothing much happens. Not sure what he expected, but them sitting in the trees staring at him wasn't it.

"How much money did I blow on what's her name?" Pop asks hearing Joe come back through the house.

Stops Joe dead. Isn't going to look at him. "Couple of hundred bucks I think. Unless you gave her your debit card and the pin number. We'll have to check the bank statement."

"Don't let it be said that youthful foolishness ends with age," Pop says watching the birds.

"If you had a good time, then what does it matter?"

"Don't try to make me feel better. It was stupid. I know better."

"You're just lonely, Pop. Nothing wrong with not wantin' to be."

"Losing time is, though. I get...*lost*. Forget where I'm at. Have blank spaces in my brain. Gettin' worse."

"Don't fret over it. We all have bad days. Gonna unpack and start the laundry. Leave the birds alone. Don't need 'em hanging out here all day beggin'." Joe says leaving Pop in the kitchen.

"Got your ass out of a crack a time or two," Pop mumbles out the door. "Treat 'em with a little respect, why don't you." Slings the last handful of whiffy meat to the yard and yells out to the vultures, "There it is! You eat it or the opossums will. Don't got nothing fresh. Maybe Joe will drop something off later. And stay out of the damn daylilies."

CHILDHOOD DISAPPOINTMENTS LINGER here—never being able to please his old man, or never being good enough in sports—Joe labels himself an all around general failure. He doesn't need anyone pressing the point. He takes a deep breath. What remained while they were in Miami feels richer, more involved—drawn to the back yard and beyond where the dead pine stands sentinel over the pond and the woods beyond. There's nothing left, inspiration to no one. He'd thought being back here would make him feel something...bad, remorseful, but it's not how he feels. And it surprises him. He's comforted the dead are still with him, at his control, their images sold and scattered throughout the world.

Two vultures sit sedate on the broken pine limbs unnoticed, disrespected, silent. They've ingested his secret and become carriers of them forever.

Joe takes inventory of his life, most of it a failure with few successes until now. On the kitchen table Joe sees Pop's box of bran cereal and its sidekick prunes, a later-in-life change when Joe was absent, distant, and resentful. The pruning shears, a passed-on promise to Mom not to let the daylilies die just because she did. A sketchbook he just couldn't get rid of pulled from a battered cardboard box in the shed, a daily reminder of a dream since middle school, and the dining room table with a notch in the leg where Mom slung the cast iron skillet to get everyone's attention when nothing else would because they'd learned to tune her out. Pop's walkin' stick turned lethal in self-defense, but always gentle under his hand.

From here in the doorway he can see the small photo gallery set up on the coffee table, the Salas's family shrine—most dead. Dead baby Jamie's ratty, matted bunny propped against the lamp, a clap-on-clap-off just so they don't have to disturb it.

He's caught Pop a couple of times picking up the photos as if dreaming of what could have been, or just grieving for what will never be. Joe's thought about taking the shrine down, packing it up, but it's all Pop has. It's here to stay, just like the vultures stuffed full of secrets, content to preen in the distance. They're not going anywhere and that's okay with him.

He pulls a beer from the fridge and sits at the table. Drags the curled, yellowed sketchbook to him and flips the torn cover to a charcoal drawing of Betty when she didn't know he was sketching her. She tried to tear it from his hand when she spotted it over his shoulder. Even in charcoal she was vibrant and fresh, before Ricky infested, desecrated, and drained her dry. She was ten years from her fate on this page, a non-returnable fate that, looking back now, he can see in her eyes. Her torment had been there all along, desperate to tell. She bore the scars of Ricky's rages like the tattoos on his biceps, an honor for him, a nightmare for her.

The *what ifs* sprang from the page, an invasion to eat away what good times he did have as if he didn't deserve them, had forfeited them for not noticing the truth she died for, and now, today, he's made restitution. The score's settled, with a healthy helping of vengeance on the side. Even made money on it. Good money. More money than he'd made in his entire lifetime.

EDDIE'S SLEPT THE better part of two days straight, and Roy, although concerned enough to check if he was still breathing, doesn't obsess on it. Obsession left around noon when he realized coming to Eustis was an empty endeavor and dragging half-dead Eddie around was nothing but a complication. Eddie's always been a complication, at least for Roy, as if it was his job to raise him because Bella had other priorities. At least he can be grateful she went into menopause later than sooner. Can't imagine trying to talk women into getting on the back of his tricycle to take them home to her.

It bothers him how Eddie slid right into the killing, like he was born to stalk women and charm them into his Pontiac with a promise of a couple of drinks. Eddie stopped taking them for drinks when Bella found out, her screaming at him about the devil's elixir spoiling the blood while she slit their throats.

Well, Eddie learned quick. He never asked why she did it or when it was going to end, as if it was just another chore to deal with. If anyone, she might have confided in Eddie, being her favorite and all. She might have thought he would understand in some deep spiritual way, but stupid Eddie never did say. Or if she did tell him, he never shared.

As for Roy, just digging the holes…must be two dozen out there now, not counting the one Bella's in, and Eddie if he hadn't crawled out. But hell it's over now. Might not even go back. Vegas is still an option if Eddie ever wakes up. But what if he's not sleeping? What if he's slid into one of those comas and drifted to vegetable land? Then what would he do with him? Can't just leave him in this motel room. Maid will catch on sooner or later and get tired of cleaning around him. Not like he can drop him off at the pound and hope for the best, tell relatives Eddie's living on a nice farm with a good family. Where could you drop someone like Eddie if he has a condition? Not sure he has one. Roy steps up to the bed and twists Eddie's left nipple real hard.

Eddie snaps straight up like an opened switch blade, grimacing, eyes wide. Knocks the snot out of Roy with a balled-up fist. Okay, so Eddie's not comatose and Roy pinches his nostrils shut to staunch the blood flow. Eddie rolls over and goes right back to sleep. Sleeping sickness? Can a bullet cause a guy to get sleeping sickness? And where the hell is Ricky? What mess did he get sucked into just to disappear—Ricky, who was the only one that seemed able to handle Bella.

Bella, Belladonna. Eat the poison and die, Bella. Her Mama named her right, means "Beautiful Lady" in Italian. That's what he read somewhere. Belladonna, nightshade, death on the tip of your tongue, shuns the light, Bella, her eyes just like those shiny black berries of seduction. It's said the root is the most toxic part and Bella's roots run deep.

Women used its dope to dilate the pupils, making eye contact more intense, and Roy remembers Bella's eyes staring into the eyes of her victims seconds before she'd strike, like a cobra's. But Ricky missed the worst of it. He was mostly gone by the time she started sharing her visions. Good excuse, prison. Why didn't he think of that? And why is it his job to take care of everyone else?

There's only one person who seems to have information on Ricky. At least where he lived. Roy digs through his wallet and pulls out a card with Detective Croy's number, picks up the phone and dials. Gets an answer on the second ring and for some odd reason that impresses him.

"Detective Croy, Roy Vega. You come by the house …Right, well gotta be careful these days…Find Ricky yet? No I haven't…His phone's been cut off I think…You did? Didn't tell me that…Yeah, water under the bridge now...Know where he lived?"

Roy grabs motel stationary from a drawer and writes fast. "Thought I could send a friend of mine by to see if…really... Who got their stuff? I understand. Where did Ricky live? What about his stuff? Sure. I hear anything I'll give you a call."

Roy drops the receiver in the cradle. *When hell freezes.* At least he's got a lead. Glances at Eddie, debates whether to leave him here alone. Only be gone an hour or so. At least needs to get the hell out of this room for awhile. And bring back real food. He stuffs his wallet back in his pocket, pulls on his boots, and shoves his shirttail in his pants. Writes a quick note and punches it through the light switch on the lamp by the bed. A quick glance around the room and Roy takes the do-not-disturb sign; places it on the outside knob and heads for the car.

He knocks on the battered door, hits it eight good times Place is dumpier than he thought it'd be. An old battered Chevy Nova sits in the drive bleeding oil like a forgotten deer kill. Roy gets out of his car and takes his time going to the door, checks the faded house numbers against the numbers on the paper in his hand. A ratty section of yellow crime scene tape is still tethered around the flimsy aluminum porch supports. Figures it's probably the right house.

He knocks on the battered door, hits it eight good times before looking in the windows then slipping around to the back. Grass is overgrown and brown at the top—no water, snaps of early autumn frost, zero attention. House looks much the same way, not what you'd call *curb appeal*. Wiping his palm across the filthy glass, Roy peers in the back window. He can make out a table, chairs, one end of the kitchen, items on the surfaces as if still in use. He turns from the window and starts, almost tramples a skeletonized old lady brandishing a toilet plunger, cigarette smoldering from the side of her mouth. She reaches up, plucks out the cigarette and pokes him with the rubber end of the plunger. Her thin lips peel back from tobacco stained teeth, the bottom two missing.

"Whatcha want!" She leans closer giving him the stink eye, cocks her head to the left as if it's the better eye because the right's all but fogged from cataract. "Betta answer now for I beat the godlessness outa ya." Plunger rises above her shoulder.

"Looking for my brother Ricky Vega."

"Vega! Don't knows no Ricky. Know a Betty Vega. Good woman she was, too. You kin?" Plunger drops a few inches.

"My sister-in-law."

"She was, huh?" Old Lady drops the plunger to her side, sticks the cig back in her mouth and starts walking barefoot through the back yard. "Damn shame what happened. She didn't deserve it, can tell you that." Shakes her head stepping along a narrow pathway on the side of the house.

"So, what happened to her?"

"You don't know? Thought you said you was kin?"

"Cops didn't give me details."

"Yeah? And now you want it from me?" Spins around facing him, pulls the cigarette from her mouth blowing smoke in his face. "Beat her to a bloody pulp! That detail enough?"

"They know who did it?"

"Hell if I know. You'll have to ask the cops." She waves off with the plunger, starts back down the path, stops to slap at her ankles eaten up with flea and fire ant bites. "Yard's a mess, I know it. She used to keep it up. You come for her things?"

Roy trails behind, watches with certain fascination the way her shoulder blades float across her back like emerging wings. He can count each individual vertebra from under the thin see-through spaghetti strap top. "Cops said someone got her stuff already."

"Don't know nothin' about that. Furniture's hers. Car's hers. Wasn't sure what I was gonna do with it, to tell you the truth, until you come up. Got another two weeks paid up on the rent, then I gotta put it in the paper." Flicks ashes to the wind.

"Cops said she had a friend who got her stuff. Joe something."

"Yeah, that's right. Thick as thieves those two. Haven't seen him in a couple a weeks, though. Think he might have got her stuff now that I think about it. Makes sense wouldn't it?"

"He live here at the house?"

"No one lived with Betty. Not a soul." Takes a draw from the cigarette.

"I'm assuming you're the landlady."

"That'd be a safe bet. Live right over there," points the cigarette to a run-down frame cottage with peeling paint, cats crawling the porch like roaches. "Why you want to know about Joe?"

"I'm pretty sure my brother was staying here. Wondered if this Joe fella knew anything about it."

"Well, if he was, Betty said nary a word to me." She reaches down and slings a branch into the neighbor's yard. "How long you staying?"

"Just long enough to get things settled."

"Where you stayin'?"

"Motor Lodge on Bay."

"One with the pool in the front?"

"Yeah."

"Devon's place. Not so bad."

"You know it?"

"Hell, I know everybody and everything if it's been here longer than ten years. I was born and raised here." Flicks the cigarette to burn out in the yard.

"Good for you."

Landlady reaches into her pocket and pulls out a ring of keys. Gives them a good shake and fingers through for the right one. "You can stay here for a couple a weeks, but one condition."

"What's that?"

"You clean it up. Get it ready for rent. Betty would a left it neat and clean. Not neat and clean, now. Bedroom's kind of a mess. Other places. Cops gave me a number for one of those…" She stops in threshold trying to remember, "What the hell do you call it?" Looks at Roy like he has a clue where her brain's going. "They clean up crime scenes like on TV." She's staring at Roy like he has to have the right answer or he doesn't get the place after all.

"Never needed one. Can't think of it," he says shrugging and stepping closer to push her in.

"Whatever. And I did call. Want too much money. Said I'd do it myself. But I didn't and it's gotta be done. You want the place or not?" She's dangling the keys like a dog treat.

Roy takes a quick glance around. Doesn't seem so bad. "Sure. Do what I can."

"Then, here. You can sell the stuff, or if you don't want to be bothered, donate it to me. Place will rent faster furnished anyway." She starts out the door. "But get the car out. Don't want it lying around. Code enforcement will slap it with tickets and make me pay to have it towed. So, do it soon."

13

a shot of mens rea, hold the olive

CROY'S MORE THAN a little confused after the visit to the VA hospital. The head of nursing, a Mr. Tabb, immense hawkish nose and slits for eyes, fidgeted throughout the interview, an obvious fidget, picking things up off the desk, moving them around as in a weird game of chess and the players were pencil cups, staplers, pens, folders. Even a photo of what Croy thinks was a character from a Star Trek movie—could be Klingon—was enlisted into service.

During the whole interview, Mr. Tabb bemoaned his future in hospital administration with the weight of at least five suspicious deaths on his head, might be more. Investigation wasn't over yet. The one common denominator was a Mr. Keys. It was going to be a political nightmare, he'd said. Once the media got wind of it, families of the dead would move across the litigation landscape like a wildfire. Mr. Tabb would be the first to go. They'd accept nothing less. He just knew it. He told Croy that as he scanned the room thinking of what items to pack first even though no one had mentioned re-assignment, much less termination.

"I'm no fool, you see. This is huge. What else can they do but pass this scalding potato to me?" he'd whined.

Croy had asked him if anyone complained or had suspicions.

Not at first, he'd said. But while interviewing the rest of the staff that worked with Keys, a pattern did emerge. Keys was too accommodating. And he was always the last one with the patient before they…you know, *passed on.* They were still looking for patients that were released—to question for any strange behavior on Keys' part—but that was unlikely since most patients were heavily sedated for their tests and *procedures.* It was a busy hospital. It would take time going through files for the five years Keys worked there. If he hadn't disappeared, no one would have been the wiser. They wouldn't have had to check the meds list and noticed the missing Epinephrine.

"He did all that, you see." Mr. Tabb leaned over the desk as if divulging a secret, the tip of his ballpoint pen pressed to the photo of the Klingon warrior. "You know how he did it?"

"Suffocation?"

"Not a chance. Keys was craftier than that. Take another guess."

"Poison?"

"Traceable, but you're close."

"Air bubble in the vein?"

Mr. Tabb waved an impatient hand, glanced at the door and leaned closer. "The missing *Epinephrine.*"

"Use that to treat allergic reactions and stabilize the heart, don't you?"

"Exactly! It's brilliant."

"Not following." Croy had leaned into the desk without realizing it, almost nose to nose with Mr. Tabb, way past his safety bubble.

Tabb whispered with heavily minted breath, "He'd give the patient just enough Epinephrine to throw them into arrhythmia. They'd code, and the team, thinking the patient was having a heart attack, would shoot him with a heavier dose killing them." Mr. Tabb slammed his hand on the desk making Croy jump. "Brilliant!"

Croy sat back in his chair, eyes locked on Mr. Tabb's.

Tabb hissed, "Then he escapes just after killing the last one. In the dead of night during the hurricane. What do you think of that?"

"Did you know he wasn't coming back? Did he take anything with him?"

Hooked finger over his mouth in thought, Mr. Tabb said, "Left a few personal things in his locker. An iPod and change of clothes. It's not unusual. The staff keeps extra clothes in case you're wondering. We all do. Just in case. Anyway, his truck was still in the parking lot. Police think he had a second vehicle or someone picked him up."

"Really? But how did you know he wasn't coming back?"

"Well, now that you put it like that, it was sloppy to leave the meds exposed. He was the last one to sign them out. And the staff did remember he said he was coming back after checking up on his place, but…you know, he never did."

"Why did it take so long to report him missing?"

"He took comp time. He had four days off on top of his two regular days. We just assumed he decided to go home and then the discrepancy in the meds came up."

"Does Keys have any enemies?"

Mr. Tabb moved the pencil box from the right side of the desk to the left. "I imagine he will now. And I'm just thinking about notification of the families…how does one broach the issue, say 'Sorry to say, your loved one was most likely murdered, but they were on death's door anyway?' How many of the families have their lawyers on speed dial?

"They'll want heads to roll. Someone to pay. Murdering war heroes is punishable by death and nothing less will do. Except maybe a seven-figure payout. I can already imagine the flag waving and American eagle posters picketing the hospital. But it's the principle of the thing!" He half stood up with a balled fist in the air, *"We won't put up with killing off our war heroes no matter how far gone!"* Mr. Tabb put his hand on his chest and sat heavily in the chair.

It was all Croy was going to get. He'd have to connect with the local police department for any updates. This wasn't going where he thought it would.

GLAD TO LEAVE Arnie behind who'd almost begged to go. Reminded Croy of a dog he had once that begged for car rides, excited just at the sound of the car keys. It might be hard explaining the slight detour and pit stop at the public park on the way home. He doesn't think Arnie's open minded enough to let it roll off his back. He'd blab to the whole department the second he hit the security door, then call everyone he knew.

Croy tries calling Bella's number the whole trip up, isn't hopeful for cooperation, and creeping up the drive to her place only reinforces that feeling. Four or five turkey vultures drift the thermals in the distance. The blue Suburban's still here, the canvas cover crumpled in the sand holding stagnant water and mosquito larvae. He sits in his car a good ten minutes, carefully rolling up his shirt sleeves and extracting two pair of latex gloves from a box under the seat.

Same crap is all over the yard—a Chevy carcass, broken down riding mower, an ancient rusted out stove— gardening implements that haven't seen a weed or vegetable in decades.

It's too quiet. No dogs to bound from under the porch and imprison him in the car, no motors running from weekend honey-do lists gone awry, no radio or TV blaring. He hates the quiet. It means something is about to break and he won't get to sleep for days. But this time it'll be the local's problem. Not his jurisdiction.

Croy leaves the car door open, just in case. Steps up to the front porch, half expects Roy to pop through the front door with a twelve-gauge pretending to be the UPS guy, or maybe the TV satellite installer as a cover for his own identity, but the place doesn't look like a living soul's been here in weeks. He remembers the lush green plant on the porch the last time he was here, now askew in its pot, brown and crispy.

Croy knocks on the door just to say he did—if accused of snooping—and quickly slips around to the side of the house where the Suburban rusts in the sun. Tag is missing. He tries the driver's door and finds it isn't locked. Pulls it open to organic rot, hot stale air and mold. Items of clothing litter the floorboard in the backseat. He's certain they're women's clothing. Resists the urge to touch them. His forefinger and thumb are furiously rubbing together, itching to touch them. Glancing up, he notices two vultures at the top of the tree line behind the house trying to navigate the thin top branches. One of them air-walks through the canopy then takes flight to the roofline seemingly triggering a breeze carrying the faint scent of decomp from the back of the house.

Croy's nerves buzz. A murder of crows takes flight into the woods, vociferously berating the intrusion. Stronger winds turn the air clean. Stink might be that of a large dog, maybe dead livestock in a nearby pasture. Croy suspects it isn't animal decomp.

Close inspection of the house, the back porch, immediate yard, small tool shed reveals nothing. Hands on his hips, Croy stands in the sun watching the bird's behavior and their annoyance at his presence. Standing on the back step, he pulls a pair of the latex gloves from his inside jacket pocket and waits.

They appear in the sky, a loose dark funnel spinning in slow motion on the thermals. Within minutes, they become more distinct, as if on a mission about three hundred feet beyond the woods line. He observes the first wave of birds descend and disappear behind the trees as the second wave moves in. Croy knows for sure it's something bigger than a dog—too many birds for something small. It has to be a large carcass or just more of it. The third wave dips and circles just above the tree line waiting their turn.

Croy snaps on the latex gloves, inhales, holds his breath, and walks out into the woods.

TWO WEEKS WORTH of mail so crammed in the box the door won't shut, a congestion of bills and advertisements, all of it junk mail to Pop. Other than his VFW newsletter and AARP, not much of it excites him. Uses the walkin' stick to shut the mailbox and shuffles back up the driveway and into the house. Never notices he's being watched from the house next door.

Each piece of mail shuffles through his hands, one stack to keep by the recliner, the rest for trash. He comes across the bank statement and slits the fold with his knotty thumb. Dreads what he'll find. Maybe an empty bank account thanks to Starlight-or-Star Bright and her sticky-hand ways. She might have drained the whole damn account, thanks to him. Pulls it close to his face, tilts it to the light. Reads the name and address on the envelope. Reads the statement again, then reads the name and address again.

"*JoJo!*"

"What?" Joe's lumbering through the living room with an armload of dirty laundry. Doesn't want to talk about the birds anymore. Doesn't want to feed them, either.

"Something's wrong at the bank."

Joe stops, peers over the lump of fabric in his arms, dreading what'll come next. "She get it all?"

"Who?"

"Your stripper lady friend, there."

"Not unless she put money in it."

"What?"

"I think the bank made a big mistake. Must have mixed us up with someone else's account."

Joe's hand uncoils from under the laundry and snatches the statement from Pop. "No mistake. Direct deposit. Sadie said they do it that way now." Hands the statement back.

"But JoJo, there's, there's…almost a half million on this statement if I'm reading right."

"Yeah, that's about right," Joe says disappearing into the garage.

Pop's chin tilts up to speak, but his eyes stay glued to the numbers on the paper as if they'll disappear when he looks away.

"Where'd it come from?"

Joe's head pokes through the garage door, his hand clutching a box of laundry powder. "Art work, Pop. It's what they paid me for it, minus Sadie's commission."

"But it's, it's almost a half-million dollars!"

"Machine's going. Gotta put in the soap." Joe disappears through the door again.

Pop sits heavy in the recliner. The walkin' stick flops to the floor. The statement's shaking in his hand, his eyes rereading over and over. "It's almost *half a million dollars.*"

"Can take a trip," Joe says walking through the living room again.

"All this just for those paintings you did?"

Joe stops. Turns. "Yeah, Pop. Just for those stupid paintings. Not for sweepin' floors or washin' windows. Not for waitin' tables or construction, or sad to say, not playin' baseball like you wanted. Just from those few stupid paintings I did in the shed out there."

A weird twitch takes hold of Pop's right eye, tugging at his brow as if it's trying to pull out his eyeball. He slaps at it with the heel of his palm. "I don't understand. Those paintings were worth that much?" Worries maybe the eye tic's from nerve damage.

"Were to someone. Got a hundred thirty-five thousand for old Ricky, there."

"You don't even know who bought 'em?"

"Not really. They go through Sadie. She handles it all. No need for me to know who bought 'em. Just glad they like 'em. Even better when they buy 'em." Joe disappears back into the garage.

Pop struggles with a million questions all at once. He's afraid to ask. Afraid of the answers. Answers he thinks he knows. Yells, "This the end of it?"

"End of what?" Joe yells back.

"You gonna do more art work? Like the last?" Pop can hear rushing water and the lid smack down on the washing machine. Joe moves through the living room again to the bedroom ignoring Pop's question.

"I asked you a question!" Pop yells, bank statement trembling in his hand.

"Not given it a lot of thought, Pop. Don't you think we got enough money for awhile? Not like we're gonna starve. Speaking of starvin', we need to go to the grocery. Why don't we catch lunch at the diner?"

Little bits of paper cling to the thigh of Pop's pants. He picks at them, noticing his tremor's getting more pronounced.

"You okay there?" Joe's staring at him. He's noticed it, too.

"Diner's fine with me."

"DO THEY SWARM like that all the time?"

"Ever since asshole Joe Salas moved on in there," Dee Dee says stuffing tissue in her purse. She adjusts her bra through the pink muu muu, hooks the purse over her shoulder and heads for the door.

Still nude, Marge peers covertly through the verticals on the sliding glass doors. "How long do you suppose they'll hang around?"

"And how should I know? At least we know what's been eatin' them cookies."

Marge turns and takes a long look at Dee Dee. "They have not, and are you really wearing that out?"

"What's wrong with this?"

"Nothing if you want to wear a sign that screams, *hey men, I'm a terrific old fat bore!*"

"No, you didn't. You did not just say what I think you said. You lay your naked ass in front of a man and can't keep him on the place, and throw food in the yard like some damn crazy person. You got you some nerve, girl." Dee Dee opens the front door. "I'll get you more booze. And stay the hell off the phone sex sites."

Marge flips Dee Dee the finger while peering out the verticals again.

SHOWERED AND DRESSED, Marge uses her time rummaging through Dee Dee's drawers. Not in a desperate hurry. She doesn't cull much, nothing to explain the way her sister's been living beyond the dog. Pictures of the dog, personal effects of the dog, birthday cards to the dog—God, no wonder she's alone. Only other photo is of her and Dee together while still at home, naive, thinner. Seems like an eternity ago, before they escaped and drifted away.

She finds a vibrator in the drawer by Dee's bed. Dead battery. That's a bad sign. Empty med bottles. And not the over the counter sleep aids, either. Serentil. Heavy ammo for disturbed people. Marge hears a car door slam and peers through the bedroom window. She watches a guy unload bags of groceries next door. Must be the guy, she thinks and makes a beeline to the front door.

ON THE THIRD trip back to the car, Joe sees a woman standing at the trunk of the Buick. At first glance he thinks it's Dee Dee, but closer realizes it's not. She's examining her nails, waiting.

"Can I help you?" Joe slows, feels the familiar sensation of battle rise in his chest.

"Wanted to see you for myself. You asshole Joe Salas?"

"What?"

"That's right. She calls you, 'My no-good neighbor, asshole Joe Salas.' I just had to see for myself, but I gotta say, there's not much to you, is there? I was expectin' some big ol' thing. You're just a puny little ol' thing."

Joe retrieves the last bag of groceries. "Who are you?"

"Marge Turner, sunshine. And just what the hell did you do to my sister?"

"I didn't do anything to her." Leans over and slams the trunk. "She's got mental problems. Ask the cops."

"Oh, I knows all about 'em. Been talkin' to that nice Detective Croy. He comes by asking questions about you. Guess you don't have 'em all fooled. Sure as hell don't have me fooled. But I'm a hard one to pull the wool over on."

"Good for you. Now if you'll excuse me," Joe turns for the house, "tell your sister to remember what I said."

"And that is?" Marge has her hands on her hips, a psychological intimidation method to make her seem even larger.

"She'll know," he says walking up the driveway.

"Oh, she will, will she?"

Joe stops and turns. "What's your favorite color there, Marge?"

"Red. Red hot poker red," she says holding up her polished dagger-like nails.

"You have any scars?"

"*What?*"

"I'm an artist. I think you'd make a great model. You should pose for me sometime. You got great bone structure."

"*What?*"

"We'll get together real soon, Marge." Joe raises his hand, smiles, and disappears into the house.

elysium spa and resort

HE'S NOT EXACTLY the same. Eddie's awake and alert. Sort of. Hasn't said a word since Roy checked him out of the Motor Lodge. He looks more like he's suffering a hangover, but his color's back and the wound on his head is healing up.

"You hungry? You gotta be. Don't think you've eaten anything worth a shit in almost a week. Want me to swing by *Sonny's* and grab a couple orders of ribs, maybe pulled pork? You like the pulled pork."

Eddie shrugs and stares out of the passenger window lost in the drone of the Pontiac's motor.

"We got the place for a couple a weeks free. Think that's plenty of time to find Ricky?" Glances at Eddie then back to the road.

Eddie mumbles a sound like "whatever," shifts so his head rests on his arm propped against the door.

"Come on, Eddie, say something. Fight if you want." Glances at Eddie again.

"Nothing' to say."

"How much you want? Double order?" Roy rolls down the window at the drive thru.

"Whatever." Eddie's eyes track three high school girls walking across the parking lot to the restaurant. "Does the place have a shed?"

"Does what?" Roy passes money to the clerk for the two bags of food. He hands them over to Eddie. "Shed?"

"Never mind."

"Are you talking to yourself?"

"It matter?" Eddie mumbles.

"You need a nap, Eddie. You're not making any sense."

Even before pulling into the driveway, Eddie sits up as if he recognizes the place and missed it. The passenger door opens before Roy can stop and Eddie hops out sprinting up the front steps. He stops, closes his eyes, tilts his head into the wind.

"Hey, what's wrong?" Roy's standing by the car a little spooked by Eddie's weird behavior. Suspects it's the bullet floatin' around in his brain again. He grabs the food from the passenger seat and jogs up the steps to unlock the door. "Landlady said we gotta clean it. That's the deal."

Eddie's hesitant at the threshold like a yard dog chancing the doorway knowing he'll get beat if caught inside.

"What the hell is wrong with you?" Roy moves past him and stands in the living room silhouetted from the setting sun behind him. Makes it look like he's on fire, at least from Eddie's perspective.

"Just hungry. Let's eat."

Remnants of Betty's life still linger: her furnishings, house wares. Her blood.

Eddie, legs folded under him on the sofa, ignoring his surroundings, gnaws a smoked rib from the bag.

Roy's forgotten about eating and drifts from room to room reading the evidence in Betty's brutal death. Most of her personal things are gone except the turntable. He flips the switch and drops the needle on the spinning forty-five. Patsy Cline bellows *Walkin' after Midnight* from the RCA speakers. He leaves it to play through as he moves into the bedroom.

The bed's been stripped, but no one's cleaned the headboard. A fine crescent-shaped dried bloodstain remains painted on the light wood finish and neighboring wall as if a child had misappropriated mommy's nail polish and flicked the brush much like an insane artist digging for inspiration.

The wall's going to need a paint job. Roy's chest tightens, feels much like the *Bella demon nights,* twisting and quivering at the sight of blood. He thinks staying here might be a bad idea.

"You gonna eat any of this?" Eddie asks. He's standing in the doorway with a half-eaten rib in his hand, barbeque sauce smeared across his face, reminding Roy of a couple of nights when Eddie had a little time with one of Bella's girls after she'd finished with her. He was too exhausted to care what Eddie did, but he'd found Eddie crouched over the body like a dog on left-over's, face smeared with blood much like he looks now.

"Not hungry. You see this mess?"

Eddie surveys the room's condition and shrugs. "That mean you're not gonna eat yours?"

"Maybe later. We'll need to get some paint and cover this wall. I saw sheets in the closet." Roy stands in the middle of the room taking inventory, hands on his hips. "I can't stay in it like this."

"Never bothered you before."

"I never slept in a death scene, Eddie."

"That's a lie. You spent nights in *the bunker.* Ma said so."

"That wasn't voluntary."

"Right. You managed to slip out of most of them, didn't you?"

Roy turns on his heel, "I had to dig the damn holes, Eddie! Two and a half to three hours of diggin' while you did what, Eddie? Seems to me you got off pretty damn easy."

"She needed me to help her."

"Yeah, right. Think you helped yourself more like it."

No comeback on Eddie's part. He stands in the doorway holding the half-eaten rib that could have been human as much as hog and it wouldn't have made a difference to him. It's what Roy thinks. What Roy believes. It nauseates him seeing the red coating smeared across Eddie's mouth and how maybe Bella's spirit's not really that far off after all.

Stripping the last shreds of meat from the bone, Eddie says, "I'm gonna get the paint. You have fun with that." He tosses the bone in the bag, sucks sauce from his fingers, drops the needle back on the forty-five again and heads for the car.

CROY EXPECTS TO find something human, but what the earth exposes is too obscene. Obvious signs of predation. Crows, hungry and disgruntled at being forced away from an easy meal, cling close by on sapling branches for the first chance to return. Croy isn't leaving anytime soon.

Soaking rains and the driving frustration of ground scavengers have left five, maybe six depressions in a clearing about three hundred feet behind the house—four by six, if he calculated the diameters right. In the depression closest to him protrudes a partially denuded forearm, skin still covering most of the hand itself. A pretty Fossil watch twinkles around the radius.

Picking at the arm is a very large vulture with bald patches as if it's a regular participant in wagered dog fights, scars replacing missing feathers on the neck. Must be the Grand Poobah of vultures from the way the others just hang back in the treetops waiting their turn. If they'll even get one. Poobah's attracted to the shiny watch, picks at the links trying to pull it from the bone.

"Okay, that's evidence," Croy mutters, looking around for a stick to chase Poobah off. Croy gets a good grip around an oak branch. "Shoo!" Smacks the branch against the trunk of a tree to show he means business. *"Shoo!"*

Vulture turns. Looks. Head weaves as if to evaluate the threat then goes back to picking at the watch.

Croy's got a distance of six feet between him and the bird. A big bird. A big filthy bird with germs on it. His free hand unconsciously feels for the hand sanitizer in his interior jacket pocket as if it is a secondary weapon. He's relieved to feel it still there. In case of an emergency. Smacks the ground with the stick. *"Shoo!"*

Bird ignores him, gets the watch band hooked in its bill and pulls. The arm bone bends with it.

"Damn it! *SHOO!*" Croy wields the stick to make himself appear larger, more intimidating. It only serves to annoy the bird now facing off with him—ruffled feathers, spread wings, open beak. Croy pokes it with the stick. Bird snags the end of the branch and won't let go. A minor skirmish ensues over the stick. Croy's impressed with bird's strength. He pulls the stick back. Bird follows. It's too close. Croy shoves the stick back. Bird doesn't appear to have a backup gear. Croy steps back, pulls the stick back. Bird pulls back. Bird lets go of the stick for the shiny watch. Croy smacks the bird on back with the stick. Bird spins and hisses. Aren't they supposed to fly off? Croy pokes the bird, again. Bird snags the stick, drops it, spreads its wings, charges.

Croy steps back. Bird makes some weird grunt of victory and returns to shiny watch. But Croy's undaunted, picks up a chunk of broken cement block and hurls it. It only serves to piss the bird off.

Weren't vultures supposed to fall over and pretend to be dead? Croy seems to remember those facts about vultures. Not working so much here.

Stick in hand, Croy approaches the bird again. Placing both hands around the stick like a baseball bat, Croy aims for the head. Good foot position, proper stance, Croy swings the stick.

Fast bird. Acts like it's been through this before. The bird spins and suddenly becomes all wings and beak. Croy drops the stick and runs. Really fast bird. Croy can see it just over his shoulder, on his heels, neck stretched, open beak, inches from his pant leg. Croy makes it up a tree, tearing a nice hole in his trouser knee.

Bird circles around the tree, wings spread, hissing. Shiny watch catches its attention again.

Croy slides to the ground, pulls off the shredded latex gloves, checks his pants. Thinks this calls for more compliance on bird's part. Snaps on another pair of gloves. He picks up the stick ready for a fight.

Croy confidently marches back to claim his territory.

Bird almost has shiny watch off the arm. It's now snagged around the hand. One or two more pulls and the bird will have it. Probably fly off with it into parts unknown, add it to some nest on the edge of a river bank where it'll eventually drop into the water and disappear into tannic sediment forever.

Croy charges the bird like a jouster, hopes the screaming and surprise attack will disorient the vulture enough to send it into the trees. He's thinking all this while picking up speed, the scream rising in his throat, tree limb held above the shoulder in a death grip.

Bird must have seen this coming. Perhaps even practiced. It turns open winged, bounces twice and becomes airborne. Just about face height. Croy can't stop fast enough. His stick glances off the left wing and Croy has feathers in his face, feels the strength of the wings and a talon now attached to his shoulder. There's a lot of yelling and screaming, fists flying, decomp being smeared on Croy's good suit. Bird drops to the ground hissing and suddenly pukes human remains and road kill on Croy's new shoes. Backs up as if challenging him to come at him again.

In one fluid motion, Croy sweeps the right side of his jacket aside, draws his 9mm, aims and pulls the trigger. Bird tilts, flops on its side, wings flapping. Birds still lingering in the trees free fly in every direction.

Croy looks down at his shoes, shoots the bird again, holsters his weapon and inspects his jacket.

In the trunk of his car are two spare changes of clothes, shoes, and large tackle box of cleaners and hospital disinfectants. Croy slips out of the shoes and socks, takes off the jacket and places everything in a Ziploc Big Bag. Uses four out of the seven disinfectants and a half pack of wipes to clean up with.

Calmer and a little victorious, he returns to the grave site, notes scavengers have dug down a good two feet to what appears to be the side of a face—a forensic anthropologist's moment of euphoric elation at such a discovery. Croy isn't euphoric, but there is a certain reward much like a dog that's been slipped a treat for a good find.

At the next depression, nothing's exposed, but the odor of human rot at his feet is unmistakable, like old cemeteries where the lids have rotted and caved. He moves from one depression to the next. Counts eighteen in all. Croy slides his cell phone from his jacket and dials 911.

EDDIE GRABS A can of whatever paint is on the shelf at the hardware store, no tinting, pays for it and slings it on the seat along with the tarp, duct-tape, and a brand new shiny buck knife.

Once in the car, he pulls the tarp from the package, tears the cellophane from the duct-tape, and opens the blade of the buck knife. Thinks Bella would have approved.

Eddie starts the engine, cranks up the radio, and heads east on SR 441.

NOT MUCH LEFT of his headache but a low steady throb. Eddie's driving through town a good ten miles an hour under the speed limit, both hands clutching the wheel, face close to the windshield.

Now and then he feels his bare neck, mumbles and turns the radio to a heavy metal station. Cruising strip plaza parking lots, Eddie sings, catching his reflection askew in the window panes as he drives by. Wonders what happened to his gold chain and when the last time was he remembers wearing it. Thinks he had it at home. Things get fuzzy after that. Thinks Roy probably hocked it for cash. Always was jealous of his bling. And his singing talent.

Eddie pulls into a discount store and checks his empty wallet. Still has a credit card.

Twenty minutes in and out, Eddie's got a brand new gold herringbone chain around his neck, and a gold stud earring. Checks the whole look in the rearview, sucks his teeth and grins to see if any meat is caught in-between. His shoulders start rocking and head starts bobbing to a heavy metal station blaring from the radio, imagines himself on stage fighting off chicks who want a piece of him because he's so damn talented. Yep, he's back in business. Thinks he looks hot. Hell, yeah.

15

nolle prosequi

"JOJO! COPS ON the phone." Pop holds the receiver above his head.

Joe appears and sweeps it from Pop's hand. "What's it about?"

"They didn't tell me. Want to talk to you. Maybe your girlfriend called 'em again." Pop grins and settles into a chair by the back door with a glass of tea. Turns up his hearing aid. It doesn't do him a lot of good since Joe isn't on the phone more than a few seconds and that takes all the fun out of eavesdropping. "What they want?"

"Say I can come get Betty's things. They're holding 'em down at the station. Say I can sign 'em out.

"How much stuff they have?"

"Like I said before, her clothes, papers, stuff like that."

"That mean the case is closed?"

"I don't know what it means. Don't think they were looking real hard anyway."

Joe sweeps the car keys off the counter. "I'll be back to start dinner."

JOE'S ALONE IN a small reception area—six chairs, corner table with an anemic plant crawling the wall for light escaping from under the mini blind above it. In a basket on the floor, magazines with missing pages, graffiti scrawled with various versions of obscene language in both Spanish and English. Seems an unofficial poll was taken on the value of law enforcement and how they can serve themselves.

Arnie lumbers through the double glass doors, five boxes loaded on a dolly and a sheet of paper tucked under his arm.

"You Joe Salas?"

"Yes, sir."

Arnie parks the dolly at Joe's feet and hands him the sheet. "Sign here."

"This mean the case is closed?"

"Unsolved murder cases are never closed. This stuff had no investigative value so we turn it back to the family. You're the one who's supposed to get it, so here it is."

Joe signs the sheet and hands it back.

"You can probably take two boxes at a time. Sorry, but I can't let you have the dolly. Had other assholes steal it."

Joe nods, pulls two boxes off the dolly. "You have any suspects yet?"

"Looking hard at her ex, but he's in the wind."

"Maybe his family's helping him out."

"We're following that."

"You assigned to the case?"

"Not directly. I'm not assigned as a primary to any cases," leans over and half whispers, "pulling the pin in…" checks his watch, "Two months, three days, six hours and forty-two minutes."

"Sounds like you're ready to leave," Joe says shoving the door open with his hip.

Arnie grabs the door and gives it a push dragging the dolly along with the last three boxes. "Been ready. This place sucks the marrow right out of your bones. Drop those on here. I'll walk you to your car." Arnie's desperate for a cigarette.

Joe sets the boxes down and steps back. "Who has the case then?"

"That'd be my partner Croy."

"Yeah, we've met."

"That's right. He said he'd interviewed you. Being a friend of the victim and all."

Joe stops at the Buick and unlocks the driver's door. "Maybe he'll find Vega and send him to the chair."

Arnie knocks a cigarette from the pack and sticks it in the corner of his mouth, "They don't use the chair anymore. Lethal injection. More *humane*." Pulls the cigarette back out. "And from what they found in Alachua County, I'd say there's a good chance of that." Sticks the cigarette back in and lights it. Sucks a strong drag deep into his lungs.

Joe's standing with the last box poised for the backseat waiting for Arnie to spill it. "Why is that?"

Exhales, "Bodies. Dozens of them." Glances around the parking lot and leans over. "Croy found them this morning at the Vega place. Just like right out of a horror movie."

"So that's where Ricky was living?"

"We're not sure. It's his mom's place. He has two brothers that live there, but haven't located any of them."

"Think they're dead, too?"

"Don't know. All female victims so far. And Croy just talked to one of the brothers a few days ago. Look more like suspects. Some of the graves are years old. You'll be hearing about it on the news tonight. This is big. Statewide big."

"I guess so. Well, I gotta get back to my Pop." Joe dumps the last box on the backseat, shuts the door. "What about the apartment?"

"Miss Vega's?"

"Yeah. She's still got more stuff there," Joe says sliding behind the wheel of the Buick.

"Oh, you can have at it. We're done with the place."

Nothing more said on Joe's part. He half waves and drives off leaving Arnie to loiter in the parking lot long enough to finish the smoke and scrub the butt into the asphalt.

Joe's read through a quarter of Betty's diary during dinner. Pop's neck stretches now and then in hopes of catching a peek at whatever has Joe's attention. Must be real good. Boy hasn't said word one the whole time other than pass the bread. He wants to ask, but the scowl on Joe's face and the box it came from makes him think better of it.

After dinner, Joe drops his plate in the sink and disappears to his room behind a closed door. And it's only six-thirty.

Pop takes the quiet time to go through one of the boxes Joe's brought home. Clothing mostly, some he remembers seeing Betty in when Joe brought her over. They'd sit around out back in lawn chairs and drink beer. He misses hearing people laugh. Not so much to laugh about now.

JOE STRETCHES OUT on the bed, opens a diary reading all about Betty's life starting from her senior year in high school. Wrote that she thought Ricky Vega was cool. Makes Joe want to gag just reading it. Ricky had her so snowed.

From what Joe can tell in the writing, she'd begun to make excuses for Ricky's behavior right from the very beginning. Verbal abuse at first. She blamed herself. Wrote she'd said the wrong thing to upset him or caught him at a time he wasn't feeling well.

She must have slathered on lots of grease to make that lie slide down her throat. It was always her fault for Ricky saying hateful things. Her fault he punched her in the face. Her fault he bashed her head into the wall. Her fault he broke her wrist, and ribs, and collar bone.

"But he's so sorry, says he'll change." she'd written. *"Says he didn't mean it."* And for the next week, according to the diary, he was a great guy. Until the next time.

She'd walked into the marriage eyes wide-open. Thought she could change him, make him a better person. And when months followed days and he didn't change for the better, it was her fault. She wasn't trying hard enough, wasn't good enough, was too ugly, too fat, nagged, asked questions that were none of her damn business. Everything she did was wrong and he'd made sure she'd never forget it.

Joe can't read anymore. It's too hard. And he's angry. At her. Any given day she could have come to him and explained and they would have found a way. She didn't need to live like this.

And he's angry at himself. He'd seen the bruises, busted lips, signed off on her feeble excuses of how they got there when he knew deep in his gut Ricky was responsible, but he crept away like the coward he is. Like the coward Pop said he was years back because he wouldn't play baseball after the curve ball knocked him out and sent him to the hospital like a little whoosie.

Pop didn't look him in the face for days. *Who-Ass, Who-Ass, Who-Ass. Look, the little Who-Ass can't play ball, look the little Who-Ass can't keep a girlfriend, look the little Who-Ass can't hold a job, look the little Who-Ass can't help a friend, look the little Who-Ass can't save his family. Now they're all dead!*

It's enough to send Joe out of the house into the dark to drive around the city until the rage subsides.

IT WASN'T LIKE he's expecting Pop to still be up, but with the lights burning and the TV on, Joe's at least expecting life in the chair. It's empty, as with the beer bottle—been hitting the stuff pretty hard—and jars of various missing pickled products, bits of product floating in flavored vinegar water, glass jars for the recycler. Joe clicks off the late-night TV comedian—lost his humor in reminiscing on Betty's life—and checks Pop's room to be sure he's taken out his falsies. Leaving them in causes swelling, irritation, and substantial bitching on Pop's part, so Joe just pulls them out of Pop's mouth and drops them in the soaking glass on the bureau.

But Pop's gone. Doesn't look like the bed's been used, and oddly, the clothes he's had on for the day lie crumpled on the floor. Shower maybe? Joe checks the bathroom. Other than a shaving cream dollop on the mirror, place is empty.

Searching the house, Joe's beyond mildly concerned, grabs a flashlight from the kitchen and heads outside. Darker than he'd hoped, no moon, streetlight doesn't reach the back yard and the back-porch light has burned out. Would have been nice to replace it but he's had real troubles. Pop being one of them.

Light beam scans the back yard, past the gate—humid air pushes against him. Some distance off a dog's hysterical barking echoes three or four blocks out if Joe calculates right. A warning surges in the back of his brain. Not sure why, doesn't make sense, but Joe hustles down Fairview Street eyes peeled for movement, and as if by magic, there Pop is under the street light looking straight up wearing nothing but his underwear. Left hand on his hip, his right hand rubbing his doughy stomach, he's just standing there, no mind to a thing in the world.

Joe's approach is cautious and he's careful not to spook the old guy. Doesn't think he would, but better not chance it, and he steps up next to him and looks up. Four or five moths circle the high-pressure sodium bulb, a fascinating game if one was tired of watching mold form on the sidewalk, but Pop seems hypnotized by it all.

"Hey, Pop. Whatcha doin'?" Joe says it softly, unlike the need to rant he really feels. Pop just stares. "Probably need to get home now."

Okay, so Pop's in one of his spells, at least Joe thinks he is. Pop looks alert. "I think they've slung the papers. What do you say we go home and get it?"

Pop turns and stares Joe in the face. "Can we take them, too?"

"Take what?"

"The fairies."

"They're moths, Pop. We have those at home."

Obediently, Pop steps in line with Joe and silently follows him home. Walking up the driveway, Pop picks up the paper and heads for the house. Asks, "What are you doing up so early?"

"Looking for you."

"Why were you lookin' for me?"

"Seriously? You don't remember any of it, do you?"

"Yeah. I get the paper very morning."

"I found you four blocks from the house, Pop. Were you looking to take the neighbor's paper?"

"What are you talking about *Who-Ass?* Got the paper right here."

"I see that. Never mind. I'll start a breakfast."

IT WOULD REALLY be nice if you were gonna be out all night you'd clue me in."

Roy's standing on the porch looking down at Eddie's bald spot highlighted by the bare porch bulb, isn't impressed with the can of latex house paint in Eddie's hand, but does notice the new gold chain around Eddie's neck. Moths and other winged night flyers circle Roy's head, smash into the bulb, hit the floor, buzz in circles.

"Where'd you find that?"

"Didn't. Bought it."

"With what?"

"Credit card."

"Credit card! Damn it, Eddie. Didn't want a paper trail the cops can tracc!"

"Shouldn't of hocked mine then," Eddie says pushing past Roy.

"I didn't hock your damn chain. It just fell off. No one's fault. How much it cost?"

"Just a couple hundred on discount."

"Couple a hundred! What else don't I know about?"

"There's probably lots, Roy, but I'm really tired now. You make the bed up in there?"

"Not until we paint over the blood."

"Won't be tonight. I get the couch 'cause I'm still recovering."

Roy shakes his head in disbelief, at Eddie's audacity milking something like a minor bullet in the head. Sounds more and more like Bella and her migraines. He picks up the can of paint and heads for the bedroom. "You get brushes?"

Eddie's already fast asleep on the couch and when he's like this there's no re-animating him. Roy sets the can on the floor and goes out to the Pontiac hoping Eddie's head wasn't so far up his ass he forgot paint brushes.

Nothing on the front seat. Nothing on the backseat. Roy goes back inside the house and not so delicately fishes the car keys from Eddie's pants. Eddie doesn't even move.

Back at the car, Roy smells a woods fire not far off. He unlocks the trunk, jerks back as if a snake has caught him in mid-strike. She isn't more than seventeen, could be younger, and he doesn't need to check her pulse to tell she's dead. The grotesque smile carved in her throat looks familiar, bears Bella's signature down to the position of the hands. Roy drops hard on the ground, most of the air in his lungs expelling in a great whoosh. And for a good ten minutes he sits in the dirt behind the Pontiac trying to collect his thoughts, thoughts that buzz and buzz like invading hornets.

"My Mama's dead," he mutters at the trunk, as if Bella herself might slide out on her belly, take his throat in her hands and squeeze. Eddie's gone out on his own, no supervision, could have been seen by anyone and he's too stupid to care for the details. Just goes into things without thinking, cries about it when it blows up in his face as if he's the victim. That makes Roy mad. Mad for the girl in the trunk, and then it dawns on him in a pure thought. Eddie was *bloodless.* Not a drop on him. Clean as if waiting on a date all shiny and new.

The screen door snaps off the top hinge when Roy bulldozes through, and it only takes five steps to reach Eddie on the couch. Roy manages the first punch on the top of Eddie's head and a second that catches the front teeth—Eddie sleeps with his mouth open—front tooth slits Roy's middle knuckle. It's hard to tell whose blood's whose, and they end up sprawled on the hardwood floor punching it out.

Eddie's half awake, fightin' back, not sure against what. It's all he can do to fend off the pummeling, hearing Bella's name over and over, and after three or four minutes of it, they're both lying exhausted on the floor.

"What's wrong with you, Roy?" Eddie uses his shirttail to staunch his bloody nose and lip. Roy does the same as if they were taught to use their shirttails when they got bloodied.

"The girl, ass hole."

"What girl?"

"What girl? Are you kidding? The one in your trunk!"

"Na ah." Eddie's sure Roy's gone off the deep end, maybe having a nightmare and taking it out on him.

"She's out there right now! Go look."

"I don't wanna."

Roy jumps up grabbing Eddie by the collar and half drags him across the floor to the door. "Go look, damn it. She's right there in the trunk where you put her!"

"I didn't, Roy. Wasn't me. And don't break my new gold chain."

"What, she crawled in there after someone slit her throat like Ma use to? Think that's just a small coincidence?"

Eddie's crouched with his head pushed through the screen door staring at the Pontiac as if it'll explain everything.

"Go!" Roy shoves him hard. "Go look."

Eddie walks on his knees to the steps and stops. "I didn't do it, Roy. Wasn't me."

"Eddie, the moon's full." Roy points to the horizon where a fat moon hides behind the tree tops.

"Doesn't mean nothin', Roy." Eddie stumbles to the car running his hands down the rear quarter panel to the open trunk, his heart pounding in his chest. One quick glance and he spins around, arm across his face.

"What are we gonna do?" He squeezes his head between his bloody hands, spinning around, desperate for an explanation. "What are we gonna do, Roy?"

Roy drops the trunk lid. "Stop freakin' out first off," he says. "We gotta figure out how to get rid of her. Get in the car."

fly spray

BLOW FLY CIRCLES, lands, rubs its hind legs. Rolls its hairy front legs over its eyes. Marge feels the tickle as it turns in a circle on her left breast and sucks sweat. Just enough movement to stir her out of the alcohol induced stupor she's been in for the last four hours.

She's been dreaming. Drifting in a lagoon off some secluded island, tiny colorful fish nibbling her toes, probably attracted by her fabulous nail polish—a hot looking local island boy massaging her shoulders, another on stand-by with a keep them comin' umbrella drink. In her dream she's twenty years younger, two hundred pounds thinner, a nineteen-inch waist; breasts, well, they don't change from what she has now. Local island boy's hand moves from her shoulders to her chest, teasing. The tips of his fingers barely touch the skin. Tickles.

She opens her eyes. She's not in the lagoon and the fly's grown fat and slow filling with sweat. She swats at it. It buzzes off, makes a circle and tries landing on her shoulder. She smacks it with the back of her hand and it drifts away.

From behind her she can hear activity next door and shifts her head. Sounds from the shed next door pique her interest, her brain dumping past conversations with Dee about the goings on over there and what seems to be the source of Dee's *issues*. Marge lies quiet for some time, can just make out shadows moving back and forth from the shed to the house next door.

"Somethin's going on, all right," she mumbles, and pulls herself up out of the lounge chair and yanks open the sliding glass door. "Dee! Your boy's at the shed!"

A note on the counter by the gin bottle says Dee's gone shopping. Marge is a little hurt she wasn't invited. Wouldn't have gone if invited, but the sun's sinking fast and Marge doesn't want to waste the opportunity. She waddles to her room, dresses, and pulls *a-one-time-use* camera that has maybe six or seven shots left from her luggage.

The sun is still a couple of hours before setting. Marge thinks she's got time, might not need the flash after all. She's got on her walking shoes and enough alcohol buzz to give her courage.

From what she can tell by spying through the wood slats, neighbor asshole Joe has been holed up in the shed for a good half hour. He could be doing something nefarious.

She doesn't really think so, but it's important to put an end to Dee's paranoia. Any longer and the poor old girl's going to be drooling on a straight jacket. Wouldn't that mean she'd have to care for Dee's estate? Horrible thought. Horrible sister to think it. Yet a simple power of attorney would clear the table. Then no need to move out. She knows Dee's annoyed at her living here, but is it really living, for all intents and purposes a shut-in, the constant references to the dead dog, killer neighbor, lack of any good men?

Marge's living quite nicely here, free range gin, and just enough excitement to keep it interesting. Today is exciting, her little heart treading against her breastbone now covered in loose linen. Sleeveless of course.

Shed door swings open and neighbor Joe returns to the house. Marge watches each and every step until the back-door closes. And she noticed he didn't lock the shed door. Means he's probably coming back. Too risky. She's not stupid, picks up on the small detail others miss. But risk is like having sex with the cruise ship's captain right on deck while everyone's asleep. Well, while most are asleep. There's always a little risk of discovery, but that's the excitement. Just thinking about it gives her chills.

Repositioning herself closer to the shed door, she tries to see her way in. Not likely through overgrown wild grapevines. She could sneak to the other side, strip away a section and hurry back.

The fat blowfly slowly buzzes her head. She can feel it land on the crown of her head. It squirms around. She flips her hand at it, feels it touch her finger and buzz off.

Salas's backdoor opens and neighbor Joe appears with a brown paper bag held delicately in one hand, bath towels in the other. Bath towels! What's he going to do with bath towels? Marge squats low behind the fence, quiets her breath.

POP'S CURLED ON his bed napping. Joe uses the time to fish Ricky's severed head from the back of the kitchen freezer hidden behind a small turkey breast and bagged vegetables. Corn mostly. Pop likes the corn. Getting harder and harder to get him to eat any other vegetable, but likes the corn.

Joe takes the head wrapped in a brown paper bag to the shed and closes the door. He'd watched Dee Dee drive off not long ago and thinks the timing's good to start another art project. Not that he needs the money. Sadie did say he needed to stay active. An inactive artist is an unpaid artist.

Head is plunked on the work bench. Joe cuts away the sealed plastic bag. Ice crystals glitter on Ricky's pale skin like a winter statue. Wonders how long it'll take to thaw out. He didn't think about thawing time. Doesn't think the ink will stick if the flesh is too cold, and it might ooze exudates much like the frozen fish he'd tried. What's a quick way to thaw a head? Damn, the microwave! Shoving the head back in the paper bag, Joe makes a return trip back to the kitchen.

It just barely fits. Not much extra space in the cavity of the microwave, but he's convinced there's plenty. Thinks twenty minutes should do it. He presses "Cook Time," and then must decide on poultry or meat. Selects meat. Laughs to himself thinking of Ricky as a meathead. Selects the approximate weight. Hits seven point zero. Presses *Start*.

Ricky's head makes it around the first rotation, but then shifts and jams up, his nose catching the corner, the glass tray rotating underneath the head. Joe peers in. Ricky's cloudy vacant eyes stare back.

Ten minutes into it, the inside of the microwave's steaming up. Hard to make out what's inside. A smell begins to permeate the air, gets sucked into the air vents and blows throughout the house. It wakes Pop out of deep sleep because he thinks dinner's almost done and doesn't want to miss it.

Joe's jotting notes down on a paper towel when Pop shuffles in, hair gone astray, shirt wrinkled mostly on the left side. "What's for dinner?"

Joe glances up, then at the microwave, then at Pop. "What are you doing up?"

"Smells like dinner's about ready. We got any of those sweet gherkins?" Pop heads for the refrigerator.

"Not cooking dinner. Still a couple hours away. Go back to bed." The pen starts to tremble in Joe's hand.

"Whatcha got in there?" Pop's still got sleep-face, eyes kind of puffy, eyebrow hair in every direction. Has the cold jar of gherkins in his hand ready to take to the table.

"Nothin'."

"Nothin'? It's something. Smells like—" Pop sniffs the air. "Pork."

"Nothing for you to be bothered about. You still look tired. Go back to bed."

"Why you cooking something if we're not gonna eat it?"

"I didn't say that. I said it's not for dinner. Cookin' somethin' else. Go back to bed!" Joe somehow manages to shift in front of the microwave to block any chance Pop might have in spotting what's inside, can't imagine the awkwardness in trying to explain it.

"What the hell's wrong with you? *You* need a damn nap," Pop bitches. Scuttles out of the kitchen with the pickles.

Joe spins and peers into the microwave. His heart sinks. The thawing process is mutating Ricky's face. The tissue's become flaccid and sunken in. Suddenly, one of Ricky's eyeballs explodes. Joe hits the stop button and pulls the head out with a dish towel. Steams drifts from the nostrils and ears. Edge of Ricky's left ear has turned black.

"Shit!" Hears the slight drag of Pop's bad leg close to the door again and heaves the steaming head into the paper bag.

"I think whatever you're cooking's gone bad there, JoJo." He's already through the door halfway between the fridge and Joe, who's holding the hot paper bag wrapped in a dish towel. "You got some bad pork there. Why don't you sling it out for the birds? They don't care. Might be a treat with it being cooked up and all."

"Good idea, Pop."

Joe's halfway out the back door when Pop yells, "I'm not cleanin' up whatever mess you left in that microwave there. Gonna finish my nap. God Oh Mighty what a stink."

Habit leads him to the shed. Paper bag is wet and tearing, practically melting in his hands. By the time it hits the bench, the bag disintegrates much like Ricky's skin. Joe stares down at it, the smell of cooked flesh invading his sinuses. Mumbles, "Epic fail." He throws a towel over it and pulls the maul from behind the lawn mower.

SHE'D ALMOST DECIDED to go back into the house. There's a red-orange wash at the horizon and Marge doesn't like bugs. The moment she stands to head back, Joe's out of the house in a hurry. He's carrying the paper bag again in a dish towel, holding it away from his body as if it's a bomb on countdown with only seconds to spare. As he passes, she catches a brief whiff of cooked meat. A hasty casserole for a leisurely supper while—what? Who eats in a damn shed? What kind of set up does he really have in there?

Door closes. Six or seven minutes later he emerges with the thing wrapped in a towel tucked under one arm, toting a shovel and maul in the other.

That's got her attention. No going back now. She follows him down the fence line and watches him with one eye through the gate disappear into the woods. Opening the gate, Marge watches for anyone who might see her enter forbidden enemy territory, quickly glances at Joe as he descends to the pond beyond the woods line and the dead pine silhouetted against the last rays of the sun. Marge huffs and stumbles. Prays she won't fall.

JOE DROPS THE head in the weeds, walks two hundred feet to the north and digs three holes. Thrust, heave, thrust, heave, thrust, heave. Hidden in the thick underbrush, a thrush clicks and whines for Joe to move away. He looks up and notices the vultures are circling already, some way up just pin dots against the darkening sky. He counts maybe a dozen. At least the ones he can make out. Didn't think they stayed out this late in the day. Maybe they didn't used to. He feels it's important to finish the job, then. It's not like he can talk them into not showing up.

Might be easier to smash the head while in the bag, Joe thinks. Keep the splatter down. Better keep the towel on then, too. The last bash-up made a real mess.

BEING OUT HERE is giving Marge the willies. She's imagining all sorts of multi-legged things finding her ankles, working their way up to her warm dark recesses. Crouched in the wax myrtle, she's got the camera in front of her face trying to get a clear focus on neighbor Joe. He's laid his bundle on the ground along with the maul, hiked out in the woods with the shovel, thinks he's digging even though she can't really see it.

Before long he comes back, pokes the bundle, takes the maul and smashes the hell out of it. Hard to tell from here what's wrapped in the towel, but now it's flattened with pieces of whatever blowing out from the tidy folds.

A blowfly drifts from fragment to fragment only to be interrupted by Joe's rude pummeling. It gives up, drifts along the woods line until it finds Marge's sweaty brow. Lands like a Piper single prop with a failed front wheel. She can feel it, heavy and clumsy, trying to cling to the left eyebrow. The back of her hand brushes it off. She hears it buzz in circles and watches it retreat to the flattened bundle. It prefers whatever's in that bundle more than her, she thinks.

She watches Joe shovel up the blown pieces and walk back out into the woods. He takes several trips and then collects the towel and tools and starts back to the house.

She hadn't thought about his going back home. Now she's between him and home and she's not exactly light on her feet even in good light. She stands up, steps back, and trips over a fallen log. The high-pitched shriek and subsequent *woof* of air pierces the quiet evening. She swears the multi-legged things have already discovered her hands, feels the sensation of crusty, prickly legs moving up her arms. She's forgotten all about neighbor Joe, until she glances up and realizes he's standing over her, the maul over his shoulder in the midst of a swing.

imprecate after sundown

"*WHAT ABOUT A* church?"

"Little too late now. Should have thought about that before you killed her, Eddie."

"No, to dump her. So at least her family—"

Roy pulls over to the shoulder of the road, stops and turns to Eddie. "Are you bipolar? Did your brain shift and now we're stuck with whatever gear you're in?"

"What?"

"We can't drop her at a church. The whole thing's evidence, stupid."

"Don't call me stupid, Roy. Ma didn't like you callin' me stupid."

"Fine. Why don't we just stop and have a pizza first?" Roy's neck is stretched and head cocked to make a point, hoping Eddie catches the sarcasm. For a moment he can see Eddie likes the pizza idea, but the interest fades and Eddie seems sad again.

"Hell, Roy, you think the cops got some machine, like a virus scan, and out pops a piece of paper with our names on it and where we live?"

"You ever watch the news? They have people. People who pick things off bodies. Little things like hair, dirt and threads."

"I'm going bald, Roy. I'm not dirty and look," pulls the front of his shirt out, "no loose threads. Looks like I'm covered."

Roy's eyes roll and he stares out the windshield hoping this episode of the twilight zone is over soon. "No church. It just ain't right."

"What about that state park we passed comin' in?"

Roy's clueless. Doesn't remember a park. Can't imagine Eddie having it together long enough to notice one, either. Weird the way his brain's working now. "I'm not with you there, Eddie."

Frustrated, Eddied exhales, takes a deep breath and says, "Where they have those mound things all those Indians are buried in."

"They don't have those in Florida. You must have dreamed that."

"No! Dirt mounds. Remember? We just stick her in one of those."

Roy smacks his forehead as if to kill a very large mosquito. "Why didn't I think of that? And while were at it, we'll stick pasties on her and say she was a dancer and just fell off the stage! You moron. They don't have burial mounds this far south. That's in north Florida. You're remembering when...who was it? One of our daddies took us to see one."

"Don't make fun of me, Roy." Eddie opens the car door like he's gonna get out.

"Where you going? You're not leavin' me with this body."

"Could just dump it here, Roy. Doesn't look like anyone comes out here much."

"Can't. We have to bury her. Can't just dump it like that. Even Ma knew that."

"Only 'cause she didn't want the reminders." Eddie closes the door. "You bring a shovel?"

"No, I didn't. Guess you should a planned better."

"Wasn't me," Eddie says softly.

Reminds Roy of when they were little and Eddie sulked anytime he thought he was a disappointment. Bella wasn't much help on that, either. Lots of criticism. Not much positive reinforcement. "Come on, we'll pick one up at the Dime Discount."

MALCOLM LOOKS AT Sarah and says, "This will never work."

"Why not? Just shove some brush under there so the tires catch and we're good to go." Sarah's got dried palmetto fronds in her hand, waves them at Malcolm as if to cool him off. Not that it's hot. There's a sweet breeze and the moon drifts in a quiet sky.

"It's sugar sand, *Sugar!* Can't dig out of sugar sand. We need a tow truck with a winch." He's on his knees next to a rear tire buried up to the axle out in the middle of nowhere probably days from a living soul. Doesn't realize he's said it out loud.

"It's the Ocala National Forest road. Look at it. You can tell it's used. Won't be days, and stop being so melodramatic." She hands Malcolm an armful of broken branches, "Here, shove this."

He looks up at her. She's smiling. He's not, says, "Call your dad."

In a high pitched valley girl way she knows he hates, she snipes back, "Tried that, no *coverage.*"

"Of course not. No reason in the world it would be easy. Did you lock the door at the house before we left?"

"Why are you asking that now?"

"Did you?"

"No. What I did was open every window, then the screen door. Wide open. Oh! I even remembered to leave the front door open, too. Anyone can wander in. Whoever should like that new flat screen TV."

"Why can't you just answer a simple question?"

"Just did, Malcolm. Screwing with you is more entertaining though. Like watching you now. You and the car. Who will win?"

"You can be such a bitch, you know that?"

"Yeah, well, we all gotta be good at something," she says twisting her hair around her finger.

"Oh, honey, your bitch factor is top of the line tonight."

"You so know how to turn me on, Malcolm," she says slowly pulling a strand of hair between her lips, "in that redneck sort of way."

In the distance, maybe a quarter mile down the road, Malcolm notices headlights. Flash on. Flash off.

"Someone else is out here."

"Finally!" Sarah exhales. "Well get up and see if they can help."

Now she's just sarcastic and trying to sound funny at it. Malcolm's hesitant only long enough to dismiss every instinct on the threat of having to listen to Sarah go on for the next five hours on why it's his fault they're stuck here. *Let's try something new, be spontaneous. Do it in the forest!* she'd said. Yeah, it was a hard-on at first, but then she wanted to turn the car around so they were facing the rising moon. So romantic.

Malcolm stiffly gets to his feet, brushes the sand off his ass. "Stay here. I'll see if they can help. Do your nails or something."

"You don't have to be so condescending."

"Yes, I do."

"You're picking a fight."

"I am. It'll make me feel better."

"Keep it up and I'll walk home."

"No, you won't. You're afraid of things in the dark." He snatches the flashlight from her hand.

"You're taking that? I'll be in the dark."

"Wait in the car. I'm not walking where I can't see. All we'd need is for me to get eaten by a bear out here in timberland."

"Fine!" Sarah crawls into the Toyota and slams the door. Malcolm can see she's lighting a cigarette. She knows he hates it when she smokes in the car.

The walk is not more than a few minutes under a full moon and Malcolm can make out the car that went with the headlights. A white Pontiac, both doors wide-open, the trunk popped. Doesn't seem to be anyone around. He stands a moment and hears voices back off the road somewhere in the woods.

In a small opening beneath the full moon, two guys stare down into a hole that Malcolm concludes they've dug because of the shovel and fresh mound of dirt. Before he knows it, he's less than five feet from them, trying to work it out in his head why two guys are out in the woods digging a hole in the middle of the night.

"You gotta go deep so it don't end up like Ma," Eddie says.

Roy looks up and sees the guy standing there, hands limp at his side staring at the hole.

"Hey," Malcolm says, "What are you guys doing?"

Eddie and Roy pass a look, and Roy's spine straightens. His fist tightens around the shovel handle. "Nothin' really." It's all he can think to say on short notice.

"Why are you digging that hole?"

The look passes between Roy and Eddie again. Roy gestures to the ground, "Hit a deer."

After a long silence Malcolm says, "Hole doesn't look big enough for a deer."

"Small deer."

"That your car back there?"

"Maybe."

"My car's stuck back down the road. Wondered if maybe you had a tow chain or knew some trick on how to dig us out of sugar sand." Malcolm's staring at the hole trying to estimate in his head just how small the deer would have to be to fit in that hole. He takes two more steps closer without even thinking, forgets about the flashlight in his hand.

"Us?" Roy asks blocking him.

"Yeah. Me and the wife." Malcolm thinks they'll be more inclined to help if a woman is stranded.

"How far down?"

Malcolm's eyes briefly leave the hole. Gets a good look at Roy. "Maybe a quarter mile that way," he points with a limp hand, his head slowly trying to see around Roy into the hole again.

"Why don't you go on back to the car and we'll help you out once we get this done. Eddie here's got a soft spot for animals. Didn't want to leave it out at the road."

Stupid Eddie swings the flashlight into the hole without thinking and lights up dead girl's left leg suspended in mid-air from rigor. Malcolm just does catch a glimpse of it, and a squeal escapes his lips before his hand slaps it shut. Roy steps aside, can't stop him now anyway, and as soon as the guy turns his back, Roy lands the shovel spade in the back of Malcolm's head. Drops him half in, half out of the hole as if he's inspecting measurements.

"*Why'd you do that, Roy?*" Eddie yells, staring down at the guy with his hands in the air, flashlight beam flooding the scrub oaks.

"He made us, that's why. You had to go and light her up, stupid."

"Quit callin' me stupid, Roy."

Roy grabs the back of Eddie's neck, shoves him close to the guy. "Look what you did! That's stupid, Eddie. You're the reason she's there, and now him."

"Didn't do it on purpose, Roy," Eddie ducks out from Roy's grip. "I didn't know he was gonna show up!"

"I almost had him back at his car, Eddie, and you had to light her up."

Could be déjà vu, the spirits come knocking, Bella's influence beyond the grave, whatever, Roy's watching his worst nightmare come true. He's had to kill some innocent guy that's caught him and Eddie in a Bella moment still feeding the two-headed demon he fears has jumped from her dead soul to Eddie. Thinks it's never going to end.

"I didn't know—" Eddie drops the flashlight. "What are we gonna do with him, Roy?"

Malcolm suddenly draws a breath of air.

"What do you think?" Roy pulls the .38 Special from behind his back, aims it at the back of Malcolm's head and pulls the trigger.

Eddie mutters, "Said he's got a wife."

"Yeah," Roy grabs the guy's feet, "and we'll have to take care of her, too." Turns the body into the grave on top of dead girl. "Doing a great job here, Eddie. Three in one night. That beats the hell out of Bella's old record. You should be proud."

"You think?"

Roy jams the shovel spade into the ground inches from Eddie's feet. "No, I don't. I was being facetious, *stupid*. But here I am cleaning up your mess again. Ever think I get tired of it, Eddie?"

"What do you want me to do, Roy?"

"Quit lying for one. Think I don't know you trolled the streets, picked her up and slit her throat?"

"But I don't remember it."

"Yeah, just like Ma when she first started. You forget that? You forget how it started? Because I remember it, Eddie. Her driving us around late at night and seeing some pathetic runaway huddled on a bus bench and her stoppin' and askin' her if she wants a hot meal and warm place to stay."

Eddie quickly shakes his head.

"Sure you do. First girl wasn't much older than I was at the time. Bella thought, at least I think she was thinking, how easy it'd be if she dragged us along, throw suspicions, and it worked, didn't it, Eddie? Who would finger point to a woman and her three kids? Who'd believe it?"

"I didn't know what she was up to, Roy! You're treatin' me like all them haters from back home! I didn't know what she was up to."

"I know, Eddie. I know all about it. I didn't know either 'till she brought her home with us and sent us out to dig a hole. I didn't get it either until she screwed up and come out of the place bloodied up with that satisfied look on her I'd never seen before. Like she'd been given the Ten Commandments and knew every secret in the world."

"How's that my fault, Roy?"

"It's not. But here we are. Nothing's changed. She's been dead for weeks Eddie and here we are burying another one as if nothing's changed. When does it stop? When, Eddie?"

"I, I don't—"

"Forget it. We got to get the other one before the sun's up. Come on."

SARAH'S SMOKED ENOUGH cigarettes to fog the inside of the Toyota. A nice *screw you* at Malcolm for making this all her fault. What is taking so long? Of course, he's probably giving whoever it is an ear full. The only thing he liked better than picking a fight with her was involving others. Total strangers. The stranger, the better.

A song comes on the radio and she turns it up loud, lights another cigarette, props her bare feet up on the dashboard. She rubs her legs finding a furry patch missed by the shaver. "Damn it." She hears a pop in the distance, turns the radio down, listens, rolls the window down a few inches and listens again. No sound other than night insects and opossums scavenging in the underbrush. She rolls the window back up. Losing too much smoke.

A raccoon scurries across the road in front of the Toyota, stops, stands on its hind legs, and appears as if waving.

Sarah flashes the headlights on and off just to see what it'll do. A knock on her window makes her jump, the cigarette slipping from her fingers into her crotch. She leaps up and plucks it from the seat. A flashlight beam blinds her. She rolls the window down an inch.

"Hi, I'm Eddie. Your husband's down at our car," he points the flashlight down the road. "He needs you to come on down." Light hits her eyes again.

"Why didn't he come himself?"

"Tripped. Turned his ankle. Looks pretty bad. We can get him to the hospital, but I think you'll need a wrecker for the car here."

Eddie's head is weavin' back and forth trying to get a better look at the girl, his head spinning, neck hot, fist knotted behind his back. *She has to open the door, she has to open the door, she has to open the door.*

"Damn it, Malcolm," she bitches opening the door. Never gives it a second thought. The moment she steps ahead of Eddie, he pulls the buck knife and grabs her from behind.

ROY LETS EDDIE handle the girl on his own. He seems to have a talent for killing. Filling in the hole feels like the old days—not so old, only weeks really—but he doesn't have to participate in snuffing out her life like a finished cigarette. The whole thing takes less than an hour. Killing and burial.

The couple was nice enough to have a gas can in the trunk. Roy slings gas on the interior, throws the can in and flicks open Sarah's lighter. Flips it in. Gas fumes whoosh into flames. Black smoke rolls through the open passenger window.

Eddie's behind the wheel of the Pontiac with the motor running watching flames engulf the Toyota from the rearview mirror. Roy's silhouette is in front of a red orange back light trotting back to the car.

"And why'd you do that?"

"To destroy evidence, Eddie. Cops will think it's a stolen car. Will for sure when they come up missing. Don't you ever watch the news?"

No answer on Eddie's part, he's staring through the windshield, breathing hard, hands gripping the wheel. His voice escapes in a hitch and goes silent again. Roy wonders what the hell's wrong with him.

"I remember."

"Remember what?"

"How I did it."

"Did what?"

"The girl. I remember how I killed her. It came back when I saw you light that car up and you were a shadow against the fire and I remember leaving the store with my new gold chain and I saw her standing by a newspaper rack on the sidewalk out front. I almost walked past her, but she spoke to me." Eddie stops as if it's all he's gonna say.

Roy turns sideways in the seat to get a better look at the side of Eddie's face. "Then what?"

"She asked if I had a cigarette. I said no, don't smoke. She looked sad about it. Then it was like I was outside my body watching some other guy picking her up. Like he'd been in me all this time just waiting. Yet I knew him, Roy. I've known him for as long as I can remember. He was just waitin'. He asked her if she needed a ride." Eddie turns and looks Roy in the eye. "She said yes, Roy." Turns back to the windshield.

"What did you…he do next?"

"Drove around awhile. They talked about stuff. Stupid stuff. He could smell her, Roy. She was gettin' him all sexed up. He told her he needed to wash his car and he found a place not too far away. He drove into the Self-Serve, turned off the engine and said he had to get out to wash it. She got out, too. He turned the ignition on so the radio played loud.

"No one was around. They had the place to themselves. The light in the bay was burned out or somethin' and she asked why he didn't move the car to a lighted one. He said he liked the dark, thought she looked sexy in the moonlight."

Eddie's sweaty hands are rolling back and forth over the wheel. He's slowly rocking back and forth in the seat.

"He pulls off his shirt. He knows she thinks he's sexy by the way she's smiling and she starts a slow kind of dance to the music and she points to his pants and he slips them off, too. He's naked, dancing, reaches for her. She teases, pretends she won't come. But she does. He can't believe how his fantasy is comin' true and before he knows it, she's in his arms, her fingers sliding along his arms and chest and—"

"What?"

"He cuts her. She doesn't even realize it until it's too late. And then she's limp in his arms, bleedin' out, her body jerkin' before it settles out. There's so much blood, Roy. He can feel the heat of it on his skin.

"He's got her in his arms still moving slow to the music like she's enjoying the dance. When the songs over he lays her on the ground, finishes washing the car and opens the trunk. He puts her inside on the tarp. He takes the wand from the wall and washes the blood down the drain. Washes blood off his skin. Dresses, and drives away. It was just that easy, Roy. Didn't need the tape. She walked right to me."

Roy turns and watches flames eat the interior of the Toyota, looks back at Eddie.

"Sure no one saw you?"

"This place is like a ghost town at night. I drove around for hours. It's like they roll up the sidewalks. Never even saw a cop."

"Let's get out of here, Eddie. Can't do anymore here, but get caught."

18

out of body

JOE'S MISSED DINNER again. It's past seven when he gets back to the house, the place dark. He's stripped naked except for the super hero boxers, his clothes wadded under his arm. He sneaks into the garage, dumps bloody clothes into the washing machine and gets it going. He opens Marge's little disposable camera, pulls the film out and drops it in the trash.

The glow from the TV casts an eerie quiet on the room. Pop's in his recliner sitting forward on the edge of the seat, hands on the arm rests as if he might get up but not committed to doing it.

Joe doesn't want to have to explain why he's so late and standing in his underwear. He quietly retreats to the garage and slips into a pair of pants found in the ironing basket. Thinks he can get away with just pants. Nothing strange about that. Nothing really strange about being in underwear around here, either. Better to not get anything started. Old man has picked up on enough stuff without asking questions.

"Hey, Pop. Sorry I took so long. You eat?"

Pop's in the exact same position, staring into space, nothing even remotely like a word of acknowledgement coming out of his mouth. Doesn't even look up.

"Pop, you forget your hearing aid?" It's a stupid thing to ask a guy who's deaf without it. He leans over so the old guy can see him. Looks him right in the eye. Waves his hand in front of his face. Not a flinch. Touches his shoulder, "You okay in there?" Joe takes Pop's pulse. Seems regular enough, but still no response.

Joe turns on the light by the recliner, realizes the TV's not exactly on a station but somewhere in between where there's a channel but no signal. Volume's turned way down, nothing audible but a weird hissing. A doily rests on Pop's lap, sharply folded in eighths.

"You hungry? I can whip us up something pretty quick. Eggs maybe. Some of that thick slice bacon? What do you say?"

Still no response, just eyes wide-open staring into some world Joe can't see. It frightens Joe deep in his bones, wonders who to call if the old guy doesn't come out of it. Thinking about taking him back to the VA brings up all sorts of feelings. Most he'd like to forget. Even the suggestion of it paroles memories of Key's and his unintentional death and the cascade of events out of Joe's control that lead to one death after the other. The chances of another one like Keys working there now must be remote—astronomical really—but can Joe chance it?

He throws on a shirt, grabs the car keys and pulls Pop to his feet. The old guy's body obediently follows along, but his brain's been left behind to wander in dark spaces Joe can only imagine.

Traffic's thinned out on 441 and Joe glances at Pop now and then to see if any light's come back in the eyes. Pop's hands lie limp in his lap, his walkin' stick propped between his knees. He's nothing more than a mannequin with bad taste in wardrobe waiting to be propped up in a window display for seniors. As Joe passes the Twisty Treat, Pop's head spins watching it go by.

"Let's get a cone," he says.

The Buick jerks as Joe hits the brake and slides into the Hardees parking lot.

"Not here, *Who-Ass*. The Twisty Treat. A great big triple stack." Pop rubs his forehead and realizes Joe's staring at him. "What's wrong with you?"

"You don't remember?"

"Remember what?"

"You checked out."

"Checked out where?"

"In your head."

"In my what? You been drinking?"

"No. I found you in your chair. You wouldn't speak. Wouldn't look at me. I was talking and talking and you just sat there."

"Really?"

"Really. Don't you remember what you were thinkin'?"

Pop looks through the windshield, fear rising in his chest. He doesn't remember. Not a thing. "I was watchin' Law and Order."

"How'd it end?"

"I don't know. Where we going?"

"Takin' you back to the VA."

"Hell you are." Pop stiffens and slides his right hand around the walkin' stick.

"Sure you're okay?"

"Don't make me show you, boy."

"Still want the cone?"

Pop reads Joe's face. Can't hold eye contact too long lest he see his fears.

"Like I said. Make it a triple."

a gamy excuse

PULLING INTO THE driveway, Dee Dee notices right off the place is dark, concludes Marge has fallen asleep on that damn recliner in the backyard getting sucked away by mosquitoes who've found the all-you-can-eat buffet of buffets. She'll bitch about the itchy swollen bites and make her life miserable about flaws in her perfect mocha skin.

Lights come on as Dee Dee makes her way through the house, Marge absent one room after the other. Out back, crickets and frogs call from the pond and moths attracted by the porch light swarm in dusty assault. She closes the sliding glass door, checks Marge's bedroom again, notices her walking shoes are missing. Can't imagine her sister going out for a walk after dark. She doesn't even walk during the day except from the kitchen to the backyard. Exercise? Please!

BY MIDNIGHT, DINNER'S shriveled up in cold pots on the stove. Dee Dee's in the dark, folded up in her recliner, hands in her lap, staring out the window. An ignored cigarette burns in the ashtray.

BETTY'S LANDLADY IS perched on the stoop of her rundown cat box of a house; a label removed tomato soup can in her hand stuffed with toilet paper. Her bottom lip protrudes on the right side as if she's taken one to the mouth. Crammed with snuff, she considers it a safer substitute for cigarettes—what the snuff makers claim—except for the indelicate way of disposing of built up saliva by spitting into said soup can.

She's glad to see Joe when he pulls up, though it makes her sad. She waves, tries to smile without losing any of her wad and wipes escaping drool off with the edge of the can.

"Whacha been up to, Jo?" She spits into the can, watches with her good eye as he comes up the walkway with his hands in his pockets.

"Here and there, you know. Quit the smokin'?" Joe notes the thirty or forty cigarette butts clustered in the yard in various stages of decomposition.

"Tryin' to cut back. Doc's say the emphysema's gettin' worse, but hell, what ain't," she smiles, brown slime edging her teeth. He can smell the pungent soggy tobacco from where he's standing.

"Cops said they've released Betty's things. Said I could come by and get 'em."

"Almost too late. Got some boys in the house cleanin' the place."

"How'd you manage that?"

"Said I'd give 'em the two weeks left on the rent. Now, I ain't gotta paint it." Grins as if she's gotten away with something.

"Didn't give 'em her stuff, did you?"

"Naw," spits in the can, "it's all still there. Did get rid of the car, though. Gonna cost me money an you know how I don't care to spend no money."

"Get it towed?" Joe's not so brokenhearted about the car, either. Ricky left it when he was sent to prison, took it back when he got out. Probably still reeks with his stink.

"Them boys did. Didn't say what they got for it. They're not back yet, but when they are, I'll give you a shout."

"That'd be good. Got my number?"

"Yeah. It's in there somewhere. I'll getcha."

He never cared for the old woman, but she treated Betty okay. Not like they were gonna be best friends now with her gone. Makes him want to heave, watching her sitting there chewing brown butt grease like cud. Doesn't think you're supposed to chew the stuff. Can't get out of her gaze fast enough.

BY EIGHT IN the morning, Dee Dee's still in the recliner looking out the window. She glances at the phone then cancels the idea. She's desperate for someone to listen, to care. No one cares. They'll know who she is the second the line connects; know she's the crazy one who calls about dead people, the crazy one who accuses that poor man next door of doing awful things in his shed.

She'd been feeling better. Really. Maybe Marge's visit has been a positive thing. It's been nice having someone to talk to, to take care of, someone who knew her even in the low times. Marge has had her own low times, an endless succession of no-account men and failed one-sided relationships. At least Marge tried to have one. At least she didn't hide away from life. Marge ate more than her share of life. Got most of Dee's, too.

What if she's not coming back? What if this very moment is as good as it's going to get? Her hand softly pats the phone receiver.

PHONE CALL COMES next day, Betty's landlord's humor soured since he saw her yesterday. She gives Joe a curt, "They're back, get the stuff." Then dial tone. Not the first time her attitude's shifted, but her timing's good. Joe's been reading through the rest of Betty's diary, not sure why he's enduring the saga of her requiem love affair with Ricky Vega. Not love really. More like a parasitic need. Nothing in the pages clears things up for him. Most of it seems repetitious, morose, even self-flagellating. And he doesn't really like her very much in this book. She's weak and self-absorbed. Only thing she obsesses over more than herself is Ricky's treatment. Hard to tell where one thing begins and the other ends.

Joe lays the book down, picks up a photo of him and Betty together in better times. They'd been best friends. And looking at the image he thinks he knows why. They were so damn much alike.

He's also been keeping track at the back door, the dead pine, a black vortex spinning above, counts maybe thirty vultures or more. Hard to count moving objects but not the point. He hears the open and close of Dee Dee's sliders, and muses on how intertwined her life is with his, and that if something drastic isn't done, it'll never end.

Pop's puttering amongst his flowers, dead heading the marigolds, whatever. Hasn't seemed to notice the birds. Just as well. Joe leans out the door shaking the car keys at him. "Gonna get Betty's things. Be back soon."

Pop raises a hand. Joe doesn't think he heard a word he said and that's just as well, too.

A WHITE PONTIAC'S shaded under the live oak at Betty's apartment, not her apartment anymore, although technically still is. Joe beats on the screen door half expecting her to play tug of war with the door knob and harass him about being late. Her fishing bucket still sits empty against the wall, but the fishing poles are gone, probably lifted by street thugs looking to make easy money at the pawn shop. Door sucks open in a whoosh and Roy's standing—arm on the frame—the same way Ricky used to. Takes Joe a second to get it back in gear to explain who he is and why he's there.

"Landlady said I could get Betty's stuff."

"Old lady next door with the jacked-up teeth?"

"She said I could come over."

Guy at the door doesn't seem all that interested in the who and why, he's clearly been sleeping and pulled his jeans on in a hurry, but ignored the zipper and button fly. Jeans lay open and Joe's greeted with curly hair and a bare chest. Guy's in decent shape for his age, Joe guesses—his age, maybe older.

"You need to do this now?" Roy half mumbles because most of his brain's asleep rolled up in some dream with a hard-on and a blond in a hot tub. Could be Vegas. The remnant is hoping to follow.

"Don't think there's much left. I'm leavin' the furniture. Housewares will go to Goodwill. Mostly going for the personal stuff."

"Well," Roy rubs his head, further disheveling already disheveled hair, looks over his shoulder as if he doesn't want company to see a messy apartment, but that's what Joe thinks. Roy's actually thinking about Eddie and how he'll react finding a stranger in the house because if it was Bella, she'd shit—Eddie, who's becoming more like Bella everyday, unpredictable and scary.

"If you can be quick about it, guess it won't hurt." Instantly Roy's thinking about all the different ways there are to hurt a guy and forces those thoughts to the back of his mind in case Eddie somehow, like telepathy, can smell fresh meat in the house.

Could be the tone in the way it was said, or the remark itself, but something sparks in the back of Joe's brain, a fizzle of memory not quite dead yet. Thinks about it while collecting Betty's things.

Roy's settled prone on the sofa, arm across his face. Even that seems familiar. Joe drags his plastic garbage bag from one spot to another around the room, dumping in a knick-knack here, book there. He comes across Betty's old record player, the Patsy Cline forty-five still on the turntable. Her favorite. Machine's still on and he wonders if it's been on since EMS carried her out of here. He gently lifts the forty-five, careful to hold it by the edges and looks for the paper cover. Nowhere in sight. Probably a casualty in one of Betty and Ricky's love fights. Just being in here after reading that diary brings their lives to focus in full color.

Joe opens the small cabinet underneath holding her collection of oldies but goodies. "Have any boxes?"

Roy stares from under his arm.

"It'll scratch in a bag," Joe explains.

Roy points to the kitchen, holds the point as if Joe's stupid and can't figure out which room he's supposed to go to. "In there, under the sink."

Passing the bedroom, Joe spots Eddie laid out on the bed positioned as if being prepped for crucifixion, mouth wide-open. Moving on to the kitchen, Joe finds the box, realizes the job's bigger than one hour or two. Might take days. He pulls open the utensil drawer, finds the fish filet knife in the same spot he left it—slips that in the box for old time's sake. He dumps other kitchenware with it so it doesn't look strange in the box alone. Returns to the living room.

"Look, this is gonna take longer than I thought. I'm gonna need to come back with more boxes. Sift through this stuff. I can come back when you guys are out of the place if you want."

Roy peers out from under is arm again. "You're turning into a pissant. Do what you have to. Not our shit. We'll be gettin' out of here in a few days anyway."

Seeing him lying there, using the phrase *pissant*, Joe's thrown back in time thinking his mind's paying tricks on him. "You say pissant?"

"Not meant to offend there sport. Just a saying. Nothing meant by it."

"I knew another guy who used it. But no one else until you. What are the odds?" Joe fingers through the album collection.

"Not that uncommon. That saying's been in my family for years. Nothing to it."

"Was when the other guy said it." Joe lays a handful of albums in the box.

"A person can use about any word to someone's detriment if they want to. Maybe you just took it wrong." It's a lie on Roy's part. He's just never had anyone call him on it. He learned it from one of Bella's part-time husbands. Ricky's father maybe.

Joe looks down at the box, the tip of the knife peeking between Merle Haggard and Charlie Rich. "No, I took it the way it was intended." Thinks back to an earlier comment in passing. "You said you're just staying here a couple days. You not rentin' the place?"

"Looking for our brother Ricky. You gotta know him if you knew her."

Joe slides the full box across the floor to the front door. "Don't ever remember him sayin' anything about family."

"Not surprised. Always kept personal stuff close to the vest. Ma kicked him out of the house as a kid and we didn't hear much from him after that. How you know Betty?"

"Best friends since middle school."

"Yeah, we never met her." Roy's arm's across his forehead deep in thought.

"Gonna go get more boxes. Get this stuff out of the way."

"Who's got the kid?"

Question stops Joe in his tracks. Debates in his head how much to tell the guy. "When was the last time you heard anything?"

"Three, maybe four years ago now, why?"

"He drowned."

Roy sits up on his elbows, *"Died?"*

"Guess old Ricky kept more than a few things from you."

Roy swings his legs off the sofa, seems genuinely shocked. "He never even told Ma. She was mad as hell he never brought the kid by. He went to prison before she finally got in contact with him again, and only after the cops clued her in. He never mentioned the boy died."

"Why you suppose that is?" Joe asks, knows the reason, but can't resist getting into Roy's head.

"Same reason he got kicked out of the house. Bella thought he was sneaky."

"You say Bella?"

"Yeah."

"She ever married to guy named Sid?"

"Yeah, my daddy. Why, you know her?"

Joe drops his hands. "Vega's not your real last name, is it?"

"Was Cooper. She made me change it to Vega. We know each other?"

"Your daddy and my mother were brother and sister."

"No shit?"

"And Ricky's your brother?"

"Half brother. Only claim half."

"And the guy in on the bed there?"

"Little half brother. Wow, what are the odds hooking up like this?"

"How's your Ma?"

"Passed away not long ago."

"And your daddy?"

"Hell if I know. He just disappeared one day."

Joe gestures to the bedroom, "What about his daddy?"

"Disappeared, too. Bella never could keep a man. Too hard on 'em. You're just full of questions, aren't you?"

"My pop'll drill me on it."

"You seem kind of familiar to me now that I'm lookin' at you. We ever get together?"

"Once as a kid. My mom sent me to your place one summer, but she didn't know uncle Sid and Bella were a done deal. Bella never mentioned it to her."

"Runs in the family." Roy gazes up at the ceiling in deep thought. "You're that kid." Points at Joe like there's others in the room that need to know. "One that took a header off the garage roof."

Joe pulls his head from the book shelf, stands up straight and pulls up his shirt. "You mean this?" A zig zag scar stretches under his ribcage.

Roy nods, "Yeah. You landed on—"

"Some damn garden tool." Joe pulls his shirt down. "One of you shoved me. I still remember hearing laughing on the way down."

"Sorry about that. That was stupid Eddie, but don't say it to his face. Between me and you, he earned the name."

"And I remember your Ma. She beat the hell out of all of us."

"She didn't let much slide. Said boys needed a firm hand, especially in the back of the head."

"Where you all livin' now?"

"A few counties north a here."

Joe shakes his head, looks at Roy as if he's gonna say something else, but doesn't. He picks up the box. "Won't take long to get this stuff together."

CALL THE POLICE? Don't call the police? Sit here and wait? How long to wait? Check her room again? Go outside and yell her name?

TIC, TIC, TIC.

Damn! Out of cigarettes. Who to call? How long's it been?

Clock shows almost twelve hours. Twelve hours since Marge vanished without a word or note. No high, by, or kiss my ass. What was in her head!

Say to the police, my sister's missing, not unlike her dog? The dog! Could Marge have met the same fate? Even she can't imagine asshole Joe Salas taking blame, but Marge did confront him. Told her so. If she had, what would he do?

But who to call? A small card rotates in her fat sweaty hand until the edges tear and begin to flake. She dials the number on the card, now, almost rubbed away and considers hanging up when a voice answers. Heart pounding in her chest, Dee Dee manages to ask for the help she dreads, praying she's at least given a chance to petition her concerns without prejudice.

ARNIE'S HAPPY TO answer the call. He's showered, shaved, splashed on some cologne he'd seen advertised on TV where mobs of firm young females swarm some loser who couldn't get a date with a blind girl. But, aha, the attraction is magic! Loser revels in hormone hyped co-eds.

He checks out on the radio that he's following up on an investigation—sort of true—snubs the cigarette butt in the car ashtray and flicks it to the curb from the open door. Yeah, gonna be a great morning, he thinks. With luck, might even get lucky.

Dee Dee's at the door before Arnie gets halfway up the sidewalk. She's wringing her hands in her shirttail, breathless and nervous, rehearsing in her head what to share. Seeing Arnie makes her relax, something about his non-confrontational easy going way.

"Miss Turner, what can I help you with this fine day?"

"She's gone. Not come back all night!" Steps aside to let him through the door, starts to close it then decides to leave it open.

"I can see you're upset, Miss Turner, why don't we sit down and you can tell me what's happened." Luggage litters the living room floor like castaways. Arnie steps over a piece to get to the sofa.

"Call me Dee Dee. And I'm not crazy, Detective Arnold. Her shoes are gone, her purse is here, her sweater," recites the list very carefully while pointing her finger at the ground, "like she went for a walk and not come back. Is there anything you can do, anyone you can call?"

Arnie sits on the sofa next to her, retrieves a small notebook and pen from his jacket. "Did you two ladies have a little tiff? Maybe she's mad and wants you to worry?"

"Tiff? We didn't have some damn fight. She's gone!" Dee Dee springs off the sofa and moves to the window.

Arnie nods at the luggage, "Going on a trip?"

"No, I'm not going on a trip!" She realizes he's talking about the luggage. "It's her's." It's all she says about it.

"Then what do you suppose happened to her?"

"I don't know. How the hell would I know? If I did, I wouldn't be yapping at you."

"Did you find anything strange in the house?"

"Strange? Like what?" She's staring at him, holding herself as if chilled.

"Signs of a struggle, items out of place. Maybe something that on the surface means nothing, but looking back might feel wrong?"

"Are you kidding me? If this is the best you can do then maybe you better go." Dabs at the corners of her eyes with the shirttail.

"Have to ask the questions, Dee Dee. Did she have any friends that might have picked her up, where she might have slept over?" Arnie's making a circle with the pen as if to move her along. "Maybe a nice man friend? Looks like she was getting ready to go somewhere."

"Are you out of your mind? She's not out hookin' up. She's gone!"

Arnie holds up his hands in a defensive sort of way like he used to do with his mother when she wanted to rail about his good-for-nothing father. Like it was his fault.

"I'll place some calls in the obvious places, but can't put out a missing person's bolo for another twelve hours," he says checking his watch. "You check around the property?"

"And where would that be?" Hands on her hips, Dee Dee's almost defiant, just waiting for the right word to set her off. At least that's what Arnie thinks.

Her hand suddenly slaps to her mouth and she slowly turns towards the kitchen.

"What's wrong?"

"He got her."

"Who?"

"That asshole Joe Salas. I bet you he's kilt her like all those other people, God help 'em. She said she'd got up in his face and I bet…" steps to the window and whispers, "he lured her to that shed and kilt her." Spins with her hands out to her sides, "You got to get a warrant! Maybe he hasn't kilt her yet."

Arnie raises an eyebrow, jots notes in the notebook.

"You don't believe me, do you?"

"Need probable cause, Dee Dee. Need more than your word and no one's ever been able to prove he's killed anyone. No evidence of any kind."

"You don't think I know that! After the looney bin and jail, you think I'd *forget?*"

"Look, I sympathize with you, but I have to follow the law here."

"Go after him!" Dee Dee's shrieking a wail that makes Arnie's ears want to bleed. "I know he done kilt her. If you don't go over there, I surely will!"

"No, no, no, let's not do that. I'll, I'll go have a talk with him and if I feel the slightest suspicion, I'll get the warrant." That's what he says to her. Knows there's not chance in hell of it happening, but the thought of staying in the room with her one more minute without a cigarette—does have a loaded gun—and flashbacks of life with his ex-wife. Not going to happen.

"Let me go and I'll get back to you shortly, okay?" He's studying her pinched face, knows she's on the verge of losing it and mobilizing on the neighbor's house. "Don't do anything rash. I'll be back."

"You got you twenty-four hours," she snaps pointing to the door.

white flies

CROY'S BACK AT his desk, reports spread across sanitized surfaces in brain-numbing organization. On a yellow pad is a list of names, locations, dates, all the way through to the following three pages. Arnie takes it all in as he slides to his own desk, his ears still ringing.

"Heard you found a whole graveyard."

"Seems to go back a decade or more from what the medical examiner could tell on sight."

"One of the Vega boys a serial killer?"

"If they are, they started in their early teens from the body count."

"Where are they at?"

"If I knew, I wouldn't be here."

"I had to pay a visit to your girl."

Croy glances up. Squints.

"Miss Turner."

"Yeah? She remember anything?"

"Nope." Arnie staples papers together, drops them in the out box. "Say's her sister's missing."

"And let me guess. The neighbor's killed her."

"You got it. I told her I'd check on it. Not going back there alone."

"What do you think happened to her?"

"Hell if I know, but someone's planning a trip. There's luggage all over the living room. Weird, those two. I sat in the car and watched the Joe fella's house for awhile. Old guy, guessing it's his father, does yard work. Doesn't leave the house. Joe, he was gone until late, brought boxes of stuff from the car."

"Oh, yeah?"

"Yeah, I released the Vega effects to him while you were gone. He's probably been collecting her stuff from the apartment. Nice enough fella."

"How'd you know that?"

"Talked to him. Easy going, doesn't seem to be hiding anything."

"No. I mean how did you know he's getting things from the apartment?"

"Oh, the landlady called. She wanted to know if it was all right for him to take the stuff."

"Have you re-interviewed him yet?"

"No. Didn't think there was any hurry. Why?"

"I need to tie up loose ends."

"They have medication for that, too."

Croy squints again, fishes through a drawer and pulls out a notebook.

"You got a call," Arnie says handing Croy a pink paper. "A Miss Sweets. Said she was going to come by the station. We finally get to meet a special someone?"

Croy struggles to maintain composure and breathe. He reads the message, recognizes the name. His mind backtracks trying to figure out how Sweets got his number. He doesn't give anyone his number unless work related and Sweets is definitely not work related. He quickly pulls out his wallet and counts his business cards. Counts those and every other paper in the morning before leaving for work. One's missing.

"Did you look around her place?"

"Her sister isn't there."

"How do you know that? Because she said so?"

"Why would she lie about it?"

Croy tilts his head. Stares. Bats his eyes.

"You think she knows more than she's saying?"

"I don't know anything. That's what we detectives do, Arnie. We find things out. We make sure people are telling us the truth, and we do that how?"

"By checking their stories," Arnie says a little deflated, deflated because he's going to have to go back there. Mouths the words *I don't want to go back there.* "Fine. I'll go look around." Turns with his hands grubbing through his pockets for his car keys. "I don't have to talk to her again, do I?"

"Do what you want, Arnie. I'm just saying, look at me. I went to ask a woman a few questions at her house and look what I discovered. You never know."

"I don't want to find a graveyard, Croy. I hate dead people."

"And they're real broken up about it, Arnie."

"Just two more months and I'll never have to have this conversation again." Arnie pats his jacket. Moves papers around on the desk.

"On the sink."

"What?"

"Your car keys. They're on the bathroom sink."

"Yeah, I knew that."

ARNIE'S NOT SURE Dee Dee's home. Hopes she isn't. He parks four houses down and walks between the houses to the back-fence line where the Forest Service has cut a fire break. With luck she's napping and not pinned to a window watching him rustling through the brush.

It doesn't take long to find his way down to the pond and the foot of the dead pine where briars and stick-tights collect thick on his pant legs. It's distracting having them stuck in the fabric, and he becomes frantically involved with their removal as if it's an infection raging up his leg. By the time one leg is free of beggars he's out of breath and spots a fallen tree stump that lies shaded under the spread of an oak tree. A cool place to sit and pick.

Halfway through the endeavor, Arnie catches a whiff of rot, slaps at flies buzzing around his head. He turns to the left and then to the right, suspects a raccoon has met its demise while hunting water. The stink's overwhelming and forces Arnie from his comfortable seat, the stick-tights forgotten. He glances over his shoulder, sees the partially eaten corpse of Marge Turner, and his feet twist against the log sending him over it backward right on top of poor Marge. Corpse ribs crack, one jabs Arnie in the side, feels like it's broken the skin. Disrupted flies swarm and buzz in mass, crawling Arnie's face. One slips between his parted lips.

Arnie scrambles off Marge's stinking remains. *"Holy God! Holy shit. Oh, my—"*

He strips off the jacket, uses it to feverishly wipe wet rot from his hands then slings it to the ground. He's in a panicked hippety-hop turning in circles and suddenly pulls his gun and points it shaking at the corpse, then at the woods line.

Takes awhile for him to calm down. Gun still trembling in his hand, Arnie dials 911 on his cell phone.

Forty-five minutes later, Arnie and Croy are standing over the body noting what's left of it.

"No clothes," Arnie says squeezing the last of Croy's hand sanitizer in his hand.

"What?" Croy snaps on a pair of latex gloves, crosses his arms, and inspects with tilted head.

"The body. Not wearing any clothes. Think someone took the clothes to hide evidence?"

"Arnie, did she have clothes on the last time we saw her?"

"No. But she's way out here. Why would she just be wearing shoes?"

"Would you want to walk around out here barefoot?"

Croy picks up a stick and pulls at the hair. "She was a nudist, Arnie." The scalp and hair slides off the skull like a wig.

"Gross. Why'd you go and do that?" Drops the empty bottle to the ground.

"To see this," Croy points out a massive fracture in the back of the head where skull bone is jammed into sodden brain matter. "Impact with a very heavy blunt object."

"Think she fell and hit her head on the log?"

Croy turns, head tilted at Arnie. Pauses in hopes Arnie's brain catches up with the evidence.

"Right. Looks like a homicide to me, too. Think the neighbor did it?"

"Don't pigeonhole it. She wasn't dragged down here. Probably not carried, either."

"I couldn't have dragged her down here in my good years. Don't think old skinny Joe up there did, either. No drag marks."

"She came down voluntarily. Don't think Joe would have been able to lure her down here. Someone got her."

"Looks like the varmints ate good. Not much soft tissue left."

"And that's going to make our job a whole lot harder."

EDDIE'S UP WHEN Joe returns with a backseat full of empty boxes. Joe throws four or five up on the porch and just walks in. Roy's rolling fresh paint on the bedroom wall, offers a nod when Joe passes to the kitchen. Joe still can't bring himself to look in there, damn near shuts his eyes walking through the hallway where he found Betty beat to a pulp. Someone's cleaned the mess on the floor, but bloody handprints still smear the door jams and baseboard.

Joe doesn't waste any time stacking dishes in the box, never hears Eddie settle by the doorway to watch with certain interest as if Joe's a wild animal and Eddie wants to see what it will do in confined spaces. He's got his finger hooked under the prized gold chain around his neck, sliding it back and forth across the joint in his forefinger because it feels smooth on his skin.

Joe looks up and sees Eddie standing there, but doesn't engage in conversation. Being reminded of the past when they were all kids has hit the refresh button in his brain and he's recalled in detail the hateful little bastard called Eddie. The whole time he was visiting Eddie and family was more or less an infected boil on Joe's ass. Eddie played mean tricks, the kind to draw blood if he could, and set him up to fall under the weight of Bella's fury and any tool she could find to use against him. It wasn't until just before he left to go home she beat the shit out of all of them. Didn't seem to care he was bleeding profusely from the fall off the garage roof—just beat him harder for messing up the front room when he came in for help. No wonder he didn't talk about the trip when he got back home. Not a word.

"You remember me, don't you?" Eddie's put on his mirrored sunglasses so Joe can't see his eyes. Keeps folks off guard when they can't look at your eyes, what he heard once, was always impressed by cops with mirrored sunglasses, like they had super powers no one else had.

"Not likely to forget," Joe says sealing the box. Drags a second box to his feet and opens another cabinet.

Eddie squats on his haunches and tilts his head down to see over the top of the sunglasses. "Still look like that little faggot we messed up in Shelby. What are you doing these days?"

"Oh, nothin' much, Eddie. Still that little faggot you messed up in Shelby," Joe says pulling glass casserole dishes out and stacking them in the box.

"Yeah, I remember. You were a dopey kid. Roy said you ain't changed much. Just got old."

"That's about it. Heard your Ma died."

"Who told you that? How did you find out about that?"

Joe turns. "Your brother. Why, was it a secret?"

Eddie rises to his feet, pushes the sunglasses against the bridge of his nose, and says to change the subject, "You talk to Ricky? 'Cause we been huntin' him high and low."

As he's sealing the box, Joe smiles to himself. "Not since Betty died."

"Hey, what happened there? Cops wouldn't tell us nothin'."

"Ricky beat her to death."

"Na aw. He wouldn't do that."

"Oh, no? I'm the one that found her." Joe looks Eddie in the face.

"Then how do we know you didn't do it and aren't puttin' it all on him?"

"Ever heard of forensic evidence there, Eddie?"

"Yeah."

"Ricky was all over it. Betty gave a statement before she died. And he disappeared right after."

"Don't mean nothin'. She probably framed him."

Joe stares at Eddie.

"Yeah, right there," Eddie insists, his finger wiggling at Joe, "I bet that's it. She framed him."

"You're talking stupid again, Eddie," Roy says walking past him to the refrigerator. He's heard plenty while painting in the bedroom, senses Eddie's on the verge of purging everything he knows to boost an ego that's broke the chain.

"How do you know, Roy? You ain't no lawyer or nothin'."

"And you are?" Pulls the cap off a beer and hands it to Joe. "You forget about Willum? Remember him?" Leans in and gets another beer.

Eddie's hands slide into his pockets. "So, what?"

"Your fault he showed up at the house gunnin' for Ricky." Looks at Joe, "Ricky was sweet on his daughter and Eddie couldn't resist feeding her old man a little story that wasn't quite true, was it?" Turns back to Eddie, "You forget about her old man showin' up at the house to get his piece of Ricky, and Dupree havin' to come to the rescue for all of us, including you?"

Eddie sweeps a dismissive hand at Roy and disappears into the living room.

"Selective memory," Roy says after a long swig. "He really do it?"

"Don't ask if you're not prepared for the answer. What my Pop always says."

"No, really. Did he do it, or was he just convenient because of his record?"

Joe sets a crock pot in a box, "She wasn't the only one he killed."

"Not the only one? Someone in prison?"

"Wouldn't have let him out then, would they?"

Roy shrugs and takes another swallow. "Who then?"

Joe straightens up, turns to face him. "He let the boy drown."

"I don't understand."

Bending at the waist and leaning over so Roy gets the point, "I mean he dropped in a toy," extends his arm as if re-enacting the event, "led the kid out to the pool and went back inside to drink a beer." Joe straightens back up, swallows some of his beer. "Kid sunk to the bottom. Betty found him. Couldn't bring him back."

"How do you know all this? Cops never mentioned it."

"They don't know about it and there's no way to prove it."

"But how do you know?"

"Because Ricky told me. The day I went lookin' for him after he put Betty in the hospital. We had a fight."

Beer bottle stops in mid-rise to Roy's lips. "You had a fight? You couldn't have come out on top of that."

"I didn't. Point is he was jealous of the kid so he got rid of him."

Roy sits up on the counter, sets the bottle down, "Why didn't she call the cops?"

"He threatened to kill her, too. Then he pulled her into that armed robbery that got her two years in lock-up, so after that she knew the cops wouldn't believe anything she had to say. It worked, too."

Joe decides to leave out the part that the kid was his. Not the point, either. Not like Ricky was coming back to dispute it. Joe continues to pack boxes as if that ends it all. He's a little surprised at Roy's reaction, not expecting it to end like it does.

From his position on the kitchen counter, Roy can see Eddie's shoulder at the edge of the living room wall where he's listening in. Did that as a kid—eavesdropping on conversations that always got him in trouble because sooner or later he'd blab to the wrong person about what he heard, more often than not getting the conversation all wrong because he'd only heard part of it and just plugged in the missing parts from his own imagination. Bella didn't mind so much as long as it wasn't her secrets, but anyone else's was fair game. One of the many special moments she and Eddie shared that they didn't share with anyone else. To this day Roy thinks that's how Eddie got rid of step daddies he didn't like. Dropped a well-placed lie about Ricky too, and next thing he knew, Ricky was persona non grata and ushered out of the house with the same shotgun used to protect him.

"Well, he's not likely to come back here then. Who knows when we'll hear from him again." Roy finishes the beer, chucks the bottle, ringing the garbage by the back door. "Eddie! Get in the car. We got things to do."

Joe's left alone in the house. He carries packed boxes to the Buick trying to shut out the memories dug up by the conversation. He holds his breath going through the house because even the odor of fresh paint can't cover the smell of Betty's pointless death.

freelancing murder

POP'S IN FRONT of the TV eating Vienna sausage from the can, using his pen knife to stick 'em and eat 'em. On the TV tray next to his recliner is an empty jar of sweet gherkin pickles, plastic once wrapped around a hunk of sharp cheddar cheese, and three empty beer bottles. Time for a refill. But the breaking news on the tube has him glued to the chair better than any titty bar. News about the growing body count two counties up. Excited reporter said some been dead for decades.

On the screen, crime scene tape stretches from oak sapling to the antenna of a local Sheriff's car, and the camera pans to a herd of uniformed cops, officials in suits with paper cups in hand, and a pack of drooling blood hounds panting at the heel of some crusty old codger—probably related to the sheriff—the dogs winners two years running in the National Detector Dog Trials—celebrities in their own right.

A news helicopter's catching a sky shot of dug and semi-dug plots covering a good half acre beyond the woods line where jump-suit clad technicians sift through a mixture of sand and decomposing bodies. Body bags lay lined in a neat row like an open-air army barracks waiting inspection.

Pop doesn't hear Joe enter the house or notice him heft box after box through the living room. Could have been a home invader with malicious intent for all he knew and Pop's eyes still wouldn't have moved from the screen. On the third trip, Joe stops to watch what's got Pop's undivided attention.

Reporter's reading from a pad in his hand, lots of facts to get out, glances up excitedly, turns and points to the activity behind him. Cut to the copter shot of bag cased bodies being carried off out of camera range.

As if he's noticed for the first time, Pop says, "Got a helluva mess up there, can tell ya." Reaches for a beer bottle, sees it's empty. "Get me another, will ya?"

"You drank all these today?"

"Just a couple, boy. Get one for yourself, there. This is a mess. A real big mess."

"What's going on?" Joe sets the box on the coffee table, clears the garbage from Pop's TV tray and disappears to the kitchen. Pop starts reciting what he knows so far, no never mind that Joe can't hear half of it.

"Last I heard, the guy there said they found twenty-two so far. They can't find the folks that live there, think they're on the run."

"Maybe they're buried back there, too," Joe says coming back in and handing Pop another beer. Pulls the cap on his own beer and settles on the sofa to watch.

"Naw, Sheriff says someone's been collecting 'em. Think the woman who lived there is buried out there, too, so they're thinking her boys have been doin' it and then finally killed her."

"Why?"

"Who knows. Maybe she caught on."

"That detective that gave up Betty's stuff said something like this was comin' out. Guess he was right," Joe says.

"Yeah? You knew about it and didn't tell me?"

"Nothing to tell, Pop. Didn't give details."

Pop gets up at the commercials and stands by the front window. Joe sees he's focused on the neighbor's house.

"You okay, Pop?"

"Cops pullin' up at Dee Dee's place again. Looks like about five cruisers and a crime van."

"How do you know it's a crime van?"

"Says so right on the side there. *Crime Scene.*" He points at the window. "What you suppose is going on there?"

"How would I know? Not my job to keep up with her." Joe gets up and joins Pop at the window. They both peer out watching a hustle of activity. Joe spots detective Croy's car in Dee Dee's driveway.

"Didn't kill her, did ya?"

Joe turns and stares at Pop. "No. And when would I have time?" He tries to laugh it off and sits back down to drink his beer and watch the TV.

Staring out the window, Pop points and says, "Guess not. There she is, but she's off her rocker again. Look there, she's fell out in the yard. Real upset about somethin'."

Joe glances at the window, tilts his head. Swigs more beer. Eyes return to the TV.

"Yep, here they come." Pop shuffles to the front door and opens it before Croy and Arnie get up the sidewalk. With an open door, they can hear Dee Dee wailing in the yard. Croy's not as crisp as Joe remembers and Arnie looks as if he'd been changing flat tires. His white shirt's soiled and the neat tie pulled loose at the knot. Pop waves them in without question.

"Cops here, JoJo."

"I can see that, Pop." Joe sets the bottle down and stands. "Detectives. What can we do for you this time?"

"Ms. Turner's sister was found dead about an hour ago out back by that pond."

"No kidding?"

Croy notes Joe's reaction. "Have you ever met Marge Turner?"

Joe can see from Croy's eyes, he already knows the answer to the question. "She came over the other day."

"What did she want?"

"Nothin' much. Wasn't happy with what's been going on with her sister. Blames me."

"Is that all?"

"That's the jist of it. Told her to have a nice day and then I came in."

"Did you threaten her?"

"Why would I threaten her?"

"Ms. Turner said you threatened them both."

"I've never met the woman before then. Know nothing about either one other than mental illness seems to run in the family."

"You've said that before."

"And it's still true. She wanted to meet me, said she was disappointed at what she saw. Said it's my fault her sister got thrown in jail and the looney bin. Then said I didn't fool her. I told her to have a nice day. End of story."

"Where were you yesterday?

"Either here or at Betty's place gettin' her things."

"That true, Mr. Salas?" Arnie asks Pop.

"Yep. When he ain't killin' people, he's right here or runnin' errands." Smiles when he says it. Then belches.

Joe looks to the floor and smiles.

Arnie's thinking about whether it's funny or not and decides it kind of is.

"Is there a place we can talk in private? Or we can do it downtown."

"Kitchen will do," Joe says leading Croy from the living room.

Croy tilts his head at Arnie. The tilt means to distract the old guy from nosing in. Arnie tilts back, smiles at Pop in an uncomfortable, *'what do I talk to the old guy about'* kind of way, stands awkward in the middle of the room craving a cigarette while Pop stares at him like he's concerned Arnie will piss on the furniture.

Joe leans against the counter, arms crossed, waiting. Croy's looking out the open back door, pulls a notebook from his jacket. Flips several pages. Reads.

"When was the last time you saw your former boss Lydia?"

"Day she fired me."

Croy's surprised at Joe's honesty. "Why did she fire you?"

"I said unflattering things about a featured artist. Said it in front of clients."

"Did he do something to you?"

"No. She did. Been promising me a showing ever since I started there, but never came through. I'd had enough and took advantage of the timing."

"Timing?"

"I was gonna quit anyway. I was never gonna be more than a clean-up guy. She looked down on me because I didn't have the hoity-toity pedigree."

"How did you do in the showing in Miami?"

"Well enough."

"What did you do about the letter she was going to send to the art committee?"

"What letter?"

"She recommended they not allow you to enter because of what you did."

"Don't know anything about a letter. They never said anything to me."

"Why haven't you cashed the check she gave you just before the art showing?"

"What check?"

"The one for two grand. She wrote it out to you. It was interesting that she never filled out her portion. We think she disappeared the same night she wrote you the check."

"Then how do you know she wrote one to me?"

"Forensics. But the check itself is still missing."

"Was it cashed?"

"No, it never was."

"I don't know what you want me to say here, detective. She never mentioned a check. I knew when she fired me there'd be no money. I was okay with it. Anything else?"

Croy stares out past the well-tended yard, past the shed and beyond. "Crime scene recovered lipstick from her office floor. Know how it got there?"

"How would I know? Maybe she dropped it."

"That would be logical except it had saliva and blood in it. Tec's said her face was in contact with the floor. A violent contact."

"What's any of this got to do with me?"

"I think you've killed people, Joe. You know it and I know it. Right now, I can't prove it."

"Then let me explain this just once," Joe says, his arms still crossed over his chest. "Arrest me or leave. This is the last time you people come over here and accuse me of murder. I *will* get an attorney and I *will* sue. Money's not an issue." Joe's eyes are piercing through Croy. Knows Croy has no evidence or he'd have been arrested already.

After a long silence Pop peers in the doorway glancing between Croy and Joe as if to see which one is more interesting. "You about finished? He's got more neighbors to kill. Been eyeing the Seymour widow across the street. So old, don't think she'll fight back," he grins.

"Stop it, Pop. They're leaving. Might check closer to home there detective. I have no reason to kill her."

"She tell ya about the fights?" Pop announces.

"No, sir."

"Ask her about 'em. Knock down drag outs they are, too. Gonna bust that slider back there one day, can tell ya that."

"We'll look into it." Arnie says.

Croy knows Joe's right. He hasn't got anything to connect him to this crime. He tilts his head and leaves with Arnie in tow. Too many homicides for one day.

"What are we gonna do about him?" Eddie's hands are cocked on his hip like a gun slinger ready to draw.

"Take off those stupid sunglasses. Who do you think you're impressing here?"

Eddie slowly pulls off the glasses looking at his reflection in the lens. "I like no one knowin' my business."

"How they gonna know your business looking at your face?"

"Sick of haters being up in my business."

"You mean people finding out you troll the streets just to slit some poor girl's throat?"

Eddie carefully folds the glasses and slips them into his front shirt pocket. "Don't want to talk about that."

"Yeah, I bet you don't."

"Well you're in it too, Roy. Not just me. You killed the guy out in the woods, not me."

"I had to because of you, Eddie!"

"He knows who we are." Eddie puts his hand to the bad side of his head like it hurts.

"Dude's dead, Eddie. Not likely to come back and complain."

"I mean Joe boy. You gonna just let him slip away?"

"What do you want me to do, Eddie?"

"He could tell the cops who we are."

Roy slips past Eddie back to the bedroom to finish the paint job.

Eddie yells after him, "He could know more than he's sayin', Roy!"

Roy appears in the doorway, paint roller in hand dripping a nice eggshell, no tint, on the floor. "How would he know the cops are after us, Eddie? You tell him?"

"No."

Roy shoves the roller in Eddie's face, "They want Ricky, stupid. They think we know where he is and probably tryin' to tag us so we'll lead 'em right to him." Roy turns and rolls a swipe or two on the wall. Most of the blood's been covered and the room's taken on a refreshing latex smell.

"I'm feelin' itchy, Roy. You got the car keys?"

"Where do you think you're goin'?"

"Out. Feel caged up here. I'll be back soon." Eddie's jittery like he's had too much caffeine.

"Think again. Grab that roller and help me. No way in hell I'm lettin' you out alone."

"Aw, come on, Roy. I don't need a sitter."

Roy slings the roller at the bucket and stomps up to Eddie's face like he's going hit him. "Yeah, Eddie you do! Because I can't trust you anymore than I could trust Ma. You got what she had. Have a little self-control. You're like a damn crack addict." Spins on his heel with his hand to his head, "I don't know how long I can do this, Eddie. I'm getting really tired."

"I never asked you to, Roy. I can take care of myself."

ARNIE SCRATCHES HIS chin, "So, what did you find out?"

"That if this guy's killed anyone, he's not likely to spend a day in jail over it. He's got a plausible answer for ever damn question. I can't catch him on anything. If we don't find a connection to this one then it's over."

"No one's that good." Arnie says.

"May not be a matter of being good. Just having things fall into place at the right time. His motives aren't strong enough, either. Unless there's something I don't know about. The Vega case has pushed to the forefront now anyway. And now this one next door."

"What about the check and all that other stuff?"

"Dead-end. Let's go interview Miss Turner."

back draft

DEE DEE'S TURNED surly and uncooperative. She's curled in her recliner with a cigarette in one hand and a glass of straight gin in the other trying to ignore the uniformed officer standing guard at the open front door. She's numbed by Marge's death, numbed that the cops think she had something to do with it. She misses her dog.

She sets the gin on the side table by the recliner, the cigarette in the ashtray and stands up. Cop by the door turns, right thumb tucked in his duty belt.

"I gotta take a piss!" she snaps. "You wanna watch?"

The cop and Dee Dee play stare down. She breaks the gaze, pulls the cigarette to her lips and inhales deeply, gestures to luggage. "And what am I going to do with all her shit? Set it out at the road?" Blows smoke at the window. "Airports give it away to the homeless, don't they? Heard they did that. No, they sell it. Don't remember where." She sets the cigarette back in the ashtray. "I could sell it. Set up me a yard sale. Wanna buy it?" Shakes her head as if it's an ordeal she doesn't want to deal with. Like facing the truth. Cop turns his back on her without an answer.

In the bathroom behind a locked door, Dee Dee clutches the sink, stares at the vacant brown eyes staring back. She opens the medicine cabinet, retrieves the bottle of Serentil and pops the cap. Six left. She swallows them all and walks back to her recliner to finish her gin and cigarette. Hums quietly amidst the luggage.

Coming up the driveway, Croy and Arnie get stopped by a patrolman coming out of Dee Dee's garage holding an eight-pound maul with a latexed hand.

"Found this hidden under tarps in the back." Cop sets it on the driveway.

Croy bends at the waist, arms crossed close to his chest, hands tucked under his arms. Leans to the left. Moves around the maul inspecting. "Bag it."

"Think that did it?" Arnie's lighting a cigarette, realizes how close he is to Croy and steps back four steps. Needs to be downwind. He's waited so long for a smoke his hands are trembling.

"Maybe. We'll go have a chat with our girl."

"I'll just be a second. You go on," Arnie says sucking deep.

Croy gives him that look with a slicing motion to his throat. Enough said.

Arnie mumbles, "Yeah, lungs like applesauce. I know."

As Croy makes his way up the sidewalk, the cop guarding the door steps out yelling for 911 on the portable radio in his hand. There's a certain look of *oh shit* panic on his face, and without realizing it, Croy's running.

Inside the living room, Croy sees the cop on his knees next to Dee Dee, giving her CPR.

"She just hit the floor. She's not breathing," cop says through chest compressions. Leans to her mouth listening for signs of breath. Starts mouth to mouth.

Croy drops down on his knees and waits for mouth to mouth to stop. Cop lifts, Croy starts chest compressions. Two-man CPR.

Arnie's standing in the doorway momentarily in shock.

Croy yells, *"Arnie, get the defibrillator out of his patrol car!"*

Seems like hours to get to the patrol car and back. Takes less than a minute. Cop pulls the small defibrillator from the bag and follows directions. "Step back."

A siren wails in the distance as a shock surges through Dee Dee's heart. It still doesn't beat.

"Step back." Defibrillator shocks her again.

"It's back. But irregular," Cop says. Gives a faint sigh of relief seeing the ambulance pull up.

"AMBULANCE PULLED UP at Dee Dee's place." Pop's neck is stretched long while his body debates whether to head for the door or stay where he's at. Doesn't want to miss anything. "Think they found another one? Who you suppose it is? Can't keep up with all the goings on over there."

Joe's quieter than usual, no comment from his end, just a pensive withdraw to the sofa. It's no surprise to him what's happening over there, was wondering how long it'd take them to find the maul. Pretty quick, he thinks, faster than he would have given them credit for. Old Marge just had to have a nosey problem. Too bad for her. But what else could he do? Couldn't let her go back home and spill her guts to her raving lunatic of a sister about what she saw. Stir all the shit up again. Not sure how long he can keep this up. He's smart enough to know eventually all things end and senses past choices are heating just under the surface. Gives him sleepless nights to worry, nightmares, the worst one last night…

Quarter to three in the morning, the fireflies have vanished. Loons out at the pond gone silent with the shift of the moon, tired now. Fog's creepin' in from around the ligustrums, filling dark voids and illuminating odd shapes by the gate leading to the woods.

Joe sucks the last of the beer from a bottle gone warm, the kitchen chair he's in uncomfortable and hard, his legs heavy stiff from hefting too many boxes in one day. But he can't seem to take his eyes off the shifting fog, watching it grow into a lean and formidable image. He wants to stand and close the kitchen door, not because bugs have found haven, but because deep in his bones he knows it's more than fog.

Details begin to shapen. Could be his mind. Could just be the beers.

Whispers. The wind, he thinks. Thinks he hears his name in familiar voice, and the fog creeps closer now collaged as human. Part human. Headless.

"Hey, Pissant, look at me. No head."

"Who's there? That you playin' tricks, Pop? Not funny."

It's not funny because Pop doesn't know Ricky's head had lay frozen behind bagged corn in the freezer until taken out and thawed. Had he known, he wouldn't have been able to look him in the eye afterward.

"Who's there?"

"Think you'd get rid of me, Pissant? You'll never get rid of me. We're connected Joe boy. Me and Keys. We've been planning, thinkin' shit up."

The fog shifts again, creeps to the open back door, the neighborhood eerily quiet.

"You're not Ricky. You're my fucked-up brain."

Joe tries to move, can't even turn his head, as if he's impaled and lifeless.

"Lydia. Remember Lydia, don't you? Terrible thing to do to an old lady. She wants something special. What do you say?"

"I say maybe I'm losing my mind and maybe I haven't had enough to drink," Joe mumbles.

"God All Mighty! Who are you talkin' to in the middle of the night?" Pop's standing by the fridge in his underwear, bed hair standing straight up.

Joe stiffens through the adrenaline surge without a word back, eyes squeezed shut. Aberration's gone when he opens them.

Pop's standing by the chair chancing a thought at getting the newspaper. "You been up all night?"

"Yeah, can't sleep."

"Might be the beers."

"No. Maybe haven't had enough."

"Don't care much for you gettin' like this. Not one bit."

"Don't worry about it, Pop. Just a lot on my mind." Joe gets up and chunks the empty bottle in the trash with the others. "Was thinkin' maybe we ought to get a new car."

"What for?"

"Buick's on its last leg there, Pop. We can afford a new one. Pay cash."

Pop stands staring out the doorway into the misty back yard. He can just make out the tip of the dead pine, the skeletal branches glowing in the moonlight.

"Might want to rethink that, JoJo."

"Why?"

"Oh, I don't know. Never know who might buy it. Who might have ulterior motives not in our interest."

Joe starts to say *what* but his mouth snaps shut and it hits him what Pop's trying to tell him. "Yeah. Might want to think it through."

Through a long silence, they stand at the door watching night die.

"Could just drive it north and sell it to the crusher. I know a guy," Joe adds.

More silence.

"Whatcha thinkin' about getting? Caddie?"

"That what you want?"

"I don't know. Could just drive around and visit car places. See what strikes our fancy. Really like those Hummers. See 'em on that forensic crime show."

"We could do that. Sounds like a date."

"We gotta stop datin' each other. Not healthy." Pop smiles.

"Could do worse, Pop. Could do worse."

JOE ONLY HIT her once. Enough to knock the last breath from her lungs. Marge had gone into some epileptic grand mal seizure after and he'd stood fascinated by the violence of it all. None of the rest of them shuttered or moaned. Ricky did gurgle some but they all died quietly and without fuss. Afterward, Joe stripped her, except her shoes, collected her clothes, the towel Ricky's head was in, the maul, and returned to the house.

His mom had a key to Dee Dee's house back when she used to check on old Elsie before she died. Pop still had it. Never gave it to the realtor when the house was sold to Dee Dee. Wasn't a conscious move on Pop's part, just a memory pushed out like so many others. Joe found it with a little tag attached with Elsie's name and address. Used it the night he killed Marge. As tempted as he was to use her for a new art project—inspecting her features and the curvature of her thick face—he'd decided to start closing off loose ends. His single worst problem was Marge, and after her, Dee Dee, so he killed two birds with one stone that night. Metaphorically speaking.

He'd slipped on a pair of Playtex gloves, washed the maul down with bleach and wrapped it in a large bath towel Marge had used to lay on when the lawn chair webbing etched her skin, stolen from her backyard. He let himself in the house with the key, hid the maul under a tarp in the garage, wadded her clothes in a plastic shopping bag with the towel and stuffed it in Dee Dee's garbage can. Wasn't rocket science. Might work, might not. But Dee Dee's history was on his side. Report after report of it.

MUCH AS HE wants to go stand in the front yard and watch the door close on that part of his life, his restraint's a powerful influence—stops him from even leaving the sofa.

Pop can't help it. He's standing in the front yard, hands on his hips, straining for a better view. He watches paramedics roll Dee Dee out to the ambulance and load her up. Waves as it leaves.

"Must a been a bad one, there. Took her out on a stretcher. Didn't look so good," Pop says limping past Joe. Stops at the recliner, clicks on the TV, limps to the kitchen. Joe doesn't seem to mind Pop's lack of attention, but less than thirty seconds into a news report, he's forgotten Pop and the drama next door.

It's Roy and Eddie's photo on the screen, DL pictures enhanced—Eddie with a cheesy grin trying to look sexy in case any cop that might ever stop him and asked for his DL turned out to be a chick cop.

"Think my stories are comin' on." Pop's got a sandwich on a paper plate, a huge warty dill pickle straddled on top. "Go get you a snack there, JoJo. Got good ham. It on yet?"

"Not exactly. Pre-empted by a follow-up on those bodies they found up north. Found some men now, too."

"You don't say?" Pop settles in the chair, pulls the TV tray up close and bites a chunk from the pickle.

Joe's brain's racing, thumb sacrificed to the nervousness between his teeth.

"Don't think this will be on long, Pop. I gotta run errands. Be back."

Pop waves the pickle without his eyes moving from the TV.

EDDIE'S BEEN GONE the better part of the night, still gone when the sun rises, slips out while Roy dozes on the sofa just in case Eddie gets ideas. But three nights without sleep has taken its toll. And Roy dreams, as if through a scrim, of Vegas, thinks he's really there, can feel the dry desert heat on his skin. He's holding a little kid's hand watching a stunning sunset. Thinks the kid's his. In the kid's other hand, a buck knife, stained and dulled by the butcher of his mother, no corpse to be found. Across his little mouth, teeth surrounded by blood not his. In the dream, Roy releases the little hand gone cold, steps back as if infected by the plague, his fear stretching into the impending dark. A great dust storm approaches, turning to smoke.

Roy wakes with a start. Smoke fills the void at the ceiling and rolls down the walls. Flames lick from the hallway and catch the edge of the sofa, eating air and memory and solid tangible things. A pounding on the front door, Roy hears it, seems stunned.

It's Joe's voice on the other side, a voice loud and just short of panic. More pounding and the door swings open and the fresh air gorges the flames into swirling vortexes from the ceiling. Joe covers his face with his forearm, yells, "Come on! The whole thing's going up."

Roy slides onto the hardwood floor on his belly and commando crawls out the door.

"Where's Eddie!"

"I don't know. I fell asleep. Tried to keep him in the house, but…" Roy sees the Pontiac's gone. "He took off."

"We gotta go before the fire department comes," Joe insists. Pulls Roy to the Buick.

"Why?"

"Your faces are plastered all over the TV. Get in!"

Every window, every door of Betty's old apartment is eaten alive by flame. The roof begins to cave as Joe rounds the corner and he's not sure what he's even doing or why it's important to protect Roy. It's a visceral thing in the back of his brain, a mitochondrial whisper he can't ignore.

Roy's gone silent as if he's had enough time to gather possibilities of getting caught. "How many have they found?" he asks, face pale, staring through the windshield. He can only trust Joe because he's at his mercy now—knowing the truth because it's found him out and all the deeds he committed for his mother who never thought a second about how all this would affect him.

"Twenty-seven, so far," Joe says.

"You know she never looked back," Roy says in a voice so soft Joe glances over to be sure it's Roy who's talking.

"Bella?"

From the tone of Joe's voice, Roy can tell he doesn't believe it. Not really. Hard to imagine a woman having such blood lust, a hunger for cruelty that might rival the worst serial offender caught on a booking photo. And who'd believe it?

"I think the only reason she had kids was to have someone to bring her beer and cigarettes, but then she got religion and turned a vile hate of men. Went through a few until she didn't need 'em anymore. Then it was just us kids left to her.

"When'd it start?" Joe makes a left on Orange Avenue and heads east.

"I guess I was around sixteen. Ricky thirteen, Eddie eleven. She'd make us ride along until she'd find some lonely runaway and invite her home."

Rain begins to pelt the Buick's windshield, the first swipes of the wipers dry and stubborn against the glass. Joe pulls into the bank drive-through waiting his turn at the teller. "All this time?"

"Until about a month ago. I couldn't do it anymore, Joe. Couldn't let her do it, either. I snapped on the last one. Realized my life was all about supporting her habit and I was a nobody standing on the edge of prison or the grave."

Joe fills out a withdrawal sheet and hands it to the teller. "So, what happened?"

"Shot her in the head. Eddie, too. But, as you can see, he came back. Maybe he can't die. Maybe she's still out there somewhere, too." Roy lays his head back against the head rest watching rain drizzle down the window.

"Eddie a little slow?"

"He knows how to play the pity ticket. He used it on Bella like a pro. Her only soft spot, best as I can tell. If she thought one of the girls she was gonna pick up was slow, she'd hand her a ten-dollar bill and move on to someone else, even if it meant waitin' weeks for the right one. Eddie and I almost prayed for the right one to show up just so Bella would get it over with and go back to normal. Whatever that was."

"So, what's his deal now?"

"Picked up where she left off. It's in the blood. What I think. Think he set the house on fire, too."

"Why? You've been protecting him all these years."

"He quit trusting me. It's been bad the last couple a days. For three weeks I've been trying to think of ways to put him down. I just can't bring myself to do it again. He'll end up dragging me to hell with him."

The teller smiles at Joe and hands over a small white envelope. *"Anything else we can help you with, Mr. Salas?"*

"No thank you. And you have a good day," he says dropping the Buick in drive. "You know for sure Eddie's picked it up?"

"Helped him get rid of the bodies."

"More than one?"

"Collateral damage. Some guy caught us burying the girl's body out in the forest. You know we couldn't let him go. Had a wife, so took her out, too."

Joe moves past the stop sign into the four lane and accelerates through the rain. "So where do you think Eddie is now?"

"Trolling like Ma used to. She taught him well. He can't help it. He'll never be able to stop."

"Where do you think he'll land?"

Roy thinks, rubs his head from not enough sleep. "I don't know. That cheap motor lodge probably. He's got an ego to feed, so he has to stay clean. Real hot on himself if you didn't catch it. Why?"

"You're an okay guy, Roy. Just jammed in circumstances you can't control. I know how it feels." They pass the *Welcome to Lake County* line sign. "Anything you're gonna look back on?"

"What do you mean?"

"I mean like when Lot's wife looked back when she shouldn't of and turned to stone. Are you gonna blow it and self-destruct by looking back?"

At first, Roy's not sure what Joe means then slowly his exhausted brain begins to knit. "I got nothing to come back to. If I disappeared, no one would care."

"That's the right answer, Roy."

The Buick slides into the Amtrak train station parking lot. Joe shuts off the engine and hands Roy the envelope. "Take this and get a ticket for as far away as you can get in a couple of days. Re-invent yourself Roy and don't ever look back."

Roy takes the envelope and opens the car door. Rain begins to soak the door panel. "Thanks man. I don't know what to do about Eddie. If caught, he'll spill it."

"Don't worry about, Eddie. I'll take care of him. You're not the only one who's got regrets. But I'm not givin' up what I've got now to pay restitution for something that came to me. They knew what they done and I gotta believe they weren't all that surprised when the end came. Best I could do was to make it quick. After, that's up to whatever God they had. Don't grieve over it, Roy."

"Maybe it is in the blood then."

"Maybe, but even if it is, we're still responsible with free will, brother. Sounds like you and me chose wisely. Be content with it and move on. Oh, the news said they found a couple of men, too. Who were they?"

"We didn't kill—" Roy looks up, the rain wetting the side of his face. "So, that's where our daddies went."

"Look, you better go. Train's coming."

"Thanks man. I won't forget it." Roy exits the car and sprints to the depot for a last-minute ticket. Joe stays long enough to watch him board the train and settle, gives a brief wave as the train pulls from the station through the downpour.

Roy thinks about being free. Thinks about Vegas.

23

erased

ON THE DESK, stuck by adhesive Croy will have to scrub off, a memo, a reminder, a message on pink paper, scrawled words and only one initial for a signature. He tugs at one corner until it releases, careful the adhesive doesn't stick to his hand because then he'd have to pull out the sanitizer.

The memo gently floats into the waste can, alone, surrounded by a new plastic liner. Croy hates things being alone, pulls a sheet of blank paper from the copier and drops it on top followed by a short sigh of relief.

He takes the short walk to the Chief's office—secretary gone—and knocks on the door.

"Come in."

The Chief's not alone. He's behind his desk, a large personnel file opened in front of him. Cecil, from Internal Affairs, stands next to him stroking gloat. It's all about him. Croy senses it, dispenses with shallow courtesies and chit chat and polite inquiries about respective family members Croy's only met at Christmas parties and award functions.

"Have a seat." Chief closes the file after sliding out a rather long narrative report from the top. Croy can read from where he's sitting that it's an I.A. report. He's seen similar ones on fellow officers' dozens of times in his career. But this one's on him, his name in the appropriate box, his rank, check marks in the right place.

"There's a problem," the Chief says.

Croy notices how the Chief purposely avoids eye contact. But Cecil looks him in the eye, a Cheshire cat eye, feathers protruding from between tense lips, dying to speak, dying to spill what he knows and what he's recommended to the Chief. All that in just one glance.

"Do you know a person named Edward Kyle?"

"Don't believe so. Name isn't familiar."

"Sure about that? Think hard."

Croy shakes his head. "No, who is he?"

"You might know him better as Miss Joviane Sweets."

Croy breathes in, doesn't answer.

"Yeah, that's what I thought. The problem here Croy is that he's filed a complaint. And it's pretty serious."

"What is it I was supposed to have done?"

"Picked him up at a convenience store and offered to take him home."

"I don't understand."

"He claimed you forced him to have sex or you were going to pull him in for an active solicitation warrant."

"It's not true. I may or may not have met the guy, but the rest didn't happen, Chief."

"Well, that's how we took it. Problem is, and Cecil will run it all down for you, is his story's checked out."

Cecil's hand pulls the report from the desk, but he doesn't read from it. He's memorized every word and every detail and waited for this very moment to recite it.

"Edward Kyle, AKA Jovaine Sweets, is a known transvestite prostitute who works primarily the OBT corridor, has been arrested seven times on solicitation and two for battery," glances up at Croy, "he was very forthcoming with his past." Pauses to savor Croy's reaction then continues, "He was at the convenience store at the date and time he claimed you picked him up. Store surveillance shows your department vehicle pulling in and Mr. Kyle coming out of the store. It shows the two of you engaged in conversation and him getting into the front seat and the two of you driving off."

Cecil lays the report on the desk, crosses his arms and glares before continuing. "We pulled the tapes from dispatch. You called in a ten-sixty, were off the air for exactly forty-five minutes and then called in ten-eight."

Chief taps the top sheet with the back of his fingers. "You know procedure. Pick someone up, you call it in, give mileage. Period There's nothing in the tape about you having picked someone up. No report of working an investigation. You were off-duty."

"It's his word against mine."

"But so far, we've caught you at the lie and not him." Cecil's grinning, "Wouldn't even give the boy a twenty for the blow job. Not very nice, Croy. Everyone has to make a living."

"That's enough, Cecil," Chief warns. "You know why this thing's so thick?"

Croy doesn't answer. It's too late. His defense evaporates.

"We've got affidavits from three other prostitutes, from here to Alachua County. God, it makes me sick reading these things." Chief goes silent.

"What about my active cases?" Croy asks.

Chief bristles, "Yes, let's talk about those cases. Let's start with the Salas monkey hunt. His attorney has contacted the city attorney. One more unproven allegation and he's hitting the city with a lawsuit. And he's got cause because you can't seem to leave him alone. Did he just become a stick up your ass?"

"I think he's responsible for the deaths of at least three people."

"And where's your proof?"

"I'm still working it."

"And now you're not," Cecil interrupts. "You have two choices. Turn in your resignation or be terminated. You can contact your PBA rep and fight it, but if you do, it becomes very public. Media public. I don't think you'd want that, do you?" Cecil asks.

Croy shakes his head.

Cecil pulls another document from the stack and slides it over to the edge of the desk. "This will get the process started. It'll take a couple of days to finalize everything. You can turn your gear in to the property room today. We won't turn you into Standards and Training. We don't want to be involved in this any longer than we have to, so maybe you can get on with some other department. Miami maybe."

Chief stands up, sticks a pen in his shirt pocket and walks around to the door. He turns and looks at Croy for the first time, "You were a good investigator, Croy, but now I just want you out."

ARNIE'S AT HIS desk placing his personal effects into a box. At first Croy thinks Arnie's packing his things—that would make sense—told to pack his partner up, but as he gets further in the room he realizes Arnie's packing his own things.

Croy pulls off his jacket and begins to disassemble the shoulder holster, badge, credentials, and other odds and ends that get turned back to property.

"Where you going, Arnie?"

"I got over a month in comp and vacation time and thought, you know what? I'm taking it and getting the hell out now. I got my hot little ticket to Mexico and I'm not letting the door hit me on the ass on the way out."

"You've heard."

"Just so you know, I got called in and I.A. drilled me. I didn't know anything. Don't think they believed me, but I don't give a shit. Gave me the push I needed to decide to get out."

"I'm sorry you got dragged into it."

"Doesn't matter. We'll both be better off. Things are changing around here too fast for an old coot like me to keep up with. You and me, we're old school originators from back in the day. Getting bad guys used to be all that mattered and we were good at it. What are you gonna do?"

"I have a nest egg saved. It's easier when there's no wife and kids."

"Yeah, that's where I screwed up. My ex still gets my cash."

"Why are you still giving her money? You've been divorced fifteen years."

"I know. And alimony stopped a long time ago, but I still help out. Her husband's in a bad way with the cancer."

"You're a softie."

"Yeah, kiss my ass."

"Love you too, Arnie."

"Where are you gonna go?"

"Had my eye on a little sailboat out in Daytona. Think I'll buy it. See the world."

"Well, when you sail past Mexico, stop by and we'll have a drink and talk about the good old days."

"Sounds like a plan."

"Oh, and something came back on the VA thing you were checking into."

"Not that it matters now, but what?"

"Patients registered there at the time of those killings. The Keys thing?"

"What about it, Arnie?"

"An Anthony Salas. Only one who left the ward alive that week. That's Joe's father, isn't it?"

"I knew there had to be connection. What are the odds?"

"I passed it on. Who knows, maybe someone with a little initiative will pick it up and finish what you started." Arnie looks around the room, says, "I'm all done here. Didn't have much, so I guess this is good-by."

"Oh, before I forget," Croy pulls a string of crystal beads from the top drawer, "I found these under the desk. I think they're your Mojo beads." Lays them in Arnie's hand.

"I'll be damned. Thanks. I sure missed these."

"You never said where they come from."

"My grandma. Bayou grandma who insisted the day I left home to keep them with me *always*. Said they'd keep me safe. I believe they have." He raises an eyebrow. "But I was sure hurt thinking I'd lost them, like I'd stabbed her in the heart. Thanks." Arnie glances at Croy, picks up the box and gives him the thumbs up.

24

I'm already dead

RAIN RETREATS AND the sun appears, but the air is still soaked from the burnt residue of Betty's white trash world. Her fishing bucket lies on its side by the edge of the sidewalk, the lip melted and curled. Roof's gone and only part of the north wall is intact. The rest, the few two by tens and a handful of two by fours, remain upright but burnt into what looks like alligator skin.

As Joe slows, he sees the stove, a small patch on one side as white as the day it was made, and the refrigerator left like a guard scorched in the midst of the rubble. He resists the urge to linger, pushes down the gas pedal to force him past the house to the stop sign three blocks down, far enough away to not want to go back and sift through it all. He turns left and winds his way through the neighborhood back to Bay Street. And one last stop.

EDDIE'S PONTIAC SITS in front of room 202 of the Motor Lodge where Eddie and Roy first landed in Eustis. Eddie's asleep, first sleep he's had in days because of the headaches and blackouts. His overnight predatory trolling has been uneventful if not exhausting, could be the rain, and it takes a good ten minutes of pounding on the door before he climbs out of his brain sewer to answer it.

"What do you want?" he bitches, the brief sunlight pushing him back into the cool darkness of the room as if his skin's close to igniting. He crawls back on the bed and covers his head with a pillow.

Joe checks the breezeway before letting himself in and closing the door.

"You know your face is plastered all over the news?"

Joe can't decipher whatever Eddie mutters under the pillow.

"I got a place no one will find you. Come on, grab your stuff." Joe kicks the foot of the bed and Eddie slings the pillow at him. "Come on now or I'll call the cops myself."

Eddie creeps across the mattress until his feet hit the floor. "Where's Roy?"

"Waitin' on us, so get your crap." Joe peers through the closed blind as if someone might be watching, notices the sun's shrunk behind the next legion of clouds as rain sweeps through the parking lot in sheets. Acting paranoid seems to be a gamble that works on Eddie. He scrambles for his shirt, car keys, and heads for the door.

"You're gonna need to leave the car here, cous."

"I don't ever leave my car. No way."

"Yeah, way. Cops are looking for it and it's only a matter of time before one of 'em spots it from the road. Had its picture all over the TV. Might have been brighter to park it somewhere else." Joe slips the door open and checks the breezeway again.

"But I gotta get my stuff."

"Forget it. No time. Don't want some fisheye spottin' you around it to blab to the cops. Whatever you have in there can be replaced."

Just the reminder makes Eddie's hand leap to his throat for confirmation his gold chain is still around his neck. Relieved, he follows Joe to the Buick and slides inside—good for Joe, the heavy rain and all. Not likely people are standing around watching the parking lot; more likely in bed screwing through the cable porn channels or sleeping it off until dark. Eddie watches the Pontiac until out of sight, seems genuinely sad leaving it behind.

JOE DRIVES AROUND for about an hour until he's sure no one's following him and Eddie's too confused to know where he's at. Not much said in that hour, Joe's kind of glad about it. Not much to talk about anyway. He doesn't like Eddie so much. But he has a family obligation, if only by his own measure, an obligation to stop whatever fever Eddie's picked up before it infests and kills them all.

Glancing over, Joe sees Eddie curled against the car door, his arm crossed over his head as if he's in pain, and if he is, Joe doesn't much care. Not going be the worst part of Eddie's evening, yet Joe's curious, curious because they're connected, not just by blood but by action. Eddie kills. Seems to need to know that Bella's gone, and Joe wonders if it's the same with him. His Mom's been gone almost three years and in that sense, they aren't anything alike, but just thinking about how they ended up gives him pause.

Joe pulls the Buick into an orange grove and cuts the engine. The rain has let up to just a misty drizzle, and heavy droplets fall from the leaves of the orange trees to the windshield in fat splats. It's interesting to watch them explode, collect, and dive across the glass. It occurs to Joe he's not exactly sure how to kill Eddie and realizes he doesn't want to get blood all over the car. Pop would ask questions, or worse, just give him looks but never say anything. Maybe say, "You gonna clean that up?" And Pop's slip ups and mental disconnects are too worrisome. Less he knows the better. But it doesn't solve his problem. Joe starts the Buick and pulls back onto the hard road towards home.

IT'S DARK WHEN they pull into the driveway. Eddie's been asleep pretty much the whole time, only popping up now and then to focus on Joe, on the car's interior then slide back under his arm.

It's okay with Joe, but now at home, he needs to get Eddie to the shed. Quietly. Doesn't want to take a chance on Pop spotting him skirting the fence to the backyard, because at the moment, Joe doesn't have a plausible answer for who Eddie is and why he's with him. No worries with Dee Dee. He does wonder if she's dead, though. Heard the words *heart stopped* from uniform cops milling around the yard, then watched things being wrapped and packed into the crime van. Makes Joe smile a little.

"Hey, Eddie. Wake up."

Only a slight groan from Eddie's end.

"We have to move fast. Roy's waitin' and he won't be happy if you give me grief."

Eddie rolls over and stares. "But how can Roy be mad?"

"What do you mean there, Eddie? Why not?"

"He's not here," Eddie sits up and looks around at the strange neighborhood. "He can't be here."

"He's right in the back here. Why do you think he can't be?"

"You been to the house?"

"Yeah, why?"

Eddie's eyes shift quickly as his brain wakes up and reminds him of what he did to Betty's apartment. And he's not sure what Joe knows and isn't smart enough to pose the questions to get answers without spilling what he's done. Maybe the flame petered out and it didn't burn after all.

"How'd he get here?"

"I stopped by and picked him up. I wanted to wait for you but he talked me into coming without you, in case the cops stopped us. He's always thinking of ways to protect you, Eddie. He wanted to be sure they couldn't get you. Says he'll take the fall for you 'till the day he dies. Wish I had a brother like that. I bet you're glad he's your brother. Real loyalty that is."

Eddie suddenly looks up hopeful, opens the door. "Is he really here?"

"Yeah. Come on. I'll get you a beer," Joe says pulling the keys and stepping out. Eddie follows him up the driveway to the side gate like a dog that's found a new home.

night soil

MAYBE EDDIE IS stupid. Joe ponders such things switching on the light in the shed. Eddie looks around at the bench, picks tools off the peg board like he gets dragged to hide out in sheds every night. Joe also wonders when Eddie's gonna start asking Roy's whereabouts, but at the moment, Eddie seems content to wander and explore.

"I know it's not much, but no one will bother you here. I'd take you to the house, but my Pop lives with me and he'll ask too many questions. Not sure he wouldn't call the cops, either. He's all wrapped up in this story out at your place and watching the TV pretty close. He's got the details down tight enough to start a book. Hiding you in the shed might be more than he can handle."

Eddie just nods and flips through sheets of drawings tacked to the back of the shed door. Facial features mostly, some colored in pastels, others charcoal, deep shadows smudged against the stark white paper.

"You do these?" Eddie asks.

"Yeah. I play around with it some."

"I used to draw too, but Ma, she said it was a waste of my time and I should try gettin' a career working at Verge's auto shop." Glances at Joe for the first time.

"He hired me right off and says I have a natural knack for engines. Guess you can tell," he grins, turns back to the pictures. "Built my Firebird from scratch. Was a junker Verge had out in the back forty. Teddy Devine, you don't know him, he wrecked it one night and his girlfriend died in it. I had to get new seats because the blood soaked through to the stuffing and Verge said in the heat, it would stink no matter what cleaner I poured on it. He's been in the business nearly all his life, Verge has, but I found new seats, well, not new new, but cleaner, ones not bloodied up, from another junker way out in Live Oak. Took me all day drivin' up and back to get 'em." Rubs his forefinger at the edge of the shaded print. "How come it won't smudge? Aren't charcoals supposed to smudge?"

"I have a can of spray. Keeps it from smearing once it's finished."

"Really? You'll show me?"

"Sure," Joe says. He suddenly realizes he wants to talk with Eddie, but at some point it has to come to an end. Eddie's end. "Damn," he mutters.

"Where's Roy?"

"Think he walked to the *Shop and Rob* up the street. Was getting' you something, but don't remember what," Joe lies.

"Skittles probably," Eddie says studying the drawing. "Gets 'em for me sometimes when he swings through a station to get gas."

That seems to be all that's needed to satisfy Eddie. He pulls off one of the colored prints from the door and sits on the stool by the bench. He's studying it, turning it under the bulb over the bench, examining Joe's technique.

"We must be related. You do it like I do." Holds it out for Joe, pointing to the center, "See here, you layer dark to light just like me. That's weird shit, isn't it?" He's waiting for Joe to show interest like a small boy hoping for approval.

Joe takes it and pretends he knows what Eddie's talking about, says, "Hey, while we wait for Roy why don't we go down to the pond and have some beers?"

"What about Roy?"

"He knows where to find us. He's bringing more beer. We all got lots to talk about. You can have that piece if you want."

"Really?" Eddie says hopeful, "Yeah, let's go to the pond. And we even got a full moon."

"Rain's stopped. You might see wildlife down there," Joe says leading Eddie out and turning off the light and closing the shed door. "Hang here for me a second while I grab a six-pack."

Joe slips into the house and goes straight for the refrigerator. The TV's playing, and through the dining room, Joe can see Pop asleep in his recliner. Works for him. He stops at the utensil drawer, slips Betty's fish filet knife in his back pocket, and returns to the backyard holding up the six-pack. "Gonna be a good night there, Eddie."

Eddie follows him through the back gate and down the path to the pond, chatting about cars, art and women, but Joe only hears brain hum. He points the flashlight to the fallen log. "Sit down there." Pulls a bottle from the carton and hands it to Eddie, pulls one for himself and gets comfortable on the log.

For a long time they just drink and listen to the loons' mourn, and the erratic hiss and cry of the cat bird, the trill of bugs. A splash in the pond spreads ripples reflected in the moonlight.

"Roy told me about Bella."

Eddie doesn't answer, takes long swigs from the bottle until empty.

"Didn't it bother you what she was doing?"

Eddie shrugs, "Kind of at first. I didn't like the blood. And I hated the screaming but you get used to it. Like hog farmers. You get used to the sounds of it."

"Don't think I could," Joe says handing Eddie another beer.

"Sure you could. If it was your Ma, you'd get used to anything."

Joe thinks about it and nods. Eddie's not so far off the mark, but it's not like he's gonna admit it and he's not sure why.

"You ever try to get her to stop?"

Eddie looks at Joe, but Joe doesn't look back. "What for? It made her happy. She isn't as bad as Roy makes her out. She had a hard life taking care of us boys and we didn't make it easy for her. Was the least we could do."

Joe raises an eyebrow. "Wow, never though of it that way."

"See, just gotta look at it from a different angle there, cous."

"Was she ever mean to you, Eddie?"

It grows quiet and for a moment the moonlight disappears behind a cloud. They're sitting in pitch clutching cold beers, the question hanging in the air.

"She didn't mean it."

"She beat you?"

"Naw. Not really. We got whipped, but not like you'd think. But she did have a mean streak and wasn't past using it when we crossed her."

"Like how?" Joe drops the empty bottle in the carton and pulls out two more, hands a fresh to Eddie.

"You don't want to hear that."

"She's not here, Eddie. And I'm not gonna tell anyone. I just want to know about your life."

Eddie pulls the cap from the new bottle and tilts it to his mouth but stops short of letting the liquid touch his tongue. Drops the bottle back down, drops his head as if thinking about it.

"Most times she just slit their throats. If she was really mad, she'd cut their heads off. If she was pissed at us, we'd have to stay locked in *the bunker* until she let us out."

"What's *the bunker*?"

"A road pipe half underground. In case of tornados, you know? Not many of those dug outs around, but my daddy had it built just in case. Said we'd be safe if a nuclear attack happened, but it never did. Never had a tornado, neither. Can't imagine having to actually live in it. Just barely big enough for four people to squat with a few supplies, but alone, you could stretch out and sleep."

"You sleep in there a lot?"

"Naw. Once though, she got pissed because I fell asleep waiting for her to finish with the girl and when I woke up she'd set the head on me. She was some kind of pissed. Ranted and hollered. That might have been the girl we gave whiskey to before bringing her home. Hard to remember now. Maybe not. I donno."

Joe shakes his head, swallows more beer. "That's cold, Eddie."

"I got over it. Then she let me do more to help her and made Roy dig all the holes. I think she knew he didn't approve of what she was doin'. She trusts me."

"Yeah, Roy told me what he did." Joe's backing off the beer, but watching Eddie's consumption. Eddie's starting to talk a little slower, his words slightly slurred, easy done on an empty stomach.

"I wish he hadn't a done it. He tell you he shot me in the head?"

Joe nods.

"Says he's real sorry about it. It sure hurt, though." Turns and tilts his head at Joe, "Bullet's still in there. He tell you that?"

Joe shakes his head, sets the empty bottle in the carton, hands Eddie another fresh.

"We're going to Vegas. Roy's always wanted to go to Vegas. I've seen shows on TV. Lot's of chicks. Chicks in clubs. Chicks in casinos. Chicks on the streets. Chicks waiting for a piece of this." Eddie breaks out into a little upper body dance. "See, no resisting this. If you was a chick, you'd be all over me," he smiles, jabs Joe in the arm with his elbow. "What do you do for a livin'?"

"Too long a story, but lately I've been doing art. Sold a few."

"You don't say? Hey, hey, you think you could hook me up?" Eddie looks hopeful. "We could be partners. Sell 'em at the flea markets. Whatcha think?"

"Might be a plan," Joe says, notices Eddie's sliding in deeper. "Why are you doing it?"

"Doing what?" Eddie drops his empty beer bottle behind him and takes a fresh. Not as cold, but not so much he won't drink it. Drank worse when he'd sneak around on Bella.

"Do you kill women because your Ma did, or because you just like it?"

"I donno."

It's not the answer Joe's hopin' for and for the first time he feels a spark of anger rise from his chest and decides he's not going to let the question go with a simple stupid Eddie *I donno*. He picks the right words to roil a reaction.

"I'm bettin' you like it. Having the power of life and death in your hands and being able to make the call. Isn't it?"

Eddie tilts his head as if considering. Nods. "Maybe."

"Why you keep going out?"

"Donno. But something happens after. I feel better."

"Better than what?"

Eddie shrugs.

"Think you'll ever stop?"

Eddie shrugs again.

"At some point you're gonna get caught, Eddie."

"Worse things than prison."

"Yeah, but your brother's gonna get dragged in, too. What about him?"

"Don't pile that shit on my back, it's not mine to carry."

"Maybe not in the beginning, but what you're doing now he's been cleaning up."

"Who gives a shit? Ma never did. So, why should I?"

Joe covertly reaches behind and wraps his hand around the handle of Betty's fish filet knife, feels the cold steel warm in his palm.

"You should care, Eddie. You're out of control. And other people don't deserve to be punished because you don't give a shit." The knife shifts right side up in Joe's hand.

"And who are you? You the police? You gonna turn me in? There some kind of bounty on my head and you're gonna collect?"

Eddie's swaying on the log ever so slightly, his eyes trying to hold a focus. "Think I'm afraid of a wimpy old fuck like you?" Eddie stands up, his stance hostile if not on the downside of useless. "You was a wimpy pissant back then, too. I see why Ma didn't like you." Leans over and bends at the waist, "She hated your good-for-nothin' family. Couldn't shed the smell of 'em fast enough." Swipes beer drool off his lips with the back of his hand. "Got rid of that sorry excuse of a man that plugged Roy in her. Roy's startin' to smell like him, too." Eddie sways and stumbles back while looking around for his beer, "Why Ma liked me better. Didn't have that fucker's stench on me."

Joe extends one arm in a gesture of comfort, "I get it Eddie. I really do. You're grieving your mother and taking hits from every side. I understand. I do." Eddie nods as if that settles it and moves into Joe's arm. They hug like men hug, Eddie patting Joe on the back, Joe patting back.

Joe whispers in Eddie's ear, "Tryin' to burn someone up's a bad thing, Eddie. Especially when it's your brother, but I really do get it. But it just doesn't change anything. Give my regards to Ricky and Bella."

In the midst of the hug, head on Joe's shoulder, Eddie's eyes widen, his mouth opens slightly. A small drop of blood trickles from the edge of his bottom lip and a push of air from his lungs brushes Joe's ear. Eddie starts to double over on the blade in Joe's hand and with one more minor thrust, Eddie steps away. He glances down, hand just below his rib cage and pulls it up to see it covered in blood.

It's odd, the expression on Eddie's face, Joe thinks. A slight tilt of disbelief, betrayal, arrogance gone astray, he's not sure what. But he looks him in the eye as he goes down, first to his knees, absent of breath, or talkin', or the singin' no one but Eddie can stand. And it's odd the way Eddie looks around as if someone or something with greater power than his own will come and save him. Joe places his finger on Eddie's forehead and gives a slight push. Eddie drops backward with a thud.

"That's the thing about pissants, there Eddie. We're always underestimated." Joe picks the last bottle of beer from the carton, takes a seat on the log, and leisurely finishes it while listening to the music of night life by the pond.

26

paper dolls

FIRST TIME HE'S ever had the luxury of taking his time. No threat of neighbors, cops, weather. Couldn't ask for better weather. In the shed, extra lighting posted from the rafters, a small oscillating fan to move the air, Joe gently cleans Eddie's decapitated head. Combs back the hair, inspects the bone structure, pinches the skin in a couple of places for texture resilience then sets it on a paper plate—one of the heavy kind, sturdy, not the weak flimsy kind that can't hold a hot dog or hunk of steak. Ink is poured in a small bowl, a brush set next to it. Joe pulls a sheet of rice paper from the roll and lays it on the cleared bench.

"You'd appreciate this, Eddie. You're gonna be the best one yet. Might keep it. Hang it in the living room so I can think of you every time I look at it." Joe carefully brushes the ink on both sides of Eddie's face and gives it a few seconds to set. He takes the paper, holds it over the face and aligns it to the center and gently lays it down. Starting at the bridge of the nose, working his way up to the forehead, he ever so gently feigns the flesh, careful not to smudge, breathing shallow.

"Sometimes things have to be done. Sometimes there's no one left and it falls on you to finish up. If you have it in you, you clean up, if not, you clean out," Joe whispers. "Gotta say, you got damn fine bones, Eddie. Damn fine."

His fingertips crawl over Eddie's face with a light touch, a tap—straight pins tacked along the side of the paper into the flesh to insure the paper doesn't slide and smear. Joe slowly lifts the paper, keeps it taut so it can't fold back on itself. He holds it towards the fan to rapid dry. Clips it to a line strung across the wall, steps back and studies. The image takes on the impression of a hooded demon, a commander in the hierarchy of a blood lust war passed down from generation to generation.

He takes Eddie's gold herringbone chain and holds it under the face to see how it looks and decides to place it on the piece once it's matted and framed. Appropriate, Joe thinks. Appropriate in the way it's ended, into whose hand it's fallen. He's satisfied today. He'll sleep tonight. Sleep hard for the first time since he can remember. Joe turns off the lights, locks up and goes back to the house.

"PACK YOUR BAGS, Pop," Joe announces down the hall.

"Where we goin'?"

"It matter?"

"Like to know. It a crime a fella wantin' to know where he's goin'?"

"Wherever you want. Anywhere in the world. You pick." Joe drags the suitcases down the hall. Sticks his head in Pop's room. Pop's slicking his thin hair down with Pommel, his neck stretched at the mirror as if a stranger's looking back.

"Could use a little nip tuck. What do you think?" Pulls the turkey-waddle skin tight on his neck.

"Yeah, Pop. Next you'll be wantin' Botox."

"Maybe we can invite Sadie to go along. Think she's a little sweet on you."

"Really? You think? Thought it was just me. Maybe I'll give her a call."

Joe moves to the kitchen, ignores whatever Pop says back. Through the open back door Joe watches the funnel of turkey vultures spiral above the pond. He throws stuff from the refrigerator that'll go bad in the garbage because he knows the vultures won't be hungry for a very long time. "Good birds."

J L Rehman lives in the
Vanishing rurals of central
Florida with a background
In law enforcement and a
Fascination of the macabre.

Also by J L Rehman

No Middle Ground

Death Impressions

Insanity Road

www.ingramcontent.com/pod-product-compliance
Lightning Source LLC
Chambersburg PA
CBHW031126210626
46816CB00015B/730